PERFECT
TIMING

KATHRYN
SHAY

Praise for Kathryn Shay's novels

PERFECT TIMING

By KATHRYN SHAY

CHAPTER 1

THE WOMAN ALEX Lansing had arranged to interview today to care for his children was late, and if he could reach her—he tried the one phone number she'd given him, but there was no answer—he'd tell her he wasn't going to consider her for the job. Punctuality was an important quality he required in a sitter and she apparently didn't have it. His life was too busy to have unreliable people surrounding him.

You're life's too busy, anyway, darling.

Damn it to hell. Sometimes he could hear Lila's voice as if she was in the room with him. And she often chided him like this, especially about working too hard. The voice had started not long after her death three years ago from uterine cancer and came to him periodically. He was half tempted to go see a shrink.

He waited for the caregiver in his home office in a separate wing of his house. Though he had a lab and private work space at Global Pharmaceuticals, the organization that sponsored his research, he preferred to work here as it was more private.

Finally, his phone buzzed and his housekeeper, Ann Kramer's voice came over the line. "Dr. Lansing, Celeste Hart is here to see you."

"I'll be right out." As he locked up the room and made his way to the foyer, he pictured the woman he'd spoken with on

Skype. Her voice had been soft and coaxing, and he'd felt… reassured by it. She'd said everything he wanted to hear. And her face, when she'd talked about his kids, mesmerized him. But she was going to need to impress the hell out of him now for him to change his mind about finding someone else who dealt better with time.

When he came face-to-face with her, that magnetic draw returned, only more intensely. He took in her dark auburn hair and clear blue eyes and felt as if he was drifting closer to her, almost touching her, though he was rooted to the spot where he stood. Instead of squirming, she studied him with interest.

When he realized he was staring, he coughed nervously. "Good morning, Ms. Hart, let's sit in there." He pointed to the living room off to the left.

"Hello, Dr. Lansing," she said then preceded him into the room. She was a tall woman, but there was a delicacy about her. Dressed in white pants and matching jacket with a pink shirt beneath the suit, she took a chair across from him in the room they didn't use much anymore. They used to spend a fair amount of time in here when Lila was alive.

Before he could comment on Ms. Hart's lateness, she spoke. "It's unconscionable to be eight minutes past our arranged meeting time." She shrugged a shoulder. On closer examination, she was well toned and feminine at the same time. "I'm not familiar with your mass transit, and I'm afraid I became lost."

Something about her dignified apology calmed him. Hell, something about *her* erased his irritation and gave him a settled feeling inside. "You don't drive?"

"Ah, no. I took a bus here."

That could be a problem. Maddy had her license and drove Lila's car, but the boys sometimes needed to be taken places after school. They often carpooled, so maybe he could work something out with his neighbors.

She added, "I can assure you, I'm usually punctual."

"You're from out of town, then?"

"Yes, a small city in upstate New York. We didn't have mass transit and we walked everywhere." She reached into a bag. "You've seen my references and résumé, but these are harder copies."

Harder copies? He took the papers. Their fingers brushed, and he settled even more, amazed at the sense of well-being enveloping him. "Thanks for these. But I'd prefer you tell me about your life." Alex knew people revealed more when they talked about themselves.

"I grew up in South America, where my do…parents were missionaries. We moved to the United States when I went to a study course at college. I attended a small, private educational institution in Rochester. I married my college sweetheart when I was twenty-one. He died in a car accident when I was thirty." She gave him a sad smile. "That's when I stopped driving vehicles. I've worked in day care or done private child sitting all my life. I…cannot bear children of my own."

He was surprised at the personal remark, so oddly phrased. "What brought you to Virginia?"

"One of my sisters recently obtained a job in Washington, D.C. We wanted to be together."

"You live with your sisters?"

"Yes." She cocked her head. "That isn't a problem, is it? I understood this job was for daytime and occasional evenings."

"That's not an issue. I work from home. My office is on the other side of the house. I have a housekeeper during the day, too, because you'll focus on the children."

She studied him oddly. Then she asked, "Do you work at home to be close to the young...ones?"

"No."

In actuality, he conducted the analysis of his research from the privacy of his home office because early in his career, when he was employed by City University, his work had been hacked, changing the entire course of his professional life. He'd left the academic setting because of the theft, though for a year now, he went to City U to teach an Ethics in Science course.

Once Global had hired him, providing state-of-the-art security, he did his hands-on research at their facilities, but old habits died hard, and he still formulated his analysis at home. The only ones allowed in his office were the kids — when he was with them, of course — and his housekeeper.

"I'd like to spend more time with my children, though."

"Sometimes," Celeste began, "when we're in the midst of our life's work, we ignore those closest to us. People adjust, so long as it's not forever."

"Tell me about your views on child care. My children's welfare is paramount to me."

"I believe children need adults to like and respect them, yet not be considered a friend. A sense of humor is important. An understanding of human needs, no matter what age."

Hmm. Again, almost his exact thinking.

"What about spanking? TV? Junk food?"

For a minute she seemed confused, then her eyes widened and she drew back. "I think spanking is barbaric, and if you hit your children, I couldn't work for you. What's more I'd advise you not to—"

He held up his hand, palm out. "I don't spank. And wouldn't hire you if you believed in corporal punishment."

"Oh, well then." She composed herself but that spark of fire intrigued him. "As far as junk food is concerned, a few indulgences seem harmless. And I confess I like the video box, but again, if you're spending quality time with the children, that wouldn't be an issue."

Leaning back in his chair, he watched her. She was one of the calmest people he'd ever met. And she came across as totally sincere. "I like your answers, Ms. Hart."

She didn't seem surprised. "I'm glad."

"I'm a bit worried you don't drive."

"I...I didn't know that was a requirement."

"It's not," he decided suddenly. "We'll compensate if we choose you. Would this job be enough for you? I pay well, but a high school student did it before and didn't need to support herself."

"I have adequate funds."

"Money isn't important to you?"

She looked at him blankly for a minute. Her eyes were pure blue, with no hint of other colors. They were quite unusual. "Of course money is important. But I have a family fund of trust — trust fund — and I don't need to work. I enjoy children. I would like to have a chance to know yours."

Again, something about her pulled him in. He knew in his gut she'd be good with his kids.

"All right," he said, despite his earlier misgivings about her punctuality. "Let's give it a shot. I need someone tomorrow at four and the young woman I have until the end of May is busy. I was going to cancel my meeting, but now I won't have to."

She smiled mysteriously. For some reason, he felt as if she knew he'd do exactly what she wanted him to.

• • •

THE DAY AFTER the interview, Celeste braced herself when she rang the doorbell to the Lansing dwelling. The wonderful sun had been beating down on her as she walked from the transit stop, and the air surrounding her was blissfully warm. She'd been in this time period for six weeks, and thinking about the constant gray air out of inside in the 26th century, she knew she'd never stop relishing the light of day. She still didn't take for granted the sun, the trees, which blew in gentle breezes, or even the wood this house was made of.

The door opened. The small, silver-haired woman from yesterday stood before her. Ann Kramer, the keeper of the house. "Hello, Ms. Hart."

"Mrs. Kramer. Nice to see you again."

"You, too. Come in. Dr. Lansing's waiting for you in the office with the children."

Celeste stepped into the small space called a foyer. Today she'd dressed in a yellow, cotton blouse that bared her arms and a skirt that did not cover her legs. She loved the feel of the material on her skin. In her hand, she held what the women of today carried…a purse…and followed Ann Kramer from the large entryway, across a real stone floor down a wide corridor. This house was even larger than Jess Cromwell's dwelling. They passed rooms on either side of a hallway, one where she'd been interviewed. Each was filled with beautiful colors and textures and different-shaped couches and chairs. Her terminology was improving though she occasionally misspoke and labeled them conformers. She entered the last room and was amazed by the deep, rich red of the walls, the burnished wood on the high ceilings and tall shelves stuffed with real books.

Alex Lansing sat at his desk. A male youngling played a game on a small handheld machine. Another worked from books and papers at a nearby table. The female youngling wasn't present.

"Dr. Lansing?"

Turning, he glanced up and covered the speaker of the phone he held. "Hold on a sec, Dad. Hello. I didn't hear the bell."

In front of him sat his computer. His research notes would be in the system. It was Celeste's task to find a way to access that work.

"Come on in. I'll be done in a minute." Back into the device, he added, "Have fun, Dad. Just don't let Mom go parasailing again. See you in a month." After he clicked off, he said, "That was my father."

"Are they enjoying their Mediterranean cruise?" Mrs. Kramer asked.

"Very much so." He turned his attention to Celeste. "Good afternoon, Ms. Hart."

"Dr. Lansing." Coming fully into the room, she transferred her gaze back to the younglings—she *must* call them children. Dr. Lansing said, "Kids, this is Ms. Hart."

"Hi." The littlest stood. She glanced at his donor...father. As the computeller had shown, they shared the same light complexion and blue eyes and dark blond hair. The tilt of their mouths was identical when they almost smiled. "I'm Cody."

"Hello, Cody."

The boy seemed content. Kind. Something else, too, but she wouldn't be able to intuit what it was until she touched him.

The other male stepped forward. Fascinated by his hair — it was lighter than any she'd seen so far—she moved closer and took a good look at his face. His visage was too sober for a child, and complicated vibes shimmered off him. "I'm Jonathan."

"Hello." She scanned the room. "Where's Madison?"

"She had a meeting at school today that I didn't know about," Dr. Lansing explained. "She's very active. She'll be home later, but I'll be gone. Ann can show you around before she leaves."

"Would it be possible for the children to acquaint me with the house?"

Dr. Lansing gave her a full smile. "Sure." He said to the younglings, "All right, guys?"

Jonathan stared over at his father. "Do you have to go, Dad? It's Saturday."

"Sorry son. But you'll have fun getting to know Ms. Hart. And I'll be back before you go to bed."

The resignation on Jonathan's face tugged at Celeste.

Mrs. Kramer cleared her throat. Celeste had forgotten she was there. "I'll be in the kitchen, finishing supper, while the boys take you on your tour. I hope you like chicken, Ms. Hart."

Animal product of the poultry family. Helen had cooked some, and Celeste liked it.

"I'm not fussy about food." *Because we never had any.*

"Well, good." Dr. Lansing stood.

Today he wore nicely fitting tan trousers and a shirt of brown that accented his coloring. He took a coat off the back of his chair—it was lightweight and tailored—and shrugged into it. "I'm off." Bending down, he kissed Cody's cheek. "Don't give Ms. Hart a hard time on the first day, kiddo."

"Me?" Cody's smile was devious.

Dr. Lansing ruffled Jonathan's hair, then stood back. "I'll escort you out." He waited until they were in the hallway, locked the door, then walked away carrying a chip-like thing called a flashdrive.

"So," Celeste said, "I'm all yours."

Cody grinned and took her hand. Ah, that was it, he liked to play pranks, to have fun at the expense of others. She, Dorian and Celeste engaged in some of those when they were young. This little one was…what was the word…oh, yes, mischievous.

She glanced at the older boy. He was shorter than her five foot, eight inches but getting some good form on him for being eleven yearlings. "Is it Jon or Jonathan?"

"Um, Jon."

"Jon. I know you wish your dad was here and not me. But he has work to do. And I'd like to get to know you. Would you show me your room first?"

"Okay." He brushed Celeste's arm as he headed down the hall. She was hit with a sense of sadness so strong it momentarily immobilized her. This was one unhappy child.

They climbed an open staircase made of richly grained wood, and the ceiling had glass apertures in it. Sun streamed through them and she sighed.

"I like the sun, too," Cody said, catching her reaction. She'd have to be careful around this one.

"Good. Maybe we can go for a walk out of inside."

Jon frowned. "Out of inside?"

"You mean outdoors?" Cody suggested.

"Um, of course." Megadamn, she kept making that mistake.

Jon gave her a skeptical look, one she'd seen on Alex Lansing's face, too. When he reached the entrance of a room, he stopped.

"Is something wrong?"

"Dad says a lady should always enter first."

"How sweet." She hadn't known about this particular etiquette.

She and Cody went through the doorway.

The room was similar to those she'd seen on the chips for young boys. There was a poster of a male in short leggings and a shirt that was too small for his torso, with number thirty-three on it. She remembered similar men on the video box at Jess's. They threw balls and tackled whoever caught them. She thought the game exceptionally violent and often winced when she watched a play or two.

One side of the room held shelves of books, as in Dr. Lansing's office. And pictures. She crossed to them. They weren't 3D, and they didn't move like the holograms of her time, but they were similarly used as reminders of people. She scanned them, and her heart tightened in her chest at the beautiful woman inside the frame. Her hair was as blond as Jon's, and her eyes smiled. In one, she was laughing with Cody. In another, holding Jon close against her. A final one, kissing Dr. Lansing. For a moment Celeste stared at their embrace and found her hand touching her lips. When Celeste turned, she saw Jon staring at her. "Is this your mother, Jon?"

He nodded, and the knob at his neck bobbed. The bleak expression on his face made it difficult to look at him.

"She's very beautiful."

He didn't say anything. Neither did Cody.

"Will you tell me about her sometime?"

Averting his gaze, Jon stared down at his shoes. She put a hand on his shoulder. Her skin felt scorched. So much was emanating from every pore in his body. It was a kind of pain Celeste had never experienced. She couldn't help but drain some of the negative emotion from him. She felt weakened by it, but he brightened a bit.

"It's all right, Jon, if you don't want to talk about her."

"I do." This from Cody. "I wanna talk about her, but I don't remember much 'cause I was two when she died."

"Does your father or sister speak of her?"

Finally, Jon said, "Nobody talks much about her anymore. We did at first."

"If you want to tell me about her, I'd love to know what she was like."

He nodded. To change the subject, Celeste wandered over to the bed. The covering was decorated with hats of some kind. A protective helmet with glossy decals on it. A cap. A big, wide-brimmed one; she had no idea what it was. Glancing off to the side, she saw the real things on a high shelf.

"I have a hat collection." Jon's tone was shy.

Because of the Domes, Celeste's society had no need for head coverings. "Will you tell me where they come from sometime?"

"Yeah, sure. If you stay around. Patty's leaving." Ah, the boy felt her loss, too.

Cody tugged on Celeste's hand. "Come on, my turn."

His room was more cluttered. On a big table sat a large, square box with water and…oh, my, he had flish in it. Real live flish. She'd only seen some replicas in Zoolawn. Crossing to the glass box, she stared at the little creatures moving and darting and coming up to the exterior. Her hand went to the glass. All those colors—orange, yellow, black and white.

"You like fish, Ms. Hart?" Cody asked.

"Indeed, I do."

"Cody snuck some frogs from outside to put in there, but one escaped." Jon giggled.

"What makes you laugh?"

"It ended up in Dad's bed."

Again Cody grinned. "Boy, was he mad."

Celeste laughed with them. The thought of Dr. Lansing pulling back sleeping covers and finding a slimy, jumping stoad in it did seem funny.

They examined more of Cody's space, then walked out into an open area on this floor with a video box, a second computer and books. The children called it a playroom though it wasn't self-contained. "Do you like to read?" she asked them.

"Yeah, sure." This from Jon.

"I don't know all the words yet." Cody grinned.

"Maybe we can read together before sleep time."

They bypassed Madison's room because Celeste preferred the girl to show it herself, then ended up in front of Dr. Lansing's private space.

"Maybe we shouldn't go in—" Before she could finish, Cody burst open the double doors and raced in. Again, Jon waited for her to enter before him.

Once inside, Celeste noted a huge bed, which appeared soft, even if it wasn't a conformer. On it was a cover with subtle greens all mixed together. It matched the color of a stripe around the middle of the walls. The floor was covered with wood.

She breathed in the scent of the room, and her skin tingled. Sometimes, the very space she occupied sent a wave of images through her, as they had at Craig Krueger's small dwelling. Briefly, she closed her eyes and could practically see Alex Lansing in here. Feel the texture of his clothes, see the contours of his body. Hear him breathe. A vision of naked shoulders swam before her eyes. Forcefully, she shook off the myriad feelings. Uncomfortably stirred by all the sensations, she eased them all out of Alex Lansing's masculine domain as quickly as she could.

When they reached the first floor, Mrs. Kramer was in the foyer, shrugging into an outer garment of knitted material. "I'm leaving. Dinner's on the counter in the kitchen. You don't have to wait for Maddy. She called to say she won't be home till seven."

"Thank you for all this, Mrs. Kramer." At least Celeste knew the mechanics of serving and cleaning up a meal. Alisha was right to make them learn this keeping of the house.

"Let's eat," Cody said as he ran into the kitchen. Jon followed more sedately. The sustenance was set out on the counter, and the boys served themselves. Celeste took small portions.

Sitting down at the table, she picked up the knife and fork. Cut the meat. Put it in her mouth. "Hmm." The cheesy chicken was tasty, the potatoes fluffy. She tried the round green things, and her nose wrinkled at their taste.

"We don't like brussel sprouts, either," Cody said, catching her reaction to them.

"But Dad says we have to eat them," the boy continued. "We could give them to a dog if we had one. I want a puppy for my birthday next month."

Her mind raced to keep up with him. Birthdays were an odd custom to her, because in her time, children came out of produceries and were never actually born. And what would it be like to have a drog in the home? How could she encourage Dr. Lansing to obtain one?

When they'd finished their meal, each boy brought his eating plate, utensils and drinking cup to the sink. Jon rinsed them in real water again—here she wouldn't be able to conserve it as they had at the Cromwell's. Then he put the plates in the washer of dishes. Celeste copied their actions, made the table clean and stored the rest of the food in the oven for Maddy, as Mrs. Kramer had instructed.

"What shall we do now?"

"Read to me?" Cody asked.

They went upstairs and she smiled as she watched Cody jump each step with two feet. He made a game of everything.

"I'm gonna go to my room," Jon said. "I have to study for exams."

She and Cody settled in the playroom, and he went to the book shelving — they were all over the home — and picked out a tome. *Harry Potter and the Chamber of Secrets.* She was unacquainted with the story.

"Dad keeps saying he's gonna read this with me but never gets around to it. Maddy read Jon and me the first Harry Potter book."

She began the strange tale and was fascinated by the wizards and all sorts of odd creatures that she didn't think even existed. On the soft couch, as she read, Cody inched over by degrees and cuddled into her.

Celeste's heart brimmed with emotion. There was nothing in her past that compared to the feeling of having a little boy sitting so close to her. *Motherhood* must be wonderful during these times.

They'd read four sections, called chapters, when she heard from below, "Hel-lo."

"We're up here, Mad," Cody called out.

In minutes, Madison Lansing appeared in the doorway. The girl was seventeen, but she looked older. She was tall and graceful, wore long hair with light-colored streaks in it, around a heart-shaped face. Her eyes were a dark blue.

"Hi, I'm Madison. Dad said the boys had somebody new tonight."

Standing, Celeste crossed to her. "I'm Celeste Hart." Purposefully, she held out her hand so she could read the girl.

Madison hesitated, then shook it.

Bombarded by Madison's feelings, Celeste had to grab the end of the desk to keep herself from stumbling backwards. Her own shoulders slumped, and her neck ached. Along with anxiety and sadness in this child was an overwhelming sense of weariness. Maddy Lansing was exhausted.

After Maddy excused herself, Celeste helped Cody into bed, checked on Jon, then went to the first floor and out of inside to sit on the porch. Seating herself on what she'd learned at Jess's was called a swing, she looked up at the stars. Their beauty usually calmed her, but her heart was full of conflicting emotions. The connection she felt with these children was strong already. And a yearning to ease their life—as well as their overworked father's—was stunning.

Alisha would be angry if she knew Celeste's line of thinking. Celeste wasn't here to do any of those things. Instead, she'd been assigned a task to complete, and her actions wouldn't ease the burdens of this already troubled family. Instead, what she had to do would increase them exponentially.

Closing her eyes, she forced herself to recall Rhea's announcement of what Celeste's work here would entail: *Whereas Dorian is to save the life of Jess Cromwell and insure his research continues, Celeste, you must destroy the life's work of Alex Lansing.*

CHAPTER 2

WHEN CELESTE RETURNED to the new dwelling they'd rented in Virginia about five miles from the Lansings, she found Dorian in the living space. Her friend looked cute in denims, a scooped-neck, sleeveless top and with a scarf covering her hair. She was taking down from the ceiling what was called cobwebs—Celeste didn't understand that nomenclature at all. They were told the place had been professionally cleaned, but Alisha wasn't happy with the dust that had gathered while it was empty and insisted they scour the place anyway. The scent of cleaning fluid tinged the air.

Dorian turned from her task. "Celi, hi. Let me call Alisha, and you can tell us how the test drive was."

Nord, even Dorian was using idioms. Celeste seemed to have the hardest time deciphering them.

In minutes, Alisha appeared, dressed similarly to Dorian. "How'd it go? Tell me you got the job, and I won't be so resentful of washing floors." She shook her head. "It was so much easier in our time with purified air. Having the apertures open brings in so much dirt."

Celeste smiled broadly. "I obtained the position. The two boys loved me, but Madison was remote. She says I'm not her caregiver." Celeste frowned. "She's overworked and exhausted."

Dorian took a sip of water from a cup. People of this time used *plastic* bottles, then threw them away, which was horrifying. The three of them tried to take as many steps as they could to conserve resources, and that included drinking and eating from reusable containers. "Maybe the girl needs a woman around. What's Dr. Lansing like in person?"

"A bit removed, though I read him well. He also has much conflict inside him. The loss of his spouse is saddening them all still."

"Which is one of the benefits of our time period." Alisha leaned up against a table. "No connections like that to haunt us."

"If you died, I'd feel sad." Celeste arched a brow. "As you would if I did. We have strong feelings, just not between men and women, like they do now."

A smile beamed from Dorian. "Those feelings are fine by me."

Celeste grinned at her friend. "Yeah, I hear you Skyping with Luke every night." None of them expected staid, sensible Dorian to fall madly in love with a man from the present.

"It's fun." Dorian's eyes twinkled. "And it can be sexy."

Dropping down on one of the couches Alisha and Dorian had purchased while she was gone, Celeste felt the softness of the material called microfiber. "This is nice, by the way." The new furniture had been delivered when she was out.

"Back to the matter at hand." Alisha's gaze narrowed on her. "Did you get any insight into the storage of his research?"

"He has a lab and office at Global Pharmaceuticals. As we know, he prefers to work at home. Presumably because, as the computeller told us, his previous work was stolen. I visited the office briefly, but he keeps the room locked when he's not in residence."

"Mostly, you'll be at the dwelling when he isn't; you'll be able to gain access to the space."

She nodded. Alisha's observation was true. "I'll have to be careful though. The boys are quick-witted and the girl is astute."

"Just don't forget what's at stake. We need to determine where he is in his research and what's next. Megadamn, I wish those particular chips weren't corroded. It's like operating blind." She gestured to Celeste's clothing. "Go change now. We have to finish cleaning the space before dinner."

Not a pleasant job. While she tackled it, she'd think about the Lansing children. And maybe Dr. Lansing himself.

• • •

PATTY MASON'S LAST day of work was Thursday, and Celeste began her job in an official capacity for the Lansing children on Friday night, one week after the interview. The meal had been a delicious dish called stuffed ziti, the scent still lingering in the air. Dr. Lansing didn't join them; had a date—a way of getting to know each other and a precursor to sexual release. As she rinsed the supper dishes, she wondered what kind of woman he preferred in this dating ritual. Would he and the female join tonight?

"Got the hang of that?"

Startled, she whirled around at the sound of his deep voice.

A soft smile broached his lips. "Sorry. Didn't mean to sneak up on you."

At the sight of him, her eyes widened. He was dressed in the fanciest male clothing she'd ever seen: stark black pants, a white shirt and a form-fitting jacket. He also sported a neck thing—a tie—the Cromwell men often wore, only his was fastened differently.

"Something wrong?" he asked at her long perusal.

"You look beautiful."

His face reddened. "Well…thanks. I'm not sure anyone has ever told me that." He nodded to the dishwasher. "Jon said he had to show you how to use that last time you were here."

"Yes, we never had one growing up." For obvious reasons.

"Not when you were married, either?"

"No, I prefer simple things." She chuckled. "Dorian says I *am* simple."

"Dorian?"

"My sister."

"Ah. You said you have two, right?"

"Dorian and Alisha."

"I hope to meet them some time. The boys have been asking for you to come again, though they adored Patty, and we'll miss her, but they like you Celeste."

"I like them, too." Trying not to stare at him, she glanced at the clock. "Madison isn't home."

He jammed his hands in his pockets and leaned against the counter. "She's too busy. She works too hard."

"Like you."

Silence. Oh, dear.

"I-I shouldn't have said that."

"No, you're right, I do work too hard."

"Why?"

Wide shoulders shrugged. Once again, they distracted her. "For one thing, my work is interesting and exciting. I was more detached before…." He paused. "Ever since Lila died… I don't know. It's easier to work."

Than to feel, she thought. "I'm sure it is. I saw the likenesses of her in Jon's room, Dr. Lansing. She must have loved you all very much."

He swallowed hard. "She did."

The crank of the garage door.

"That must be Maddy." He looked to the back entrance, which was down a short hallway. "I'm glad she's home."

The door opened and closed. Dressed similarly to Celeste in capris and knitted shirt, Madison walked into the kitchen with slumped shoulders and a weary tilt to her head. "Sorry, I'm..." Her eyes narrowed when she caught sight of her father. "Where are you going?"

"Out with Sherry to a benefit at the Kennedy Center."

Madison flushed with emotions which radiated from her. Her feelings practically shimmered in the air. "Dad, you said you'd help with the research for my final science project."

"Oh, honey, I forgot." He shook his head, his jaw tight and his brow furrowed. "I'd cancel, but Sherry was involved in the planning and..."

Madison's shoulders stiffened now. "Never mind."

"How about tomorrow?"

"I'm leaving with my youth group for that retreat. It's why I have to finish the research tonight."

Feeling sorry for them, Celeste straightened. "Perhaps I could help."

The teenager shot her a disgusted look. The blast of it had her backing up against the counter. "Not unless you know anything about synthetic food."

Celeste gave a small smile. "As it happens, I do. One of my sisters is a specialist in nutrition. She's done some work in the field of food supplements."

Madison remained rock-faced.

"Give me a chance. I can call her and see what she recommends."

The girl said, "Yeah, whatever," and started out.

Dr. Lansing grabbed her arm. "I am sorry."

"I know, Dad." As she walked away, Madison said, "You always are."

"You need to eat," he called after her, but Madison kept walking.

"I'll make sure that she consumes some food."

He looked pained. "Is your sister a dietician?"

"Of sorts. She has great knowledge of foods." She arched a brow. "I wouldn't lie about that."

"I hope not. Dishonesty is something I particularly abhor. I've had bad experiences with that in my work."

Because she could sense he meant his words, and because she was being utterly dishonest with him, she shifted uncomfortably. "Have a nice night."

After Dr. Lansing left, Celeste did a quick check on the boys and then locked herself in the bathing room. She whipped out the computeller and called Dorian. She purchased a cell phone but she liked to see who she talked to.

Dorian's screen came on. She was in her nightwear, a pale lavender set of pajamas. "Hey, Celi. Hi."

"Are you busy?"

"No." She glanced around. "I'm quite bored, as a matter of fact. This research into the other drugs on the market of the type Dr. Lansing is developing is tedious. And mind-boggling." She focused on Celeste. "Is something wrong? You appear concerned."

"Don't tell Alisha, but I'm beginning to care about these younglings."

"And the hunky Dr. Lansing?"

Oh, Nord. "Hunky? What does that mean?"

"It means what he looks like."

"You can't be saying what I'm thinking. In any case, not him. The younglings are wonderful. I can't wait to spend more time with them."

"Any ideas about getting access to Lansing's work?"

Which is so important to him. "No." Before Dorian could pursue her questioning, Celeste said, "I have a favor to ask. I know you researched food experiments of this time period that led to the kind of nourishment in our society. Do you happen to have the websites that came from?"

"I can find the sources with a few clicks on the computeller. Why?"

"For the oldest child's science project."

"Celeste!" she heard from upstairs.

"I think I hear one of the children. I have to go. Can I have the sites soon?"

"Thirty minutes, tops. It's not rocket science."

"Thanks. Send it to my electric-mail account. See you later."

Thirty minutes later, after dealing with Cody's distress over one of his flish, who wasn't eating, Celeste walked down to Madison's room. She hadn't had to wait long to get Dorian's information, and when she did, she used the computer in the playroom to print the articles off. She couldn't risk connecting the computeller to the archaic machine, so Dorian had sent the sources to Celeste's new email address.

Her steps slowed as she thought of her mission. She would have trouble accessing Dr. Lansing's private machine because he kept the door secured. But if he was still out on his date after the children went to bed, maybe then she could try to find a way to enter his work space. She ignored the actual

22

clutch in her heart at the thought of destroying Alex Lansing's life's work.

Once she reached Madison's door, she knocked and heard a soft, "Come in."

Celeste entered. She'd yet to visit this space, as Madison hadn't invited her in the last time Celeste had been in the house. The window was open, and the scent of spring flowers wafted in. Madison was seated at a beautiful, white desk. Her bed was made of the same wood. Shades of the color purple — dark, lavender, lilac, mauves the likes of which Celeste hadn't seen before — blended in everywhere from the floor covering to the walls and upholstery. Maddy's pajamas matched the color scheme.

"What a lovely room."

"Thanks. Mom helped me decorate it."

"It must remind you of special times."

The girl's blue eyes flashed with grief. On impulse, Celeste crossed to her and placed a hand on her shoulder.

Madison startled, then almost instantly her shoulders relaxed, and Celeste felt some of the sadness flow out of her. Celeste drew back with a sick feeling in her stomach.

"I…I have something for you."

"What?"

"Copies of the articles my sister sent me. I printed them off for you."

"Already?"

"Yes. She wasn't engaged in any activity when I phoned her, and she sent them through email on my network account. Your father gave me permission to use the computer in the playroom."

Cautiously, Madison took the papers and stared down at them. Her brow furrowed as her father's did when he was thoughtful. "Wow, this is great. It'll save me hours of work."

"I'm pleased, then."

Her eyes were wide and ingenuous when she looked up. "It's not cheating to use what someone else found, is it?"

"What did your instructor say?"

"To take notes from articles on our topics. They're due Monday. Dad was going to help me find them."

"Then I think it's acceptable that I procured them for you if your father was approved to help. And you'll do as your teacher instructed and take the notes yourself."

"Thanks, Ms. Hart."

"You can call me Celi, Madison. I told the boys that, too."

"Okay." She turned back to the desk.

"I'm going to spend some time with them. Call if you need me." As she reached the door, she was thinking about how Dr. Lansing should spend more time with Madison. It made her ask, "Madison, you're familiar with today's slang. What does hunky mean?"

The girl had looked over her shoulder. "You're kidding right?" When Celeste shook her head, Maddy said, "Great looking. Sexy. Very masculine. It's an old people's term though. Kids say *hot*."

Hmm, those descriptors described her father perfectly. Unfortunately, Celeste kept thinking about him in that formal wear until she found the boys in the playroom. "You're ready for bed?"

Cody's eyes danced. "I told Jon if we did it ourselves we'd have more time for Pictionary."

Celeste nodded. When they explained the gist of it to her, she knew she'd be incompetent at it because she'd have to draw a picture of whatever was on the card, and Celeste wouldn't know what some of those things were. But she gave it a good try. What the hellor were bicycles, and parasols and handcuffs?

Cody took evil pleasure in trouncing her. Jon tried to help. They played until nine, ate ice cream of the chocolate flavor, which Celeste thought was the best thing she'd ever tasted. Then she helped the boys to bed.

Snuggling in, Cody looked up at her from the pillow. "I like it when you're here, Celi."

"Me, too."

He bit his lip. "Can you, um, kiss my head?"

"Please repeat."

His eyes started to droop and he said sleepily, "Mom used to do it."

It seemed like the most natural thing in the world to bend over and touch her lips to his forehead. Her heart was so full she thought it might burst. Had any simple gesture ever made her happier?

When she turned away from the bed, the lighted aquarium caught her attention. Nearly a dozen little flish darted and glided through the water. The blue-striped one that Cody had worried about earlier seemed to notice her and came to the glass. She bent down and stared him in the eyes. He blinked at her — his hello — making her laugh.

She left the child's room, and peeking in from the doorway, she found Jon in his bed. "What are you reading?"

"*Old Yeller*."

"Want me to read with you?"

"I'm not a baby like Cody." She didn't need to be a sensitive to detect the yearning in his tone.

"I know. *I'd* like to read with you."

A small smile, then he scooted over. "I guess it's okay."

Celeste settled next to Jon, thinking how wonderful this position as a caregiver was.

• • •

ALEX ENTERED THE house to find the downstairs dark and empty. Supper smells—hmm, Ann's ziti—hovered in the kitchen, and he wondered if Maddy had eaten. He'd left Sherry's party early because of his daughter. Sherry had been vocally unhappy, but Alex felt like an inadequate father for letting Maddy down, so he'd come home now, at nine o'clock.

Taking the stairs two at a time, he headed down the kids' hall and stopped at Jon's open door. He found his son close to Celeste on the bed, while she read from a book. For a moment, he was speechless because the image brought back so many memories of Lila reading with Jon.

Celeste said, "And then old Yeller…" Her choked voice trailed off.

Jon grasped her arm. "Are you crying, Celi?"

Celi?

"No, of course not."

"You are."

A half smile. A pouty lip. "I'm misty-eyed. This is sad."

"Yeah, but it's not real."

"Hello, there."

Celeste glanced up. Her eyes were liquid and shining, making them an even purer blue. "Dr. Lansing." She blushed a pretty shade of pink. It…distracted him. "You said you wouldn't be back until much later."

"I know. I came home early to help Maddy."

"She'll be pleased."

"You two look like you're having fun."

"We're just about finished with the chapter."

"I didn't know you still liked to be read to, Jon."

His son shrugged. "I do. Sometimes."

"Good to know. I'll leave you to it." For some reason, the sight of Jon and Celeste, heads bowed, intent on the book unnerved him. For some reason, tonight he found Celeste extremely pretty. Huh! she thought *he* was beautiful!

Hell of a thing, he said to himself as he strode to Maddy's room, knocked and opened the door. She was folding clothes into a suitcase and looked up. "Dad? What are you doing home?"

"I left the party to help with your research."

"You did?"

He loosened the tie of his tux. "Yeah." He glanced at her desk, then back at her.

"I'm done with it."

"So soon?"

For the first time in a long time, his daughter's face brightened like a normal kid's. "Celi helped me. Her sister emailed her some articles and I got so much information out of them I finished in half the time I thought it would take." She cocked her head at his frown. "It's okay she got me the articles, isn't it?"

"Yeah, sure. So long as you did the note taking and understand what you found."

"I did. You could, um, go back to your party."

"No." He hitched a hip on her desk. "I'd rather be with you."

"You would?"

Holy hell. When had it gotten so bad that his own daughter would ask a question like that? "Yes, of course. I picked up a pint of Chocolate Decadence—your favorite. Want to share some?"

"I would, Daddy." She linked her arm with his and laid her head on his shoulder. "Thanks."

"For what?"

"Coming home."

They'd just finished the treat when Celeste walked into the kitchen. "Jon's nearly asleep." She glanced at the clock. "Are you staying home, Dr. Lansing?"

"Yes."

"Then I'll take my leave. I can catch the eleven o'clock transit."

Transit? "The bus? At this hour?"

"Yes. It's still nice out of in…outdoors. I enjoy walking at night. There are stars in the sky when it's dark."

How odd.

"Celeste, you're not taking a bus alone this late."

Madison added, "Dad, she shouldn't."

He stood. "I'll drive you home. Maddy's here for the kids."

"I could babysit more, Dad." She glanced at Celeste. "Not that I don't like you."

Alex shook his head. "No way. The boys aren't your responsibility. You already have too much on your plate." He winked at Celeste. "Besides, I think I'd have a riot on my hands if I stopped having *Celi* stay with the guys. She's won over the Lansing men, I think."

Maddy squeezed Celeste's arm. "Thanks a lot for the help."

Celeste covered Maddy's hand. "I'm glad you feel better."

Again, an odd response.

"Get some rest and have a good weekend at your camp."

"When are you coming back?" Maddy asked.

Alex said, "I was going to ask you if you could fill in for Ann on Monday. She has some doctors' appointments and I'd like to give her the whole day off."

"Yes, of course. See you then, Madison."

He waited until Celeste preceded him out the door and to the car. The peach-colored capris and a matching shirt looked nice with her reddish hair. And from this angle, she filled them out…well, nicely. She was very fit and had told him she ran outside every day.

She seemed surprised when he opened the car door for her, as if no man had shown her the courtesy before. And she sighed when she sank onto the seats. Maybe the kids had tired her out.

Nonplussed, he circled the hood and slid inside. He caught her scent then—clean and fresh, as if she used bath splash and not perfume, as most women did.

"This is a sound vehicle," she said, scanning the interior.

"Hmm."

"What is it called?"

"Excuse me?"

"What kind of vehicle is it?"

"A Prius. One of those hybrids that's better for the environment."

She stiffened. "Hybrid auto vehicles aren't enough to curb carbons. Their emissions still damage the ozone layer irreparably and, combined with other forms of air contamination, will have disastrous results if society doesn't do something about pollution."

"Do you have a science degree?"

"What?"

"Knowledge of food supplies. Your attitude toward the car. You talk like a scientist."

She scowled. "No, just a concerned citizen. I think Madison has all the potential of a scientist, though. Like her father," she added.

Was that a change of subject? "Maybe."

"What kind of research do you do, Dr. Lansing?"

"I've been working for almost a decade on a drug called Equisex that enhances sexual potency. It's groundbreaking because it's for both men and women."

"I wonder why your society needs those kinds of drugs?"

"Trying to put me out of a job?" he joked.

"No, it's just that people seem to enjoy mating, so I don't understand why you need drugs to do it."

His car veered into the other lane. *Mating? Seems to enjoy?* He blurted out, "Didn't you and your husband enjoy sex?"

"Yes, of course. I phrased that incorrectly. English is my second language, so sometimes I get words wrong. Tell me why is it that you focus on sex instead of other needs of society — poverty is appalling, energy supplies scarce and universal health care limited."

This was a common reaction to his work and raised his hackles. He could feel his pulse speed up, and he was about to go into his defense when she touched his arm. "I don't mean that as a criticism. I really want to know."

Her words calmed him down. "I agree there are a lot of problems in society. But sexual fulfillment is one of the highest priorities of people and helps alleviate the stress all those others things cause. Besides, sex is a natural drive. Doctors like me are just trying to extend people's participation and enjoyment of what's an innate need in us." He was proud of what he'd done. "And soon the clinical trials will show I've got the side effects almost obliterated."

"Some side effects of a drug can never be fully predicted. Especially with one-generation testing."

For a minute he was confused. "There are no more generations to try it on, Celeste."

"Hmm."

Again her patronizing tone pushed his buttons. "You know, the drug isn't just for older people. Because of widespread use of medicine for depression, elevated cholesterol and high blood pressure, and treatments such as chemotherapy, many people are prevented from enjoying sex."

She didn't say anything else, and it pissed him off again. "I think I'm contributing to the health and well-being of mankind."

"I can see that."

He shot her an angry glance. "What? That I believe it, or that I am?"

"I..."

In the darkness illuminated only by a few street lamps, a car darted out of a side street and pulled in front of Alex. He was forced to swerve to the shoulder of the road and slam on the brakes. Despite her seatbelt, Celeste pitched to the right and banged her head on the window with a thud. The other driver kept going.

"Celeste?" Alex grasped her arm. "Are you all right?"

Her eyes closed, she moaned. Quickly, he took her pulse at the base of her neck. Steady, not too fast. His hand was still on her arm, so he felt her trembling increase. "Celeste?"

She whimpered.

"Are you injured?"

"My head hurts." Her voice was incredibly shaky. "I never..." She trailed off, and in the light from a street lamp right overhead, he could see her pale color and bluish lips.

"Oh, damn, you don't drive because of what happened to your husband." Again, he scanned her. "You're shivering, badly. Must be shock." Undoing his seatbelt, then hers, he drew her to him, as much as the gearshift allowed. His arms banded around her to warm her up some. "I'm sorry."

Her entire body folded into him. She was frightened and disoriented, he told himself as she burrowed into his chest. His hand went to her hair. He soothed her, murmured calming words.

Suddenly, he was besieged by a myriad of emotions he hadn't felt in a long time. Joy at how good she felt. A stirring of awareness of her curves and indentations. A sense of... expectation.

Damn it, she'd been hurt. And he was acting like some horny teenage boy. He shoved away the emotions and concentrated on comforting her.

CHAPTER 3

JON WATCHED CELESTE from his place at the table. Studied her, really, so she asked, "Do I have something on my face, Jon?"

He shook his head. "It's better already. When you got here this morning, Dad was surprised at how much better your head is. He said he'd never seen somebody heal that fast, and he's a doctor. Now, the bump and black-and-blue parts are almost gone."

Remembering the stock answer she and the women had agreed on, Celeste said, "I have good genes. So do my sisters. We always healed twice as fast as anyone else when we were young."

"I think it's cool." Cody grinned around a sandwich made of butter from peanuts and a sweet gel-like substance. "I wish I was like that 'cause I always get scraped up."

"I have some salve a friend of mine developed. Next time either of you gets a cut, I'll show you how fast it works." She glanced at the clock. "Now you've had a snack; want to play outside or do homework?" Silly question, she knew. But they liked to pretend with her and she enjoyed the game.

"Hmm…"

"Maybe…"

"Play outside?" she suggested.

They headed to the backyard and she stopped on the patio. Once again—she never took this for granted—she reveled in the sun on her face, the rich loam of overturned earth and the aroma of real, live flowers. In one corner of the lot was a professionally built apparatus with ropes, and seats, and ladders and poles to slide down.

Turning, she checked for the boys. Cody was rushing over to the set. Sometimes, Jon played on it with him, but today he'd retrieved a glove and a ball, which he began tossing up in the air.

"Jon? Want to throw that back and forth with me?"

"Play catch, you mean?"

I guess I do. She didn't know the terms for most of their sports, but she'd watched some videos on their athletics, especially baseball because she knew Jon participated in the sport. The game seemed completely useless, hitting a tiny ball with a stick while others tried to catch it. The team members didn't even look like they were having much fun. "Yes, I mean play catch."

"Okay. We got an extra glove." He disappeared into the garage, and when he came out, Jon gave her a small smile. "We'll start out close. In case, you know, you don't do so good."

She hid a grin. She exercised regularly through running and lifting weights that Alisha had bought for them all to use. "That's probably wise."

Out in the grass, he tossed her the ball. She caught it easily and tossed it back to him.

Jon lengthened the distance between them, and Celeste began to throw the ball harder. Play began in earnest. Celeste ran to catch his tosses, stretched and skidded, slid to reach the ball and fell on her butt. Moisture appeared on her forehead and under her arms — she was sweating. Though it had happened occasionally in New York, the sensation was still a phenomenon to her because people of her time didn't perspire. Air in the Dome was purified and temperature controlled.

Jon seemed to be having a great time, too.

Then Cody joined in. It was a kind of fun Celeste had never experienced and she savored it, savored them — these children who she was beginning to care deeply for.

• • •

ALEX WAS DISTRACTED by the laughter and shouts in the backyard, which his office faced. He'd been up most of the night because late yesterday he'd gotten word that his clinical trials for Equisex would begin this week. The primary investigator, Charles Ravel, had finished choosing the participants. Alex rubbed his neck as the giggles from outside floated into the office. Finally, he went to the window to see what was going on.

Jon, Celeste and Cody were playing on the grass. He watched, mesmerized by Celeste. Today she wore soft, cropped jeans and a formfitting white T-shirt. Her motions were utterly graceful. She threw the ball like a pro. Her catching wasn't as good, but she could run at lightning speed. Once again, he wondered how she kept in such good shape. Really good shape. He knew from when he'd held her in the car the night of the accident she was well toned all over. And she told him she and her sisters exercised regularly.

Go out and play with them, darling. It'll be fun.

No, we used to do that with the kids.

It's been three years. You need to move on.

Chiding himself for his whimsy — he knew he was giving himself permission and not talking to his dead wife-Alex left his den, locked it and hustled upstairs to get his sneakers on and change into shorts.

When he joined them outside, he said teasingly, "Hey, you're making so much noise, I couldn't work."

Celeste's face fell. As he got to know her better, her emotions became easy to read. Funny thing, it seemed mutual. Often she verbalized exactly what was in his brain. Or his heart.

"I wasn't complaining," he was quick to add. "I liked hearing you out here having fun."

"Oh. Good."

His youngest son ran toward him and leaped into Alex's arms. "You gonna play with us, Dad?"

"If you'll have me."

"Celi's not bad." Jon, too, had an all-too-rare lightness about him. Since Celeste had come into their lives, she seemed to have that effect on his sons and his daughter. And him. "She can throw real hard."

"So I saw." He smiled at her. "Let's give her a run for her money."

Cocking her head, she looked at him strangely, and he was struck again at how often she did that—seemed confused about something he said. But the kids tugged them out to play and he forgot about it.

Alex took the bat and sent several pop flies to the two little boys. He hit a high one to a very grown-up woman, who reached to catch it, revealing a small patch of skin on her stomach; he couldn't tear his gaze from the sight of it.

They divided into teams of one adult and one kid and played a game of sorts. When he slid to home base when Celeste was covering it, they collided and fell in a heap on the ground. Her laughter told him she was unhurt, but as she sprawled on the grass, partly entangled with him, he was hit by a sharp blast of desire. He managed to turn away from them all until he got himself under control.

They played a while longer, then he said, "I think it's time to go inside and start homework."

"No, Dad."

"Aw, come on."

"Let's do as your dad says. We've been out here a long time."

"But he never plays with us." This from Jon.

The complaint cut deeply into his father's heart, though having Celeste here made him realize what the kids were saying was true. "I'll be better with that, son, I promise."

After she served lemonade, Alex shooed the guys upstairs to do their homework. Celeste faced him in the kitchen, where he was drinking some water to cool himself off.

Standing by the sink, she sipped the lemonade and closed her eyes to savor it. "Mmm."

His body reacted to the sound. Damn it. Not again. Quickly, he sat down at the table.

She grinned over at him. "Mrs. Kramer cooks your dinner meals. I can do it tonight."

"No thanks. I asked you to stay till five, and it's past that. Besides, if I cancel the pizza order, there'll be mutiny among the ranks."

"Pizza?" Her face lit up.

To the point where he laughed out loud. "Want to stay for some?"

Her blue eyes narrowed. "I shouldn't intrude on an evening alone with the children. They say you rarely eat with them."

Jesus.

"They'll love having you stay."

"If you're sure. I want to. I'll go check on them and see if I can help with their schoolwork."

"I'll call for the delivery." He watched her leave with that graceful sway to her hips and alluring sight of her ass encased in denim.

To distract himself, he stood and began emptying the dishwasher. Since Celeste came, dishes were in cupboards where they didn't belong. He was wondering why she hadn't figured out which dishes went where when a knock on the back door distracted him. He went to open it. "Ann, hello. You don't have to knock."

His housekeeper smiled at him. "I know. I saw you inside and didn't want to startle you."

He got a good look at her face. The lines there seemed more pronounced today. As a matter of fact, she'd seemed tired lately. "Are you all right?"

"Yes. Just tired. I'd like to talk to you, Dr. Lansing." Old school, she refused to call him by his first name, though he'd told her to several times.

"Of course." They sat at the table. Close up, the fatigue was even more visible.

The woman wrung her hands and he noticed how papery and blue veined they were. "You know how much I love the children. And like working for you."

"We feel the same about you."

"I haven't wanted to bring this up, but I've also had some conflicting feelings. My daughter lives in Indiana, and some-times I wish I could retire there with her and her family."

"Really? Why haven't you said anything before?"

"Because I couldn't abandon you and the children. Espe-cially after Mrs. Lansing died." He knew Ann and his wife had become friends and that Ann had mourned Lila's loss deeply.

"Did you find out something at your doctor's appointment?" He grasped her hand. "Are you ill?"

"No. I'm in good health. Actually, Celeste is the reason I brought this up."

Could Ann *dislike* Celeste so much she'd make him choose between the two of them? He was startled to wonder which woman he'd pick. "What do you mean?"

"She's wonderful with the children, and so likable. I thought maybe she could take my place. Otherwise I wouldn't have broached this."

The bump in his chest said he liked the idea of having Celeste here full time. Every day. "Either way, you should do what's best for yourself."

"I hope she'll take the job. Maybe she can move in here, even though I didn't want to. That whole third floor could be an apartment. I think it's…time to use it again."

Move in here. Hmm. The thought of Celeste living under his roof was not at all unpleasant.

• • •

CELESTE SAVORED THE spicy sauce, the thick dough and pepperoni, which she'd never known existed. Alisha had objected to them eating pizza, and the Cromwells weren't big fans either. A giggle from the end of the table distracted her and she glanced up. "What?"

"You closed your eyes when you took a bite," Jon said. "You act like you've never had pizza before."

"Of course I have."

"Now that Jon brought it up, I never saw anybody savor pizza quite like you." Alex said the words with a twinkle in his eyes. He was more handsome when he teased, if that was possible. And more sexy. She thought of the way he'd looked reaching for a ball. He was long and lean in his tan shorts and yellow shirt. And now, that late-day sun came in through the window and highlighted the gold strands on his head. The memory of him sprawled out on the grass with her made her warm.

"I...enjoy sensual experiences." She'd learned how to make her voice haughty. "All kinds."

Alex's dark eyes narrowed on her, full of something else now. Which she recognized, though she hadn't seen it on a man's face since she came here. Pure male interest, the kind of expression men whom she met to join wore.

"Maddy's always worried about calories," Jon said, chowing down a big mouthful. "And how much she weighs."

"It's important to be strong and fit, not to be skinny. Especially by those standards I see in newsprint and on the video box." Celeste wrinkled her nose. "I don't understand the attitude in today's women. I don't *get* it," she emphasized.

Alex put a glass of the rich red wine to his lips. Celeste refused any; she told him she didn't drink much. Instead, she sipped her soda, which was deliciously sweet.

After a bit, Alex faced her. "I have something I need to talk to you all about."

Celeste stiffened. "It sounds serious." She hoped she hadn't done anything wrong.

"I know we all like Ann Kramer. She's been with us since Jon was born. But she's getting older and has a daughter she'd like to spend more time with. So she's thinking about leaving us."

"Oh, no." Celeste felt her stomach pitch. "I'm sorry. She's so nice."

"Apparently, she's wanted to go live with her daughter for a long time but hasn't wanted to tell us…to abandon us, she said."

"But she wants to leave now?" Celeste asked.

Alex gaze was intent on her. "Yes, because of you."

Her heart fisted in her chest and she clapped a hand over it. "H-have I offended her somehow? If I have, I can—"

"No, it's just the opposite. She thinks you're terrific."

Everyone stared at him.

"So much so she wants you, Celeste, to take her place so she'll feel comfortable resigning."

A thousand thoughts whirled through Celeste's head. How good it would be to spend more time here. How much she liked the children and Alex. How fortuitous it was that Ann would want to leave now. Or was it?

One theory of time travel is that if a traveler goes back into the past and changes something, it was meant to happen that way. Could it be true that if she hadn't backtracked to this century, Ann Kramer wouldn't have left the Lansings? Was Celeste supposed to be here? To accomplish her goal? The paradox made her head spin.

"So, what does everyone think?" Alex asked.

"I think it's great," Jon put in.

"Me, too," Cody added. "Gosh, Celi, you could even live here with us. Mrs. Kramer didn't want to, but we have a whole third floor where you could stay."

"Mrs. Kramer suggested the same thing." Alex's voice was even.

Her gaze swung to him. Celeste tried to tell herself she was thrilled about this idea because it would make completing her task here so much easier. But by the godheads, she wasn't thinking about sabotaging Dr. Lansing's research, because she hated the idea of it. Instead, she was thinking about him and the children. "What's your opinion, Dr. Lansing?"

"I must confess. I stacked the deck here, telling you in front of the kids."

Put cards one on top of the other?

Alex looked wary. Without her even voicing the question, he explained, "It means I told you in front of the kids because I knew they'd be excited."

"Would *you* want me here every day?"

He kept his face neutral. "Yes, *Celi*, I would." He cleared his throat and held her gaze. "And I think it's time you started calling me Alex."

CHAPTER 4

BRIMMING WITH EXCITEMENT, Alex stood when Charles Ravel walked into his office at Global Pharmaceuticals to discuss the first of the clinical trials. He said to the tall, thin, white-haired man, "Good morning, Dr. Ravel. Thanks for meeting me here."

"No problem." Ravel was legendary for running a tight ship with his protocols for each phase of the trials. "I'm glad to meet you. I've been interested in your work."

That was good since this guy was not only responsible for conducting the trials but had access to and control over the data gathered. He also had the right to publish the results and submit the trial information to the FDA, even if the results weren't good and Alex didn't want them made public. "Thank you. Have a seat."

After sitting down, Ravel set his briefcase down on the other side of Alex's oak desk and drew out a folder. Staring at it, Alex was hit by the knowledge that the three clinical trials were finally going to happen: the first for safety, the second for efficacy and the third for comparison to other drugs on the market. But if Alex's baby didn't pass the safety hurdle, it was dead in the water.

Ravel put on reading glasses. The rays of sun coming in from the back window bounced off of them. "I realize you know this inside out, but we have to go over the specifications of each trial. He handed Alex an outline of the first set.

"Since this is the smallest of the three trials, we have twenty-four research subjects, half men and half women ranging from twenty-six to sixty-five. The study will run for three months."

Alex nodded.

"If the treatment appears safe then we'll have a larger number participate in the second and third trials."

"I understand."

"For the first trial, patients will meet with us six times, and different tests will happen in each one. All, of course, are geared to how safe this drug is."

"Will I know the dates of the meetings?"

"They're on the outline."

Alex read one of the columns to himself: "For Clinical Trial One on safety, checks with participants will be held June 12, July 3, July 24, August 8, September 12 and October 3."

Alex scanned the list of what would happen at each. "So, tomorrow is the preliminary physical exam, data gathering and inventory of each participant. Then they're given the instructions and drugs for the first three weeks."

"Yes. We'll have some data in early July when the dose is the lowest, but more significant results will come in on the 24th after we've upped the dosage to its suggested use."

"I don't see preliminary data, right?" Damn, he hated being kept in the dark.

The man held his gaze. "Unless the results indicate there's any danger to the participants. Then you'll know everything."

Alex suppressed an intake of breath. It was important to show confidence.

"Look, Dr. Lansing, we don't expect any negative results. From what I can tell, you're going to change the future of human sexuality with this drug. Just be cognizant of unforeseen circumstances." He stood. "I think that's it. I'll be in touch every three weeks to let you know if we're proceeding."

If. As he watched Ravel walk out, Alex gripped the edge of the desk. He'd devoted a decade of his life to this research, at the expense of his family, he was coming to see. And damn it, he wanted success now. Success that had been snatched away from him ten years ago when he was looking the other way.

He thought about Celeste's negative reaction…

Tell me why is it that you focus on sex instead of other needs of society – poverty is appalling, energy supplies scarce and universal health care limited…

Some side effects of a drug can never be fully predicted. Especially with one-generation testing.

He couldn't figure out why her obvious disapproval for his research affected him. Or even why she felt that way. Most of the women he knew found his research into sexuality, well, sexy.

Hell, why was he thinking of Celeste anyway? After his reaction to her physically the other day, he needed to keep her at a distance. She was moving in tomorrow to live in his home and take care of his children. That was all she could mean to him—though, of course, he liked and respected her. Otherwise, he wouldn't have entrusted her with his kids.

When he was ready to leave his office, he gathered his things and locked his desk and cabinets, then secured the door. Some people thought he was paranoid about security here, even though he did the analysis of his lab testing at home. But he'd been sabotaged once and wouldn't be again.

Only Lila had kept the blackness from engulfing him then. And the impotence of not being able to do a damn thing about the situation ate away at him. Nope, never again.

Hell, who cared what Celeste Hart thought? His advancements in the field of sexual-enhancement drugs were going to make mankind's future a lot brighter.

• • •

DORIAN LAY ON the bed as Celeste packed all the clothes they'd purchased together, with Helen as advisor. "I'm glad you've achieved so much in such a short time, Celi, but I'm sad that you'll be leaving our new home. I'll miss you."

"You feel bad because you miss Luke, and you don't have enough to do here."

Dorian nodded. "As I said, the research we're conducting on sexual-enhancement drugs of the past is tedious, and their methods of determining safety, even now, are archaic." In the future, the Multimed screened drugs for efficacy and safety, though, in truth, there weren't many chemicals used in their time. "I could have done this work from New York, too."

Looking restless, Dorian stared into space, then rolled off the bed. She wore a red outfit of one piece that went well with her dark hair. Her friend preferred bold colors, whereas Celeste preferred the pastels, like the light yellow of the skirt and blouse she wore today.

Dorian approached a lower table that held the hygiene products Celeste hadn't packed yet. When she opened a jar, the scent of real, live flowers wafted out. Dorian sniffed and said, "I'll never get used to the smells here."

"Some are worth forgetting."

"I know. But we have these, too." She held up the jar.

Turning from her task, Celeste cocked her head. "Why are you delaying asking me something?" She sensed her friend's internal excitement.

Dorian went to the bedroom door and closed it. "Next week, Jess is getting an award from the Environmental Research Institute in Washington, D.C. He's coming to town with Helen to receive it."

"Ah, I understand." Celeste smiled genuinely at Dorian. "And Luke wants to accompany him to visit you."

"Yes. I long to see him. The ceremony will take place in a hotel and he suggested we all attend."

Celeste gave her a knowing smile. "A hotel? A building that contains rooms for people to sleep in, as well as entertainment and meeting rooms."

"Well, if I don't come home with Alisha…"

Celeste zipped up the bag and set it on the floor. She faced Dorian. "You want my help in convincing her to allow this to happen."

"Yes." Dorian raised her chin. "Though we really don't need her permission."

"But it would be nice to have. We've always compromised and rarely cross each other despite how didactic Alisha can be." She picked up another leather satchel Helen had called a traveling case. It was smaller than the two others and held bottles and such. "Maybe we can think of something to sweeten the dish."

Dorian laughed aloud. "Sweeten the *pot*. I'll ask Luke for suggestions." Her cell phone rang. "Speak of the devil."

Celeste held up one finger and waved it in the air. "I know that one. It's when you name something, and it appears. In ancient times, people believed that if you uttered the devil's name, you would summon him." She frowned. "What an odd concept…the devil."

Dorian answered the phone. "Hello, love." She reached for the door again, and just as she opened it, she found Alisha about to knock.

Celeste giggled. "Again, speak of the devil."

• • •

ALISHA KNEW HER two friends were up to something. And she'd bet her last diamond on the fact that she wasn't going to like it. So when Dorian said into the cell phone, "I'll call you back; I don't have an answer yet," Alisha sighed. More and more, she disliked being the sensible one of the group.

Dropping down into the comfortable bed—though nothing could compete with a conformer—she studied her friends. Their outfits spanned the colors of the rainbow, in contrast to her dark pants and white blouse. "So, what are you two planning?"

Dorian's eyes narrowed. "Don't you get tired of playing the Mommy?" she asked.

"Mommy?"

"The one who scolds her younglings…children."

"I was just thinking that. If you two would behave, I wouldn't have to fill the maternal role." She looked at them. They were the most important people in her world now and she'd come to care deeply for them. "I'm just trying to keep us on task. And safe."

"We're kidding, Lisha." Celeste must have read her hurt feelings.

They weren't kidding, though. She'd have to give that some more thought. "So, what do you want?"

Drawing in a deep breath, Dorian told Alisha of her plans. After she finished her story, Alisha ran her hands through her hair. Though she still sported the short locks of their time,

Celeste's had grown the longest and Dorian could pull hers back in a clip. "Seeing the Cromwells is dangerous. I know you miss Luke…"

"Don't you want to see Helen and Jess?" Celeste interrupted. "It's been weeks. Helen could have a baby bump by now."

The truth was Alisha *did* want to see them. She missed the Cromwells, even Luke, who mostly irritated her with his machismo ways.

Lying back into the pillows, she looked up at the swirling ceiling fan. June was hot in Virginia and the moving air cooled her skin. "We'd have to keep our residence a secret."

"We'll meet them at the hotel where the ceremonial dinner is." Dorian's voice was so enthusiastic, Alisha was moved by her tone.

"A hotel? With rooms to rent? And would you be staying there with Luke?"

"I do miss joining with him."

"I miss joining, too," Alisha and Celeste said in unison. All of them rued the monogamous sexual customs of the time period and the absence of a SexLine, where immediate needs could be met with those registered in the central computeller.

"Lisha? Please," Dorian begged.

Oh, why the hellor not? "Maybe it would be okay."

Celeste grinned and Dorian said, "I'm going to call Luke." She stopped and kissed Alisha on the cheek. Alisha was used to that. Women showed great affection for each other in their time. "Thanks, Lisha."

When Dorian left, Celeste joined Alisha on the bed, stretched out and crooked her arm to rest her head in her hand. "Lisha, do you think anything has changed already in the future because of Jess's survival?"

"Who knows? People of our time could be living without Domes."

Celeste didn't say anything.

"When we finish our tasks here, everything could—*should*—be put to right for them. Let's be happy about that." Alisha was trying to reassure her friend, who felt things so deeply.

"Funny, we'll probably never ever know."

"Reverend Ryan would say we have to have faith."

Celeste thought about this time period's concept of a deity. They'd lost that in their society, too. "Do you think we could learn to believe in a God?"

"Maybe you could. Not me, though. I'm not planning for any god to have a role in our future. We have to be the ones to change it." She studied Celeste. "Are you ready for your part, Celi?"

"Yes."

"Good. As you know, I have access to Dr. Lansing's email. The clinical trials start tomorrow. The missive from Dr. Ravel confirmed it."

"Dr. Lansing said the same thing." Suddenly, Celeste felt flushed and her head began to hurt. She did not want to tamper with Alex Lansing's work, dash all his hopes and destroy what he'd labored over for a decade. The knowledge that she would made the very air oppressive.

"We'll need to act soon, Celi."

"I know."

"Our changes will have to be in the clinical-trial results. I have to find a way to alter them."

"You will." She cleared her throat. "I'll help."

"Just as long as we're on the same page." At Celeste's confused expression, she said, "As long as we're in agreement."

"We are."

But knowing they had no choice in fulfilling the tasks assigned to them didn't make Celeste's heart hurt any less for Alex Lansing.

• • •

"WHEN IS SHE getting here, Dad?" Cody asked the question from the front porch where they sat waiting for Celeste and her sisters to arrive.

"Anytime now." He checked his watch. He had work to do on summaries in his log about this morning's kickoff, as well as prepare for the summer lectures he was giving at City University, but Cody was so excited when he got home from school about Celeste's moving in that Alex was trying to entertain his son.

The front door banged open and Jon came out with his glove, a bat and ball. "Wanna play some ball, Dad? We haven't done it since that time with Celi."

Fatherly guilt came roaring back and he remembered his and Celeste's comments about Maddy.

She works too hard.

Like you.

"Sure, can Cody play?"

"Yeah, but he won't catch anything."

"Dork."

"Dweeb."

"Come on, guys, none of that." He stood and rolled up the sleeves of the blue dress shirt he still wore with suit pants. The day was mild, a slight breeze rustled through the trees and Alex enjoyed being outside. Or *out of inside*, which was the odd way Celeste described it. "Let's go."

They had fun. He hit the ball lightly toward the side of the yard where Jon hunched over, his gloves poised in front of him. He caught one fly ball and threw it back. After a few hits directly to his younger son, Cody started doing cartwheels in the grass. A couple more to Jon, then a taxi came down their street and pulled up in front of the house.

"She's here," Cody yelled. He raced to the cab just as Celeste and her sisters emerged from it.

Alex's jaw dropped. The women were…amazing. Celeste was beautiful, but together…what a picture these three made. They all wore those below-the-knee pants and T-shirts, in deference to the heat, and each carried a suitcase. Each was tall, fit, and commanded a presence that was almost intimidating. Definitely confident.

"Celeste," Cody exclaimed as he ran to her. She dropped her case and caught him as he threw himself into her arms. Alex watched them hug and felt something stir inside him.

Jon walked over more sedately and smiled shyly. "Hi, Celi."

"Hi, guys." Disentangling herself from Cody, she smiled down at him. "I was just here a few days ago, Cody."

"I know, but you're moving *in*. With us."

One sister also smiled. One frowned. At Cody's affection?

"Let's go see your dad." She took Cody's hand and tousled Jon's hair. "I'll introduce you all together."

The five of them approached Alex. He wiped the sweat from his palms on his trousers—he must be a mess—and met them halfway across the grass. "Hello there," he said to her and her sisters.

"Alex, Cody and Jon, this is Dorian." The darker haired sister held out her hand to him. When he shook it, he noted how firm, how strong her grip was. Like Celeste's grip. Then Dorian extended the shake to Jon. "Hi, Jon."

Surprised at her offering the adult gesture to him, he said only, "Hello."

Cody babbled. "Hi, Dorian. I hope you don't miss Celi too much, but we *need* her here."

"I can see that." Another smile broached her lips.

Celeste pulled the other sister forward. "And this is Alisha."

"Nice to meet all of you." Her demeanor and tone were the most reserved of the three.

Glancing behind Alex, Celeste asked, "Is Maddy home?"

"No." Alex shook his head. "She's busy with end-of-the year exams."

"Oh, well."

He noticed the sisters scanning the yard. Dorian sniffed as if she was enjoying the scent of the grass and the smell of the geraniums that hung from the porch and graced the lawn. Alisha, however, studied him.

Jon asked, "Can I carry your bags?"

Alex also added, "I can take one, and Cody can get the small case."

Looking confused, Alisha asked, "Why would you do that?"

Interesting. "Um, courtesy."

"We're used to doing things on our own." Celeste handed Jon hers. "But if you insist."

Still a bit surprised at their appearance, Alex led them into the house. "We've been hoeing out the third floor even before you decided to move in. The cleaners came Friday, and Maddy and I went out last night and bought some furniture. I hope it's adequate."

They followed him up to the third-floor space. Lila had used it as an art studio of sorts. But after she died, the kids didn't want to convert it to a playroom.

"Oh, my, this is beautiful." Celeste scanned the pretty peach walls with white accents that Alex had painted a few days ago, the wooden bed, dressers, a sitting area with a couch and TV and an adjacent bathroom. "It's much more than I need."

"It's lovely," Dorian added. "Look at all those aper—windows, Celeste. You'll love the air coming in through them."

"I'm glad you like it." He was. "I would have let you furnish the place, but I wanted something ready when you moved in."

"I'll be sure to thank Maddy and I'm grateful to you, too."

Her pleasure at what he'd done meant something to him. More, he realized than it probably should.

"All right, kids, let's leave Celi and her sisters to settle Celeste in. Would you like to stay for dinner, Dorian? Alisha?"

Alisha perked up. "We'd love to."

"Then we'll see you in a bit. Mrs. Kramer made Italian food and froze it before she finished up. I hope you like it."

He left the room last, turning back once to Celeste. "Thanks so much for moving in. It's going to make our lives a lot easier."

Celeste gave him a big fat smile. "I'm happy to be here."

As he closed the door, he wondered if this was *really* the right thing to do. He'd been absurdly happy she agreed to the move and almost as glad to see her today as Cody had been. He'd decided he should keep some distance from her since his reactions were more than he wanted them to be, but today he realized he'd failed miserably.

• • •

"I LOVE LASAGNA." Cody shoveled in another mouthful. "Don't you, Celi?"

She smiled. "I do." In truth, the sauce was a bit spicy for her, but she liked the texture of the cheese they called ricotta. Did they have any idea how lucky they were to have cheese? Real food?

Alex cocked his head. "You seem unfamiliar with the dish. Haven't you had lasagna before, Celeste?"

"Of course she has." Alisha looked to Dorian.

"Oh, yes, I've made it for her."

"Dorian is our cook." Alisha smiled at Alex.

Maddy, who'd come home just in time to eat, nodded to Dorian. "Thank you for getting the articles for my paper on food sources for the future."

"I read her paper," Celeste put in. "It's very insightful, particularly the part about conserving the earth's resources."

Everybody agreed on that necessity.

"I'd like to read it." Dorian told her. When Maddy seemed surprised, Dorian added, "Earnestly."

"That's what Celi says," Jon commented.

"Please explain."

"Most people say *seriously*. Or *really*. You two say earnestly."

"It comes from our parents," Alisha put in. She glanced at the dishes. "We'll help clean up."

Maddy stood. "No, I will. Dad, you and Celeste go sit with her sisters outside. I'll even bring dessert to you when I finish with the kitchen."

"I can help, Maddy," Celeste said. The girl looked tired again today. The end of the school year was hard on her.

Celeste made a mental note to get Maddy to relax, to rest more.

"No," Maddy responded. "You'll be doing plenty of this when you cook for us. Jon and Cody'll help me."

"Thanks, honey." Alex rose, too, kissed Maddy on the cheek and led the women out of inside.

Celeste loved the beautiful space called a patio, a real stone floor covered with comfortable cushioned chairs and couches. Alex lit a few of what he called tiki torches and once they were seated, he turned to her.

"Celi, Dorian says she makes your meals. I never asked if *you* could cook."

Celeste made herself blush. "Not like Ann Kramer. I know a few basic recipes." Seven to be exact. She'd learned only seven in the short time they'd had for that task.

"And I can come over and teach her more." Dorian seemed pleased at the notion. "I have a lot of free time now."

"Do you work?"

"I just finished up a…job and am now looking for something else. I'd be glad to spend time here with Celi."

"I feel bad for taking you away from your sisters." To Dorian and Alisha, Alex said, "Please feel free to visit anytime."

"Oh, we will." Alisha sounded happy about that. Of course, their visits would be to check up on her.

And help me access Alex's research. Again the clutch formed in Celeste's stomach, a bit stronger than before.

Leaning forward, Alisha perched on the edge of her seat. "Dr. Lansing, I understand you're a researcher on sexual-enhancement drugs."

He shot Celeste a look, then focused on Alisha. "Yes, I am. And we've reached an exciting phase."

"What's that?" Alisha pretended to know nothing but, in reality, had found out myriad details.

"The pilot clinical trial."

Her friend nodded. "Celeste says your research is very important to you."

"It's a field I've worked in for years."

Dorian added, "I find it fascinating."

His eyes narrowed on Celeste. "Your sister thinks it's superficial."

"I never said that, Alex." Though she did feel that way.

"All right, you questioned why I wasn't concentrating on world hunger or global warming."

"Why aren't you?" Dorian asked.

"Because I believe my research will contribute to the health and welfare of the future of mankind."

From the ancient fiction, Celeste knew the meaning of irony, and this was a classic case. Alex Lansing had no idea what he would do to the future if he was successful in marketing Equisex worldwide. As Alisha had reminded her, the drug initially passed the clinical trials with flawless results. And the manufacture of it served as the foundation for a future drug that would eventually be taken as a vitamin pill every day by both sexes. What no one knew was that when the drug was consumed in generations to come, it would cause thinning of the uterine walls and low FSH levels in women and prostate and hormonal issues in men. The result would be total infertility.

Unless they stopped him.

• • •

WHEN CELESTE WALKED her sisters out, Alex headed to the den. The kids were upstairs watching a movie together and he planned to join them in a few minutes. He wanted to check his email. While it booted up, he swiveled around in his chair and stared out the window. It was dark by now, but the bright moon beamed into the den. He thought about Celeste's sisters.

They weren't like normal people. In many ways, Celeste wasn't either. He'd had a chance to study them on the patio. From what he could see in their summer outfits, none of them had an ounce of body fat on them. Very unusual for women in their forties. And there was something stilted about them—the way they talked, their…observation of things. As a scientist, he caught these kinds of details in people and knew they meant something. He just couldn't figure out what.

"Dr. Lansing?" He turned to find Celeste in the doorway.

"We're back to Dr. Lansing?"

The corners of her mouth turned up. "I forget sometimes."

"Your sisters—and you, to a degree—are very formal."

"The culture in South America, where my parents worked, was formal. Very polite. We were especially taught to respect our elders." Now a grin.

"You're forty. I'm forty-five. Don't call me an elder, woman!" Jesus, he was flirting.

Her eyes widened, but she eventually smiled. Then she gestured to the computer. "Are you working this late?"

"It's not so late. I'm often up half the night."

Her brow furrowed. "Sleep is important. I've learned that eight hours is recommended, but the body can sustain itself with seven."

"There you go talking like a scientist."

"No, like an ordinary…housewife." There it was again, the hesitation on a word.

"Come on in and tell me what your husband did for a living and why you never worked outside of the home after college."

Gracefully, as she did everything, she took a chair on the other side of the desk. "Mitchell worked in computers. He was very good at it. I helped him run his business."

"What was your degree in?"

"My degree?"

"In college. What did you study?"

"Oh, biology." She shrugged. "I was particularly interested in fertility and reproduction."

That was a coincidence. "Huh. I started out as a gynecologist, then became a fertility specialist. Both my parents were in the field."

"We have a lot in common." She seemed thoughtful. "I did work in a lab for a while."

"Seriously?"

She nodded. "But then Mitchell's business began to boom and I quit to help him."

"Most women these days don't do that."

She watched him for a minute. "If you ever need any help with your research, coordinating data, whatever, I'm available."

He felt himself close down. "I work alone, Celeste."

"Why?"

"I had some bad experiences when I started out." He could hear the hoarseness in his own voice.

She moved her chair a little closer and touched his arm. The gesture moved him. "Can you tell me about it?"

Suddenly, he wanted to talk about the time when his life imploded because of a colleague he thought he could trust.

"As I said, I started out in women's health care. My mother was a gynecologist, and my dad, a urologist. But as time went on, I began to hear more and more about sexual dysfunction in both men and women. Since I'd always loved research, I decided to take a leave from my practice and see if I wanted to work in the field permanently. Ten years ago, when I began working on sexual-enhancement drugs at City University, somebody hacked into my research. We were an academic institution and I never thought that could happen. Virtual theft wasn't on anyone's radar." He shook his head, feeling a lump in his throat at thinking about those bleak days.

"Go on."

"I was making phenomenal progress in a sexual-enhancement drug that could change the way people lived their lives. Turns out, I was right. The people who stole my research, whoever they were, had big corporations at their disposal. One came out with the little blue pill, based on what I'd developed so far." He'd been so naïve to think his work was safe. "Several followed before I could regroup."

"Is that why you left leave the university?"

"After the theft, I realized I needed Big Pharma's money behind me and no distractions like teaching."

"I misunderstood. I thought you still taught."

"Just as an adjunct. A course in Ethics in Science. I think I'm good at it because of what happened to me."

"Teaching suits you, Alex."

"Really, why?"

"I'm not sure. I can see you transmitting your knowledge to young people."

"As an ancillary profession. Back then, I decided if I was going to make a better drug, I had to work at it full time."

"I'm not familiar with the term Big Pharma."

Geez, there it was again. "It's a pejorative term for pharmaceutical—drug companies."

"I see. It must be lonely working by yourself. Having no one to share successes and failures with."

"It has been. Since Lila died."

"Ah, she was there to console you."

His heart constricted in his chest. "Yes. And to repay her, all I did was work, work, work after I was robbed of my first research."

"Again, I'm sorry."

He took a good look at Celeste. She was biting her lip, and her hands fisted in her lap. "I didn't mean to upset you."

"I feel bad…that someone took your work and hurt you so much that it affected the rest of your life."

"That won't happen again. I have enough security in place to guard Fort Knox. Nobody gets in here without my permission."

If anything, his remark seemed to upset her. More.

"Have I offended you, Celeste? I didn't mean to imply I didn't trust *you*. I just don't trust anybody around my work."

"No, no, I'm not offended. Only sad for the hardships you've had both professionally and personally."

"At least the professional part will pay off." He glanced at the computer. "Hopefully, very soon."

"Good luck, Alex." She nodded to his desk. "I'll let you finish up." She stood and headed to the door. Once she got there, she turned back. "Alex?"

"Yes?"

Her throat worked convulsively. "Good night."

When she'd left, he wondered why his tales of woe affected her so deeply. He knew she cared about him and the kids, but she seemed remorseful somehow.

He shook his head. Determined not focus on her, he turned his attention back to his email.

Oh, good. He'd gotten a missive from Charles Ravel. Excited, he clicked into it.

CHAPTER 5

THE WILLARD HOTEL was considered one of the best entertainment facilities in Washington, D.C. One block from the White House, the structure was a unique blend of both historic and contemporary significance. As Celeste entered the lavish ballroom, she really couldn't understand that term as there was no sports equipment in here. The space was filled with white-clothed tables, red roses and napkins and candles. She was almost as excited as Dorian to be seeing Jess, Helen and Luke here.

Almost. "Do I look okay?" Dorian touched her hair, which Celeste had helped her style. "I wish I could have seen Luke first, without all these people around, as we planned. Megadamn those vehicle accidents."

The Cromwells had been delayed by a traffic mishap on the interstate from New York to D.C.

Celeste grasped her arm. Drained some of the nervousness. Dorian was too animated to notice, but she did calm.

"You're lovely, Dorian." She wore the sequined dress that she'd bought for their first outing to The Mix. Alisha and Celeste wore their respective dresses, too. For Celeste, that night, the events in New York seemed as if they'd happened eons ago.

"We're at table four, in the front with the honoree." Alisha led the way, and the others followed.

Celeste felt the Cromwells' presence before she even saw them, and her whole body felt buoyant. Jess, Helen and Luke were seated at a round table. The men were in suits, and Helen looked lovely in a peach dress, her long hair tied back in a clip. Luke was scanning the room but hadn't seen them yet. When he got a glimpse of Dorian, he bolted up. Jess grabbed his arm and said something to him; Luke nodded.

They hurried to the table, and everyone watched the couple reunite. "Luke!" Dorian whispered hoarsely.

Luke smiled like Celeste had never seen him smile before. "Hello, sweetheart." Drawing him to her, he hugged her. To any onlooker, they were old friends who hadn't met up in a while—Celeste noticed a lot of people in the crowd embracing. But she saw the grip Luke had on Dorian, the tender way she grasped his neck and the whispered words they exchanged.

For a brief moment, Celeste coveted what Dorian had with Luke. She longed to experience it. Would this kind of intimacy ever happen to her? She wanted that almost as much as she longed to have a youngling. Images of Alex Lansing floated through her mind and she chided herself for making the connection from what she yearned for to the man himself.

Jess stood, too. "There's my girls." He hugged Celeste heartily and insisted Alisha share one with him, too. Though Alisha wasn't as affectionate as she and Dorian, Celeste noted she held on to Jess extra-long.

Celeste's heart swelled when she circled the others to get to Helen. "Oh, Helen. I missed you so much."

Helen held her tightly. "I missed you too, Celi."

After they embraced, Celeste put her hand on Helen's stomach, which had no visible baby bump. "Hello, Jessica."

"Then she is a girl?" Helen's voice was shaky. "The doctors say they can't tell from the ultrasound yet, and I didn't want to have any other tests done."

For a moment, Celeste listened to the strong heartbeat, felt a lazy shifting inside Helen. "Yes, and she's doing great."

Helen's eyes misted. "We didn't know if you might have changed other things in the future... You were hoping to... Oh, I'm so glad." She threw her arms around Celeste again.

When the greetings were complete, they all took seats. Celeste noticed an empty chair next to Alisha. "Are we expecting someone else?"

Helen shot Luke a look. "Didn't they tell you?"

"No."

"Jess asked David Ryan to give the invocation."

Alisha's eyed widened, but she didn't say anything. However, Celeste could read her from across the table. She would be glad to see David.

Dorian and Luke were paying no attention to the conversation. They held hands under the table and focused on each other.

"Come on, Luke," Jess complained. "We want to hear how the girls are. You can exclude everybody all you like later."

Luke winked at Dorian. "Now you know what I've felt watching you and Helen two for decades, little brother."

The Master of...something for the evening came out to a voice amplifier—a microphone. "Good evening, everyone. Thanks for coming tonight to the annual dinner honoring two top researchers in the country whose work in alternative energy sources is exemplary. Dr. Jess Cromwell and Dr. Anita Nichols are making progress in both renewable energy and natural gas..."

Celeste half listened to the man. She was scanning the crowd, noticing all the dresses of different colors and how handsome the men looked. Dorian had told her who would be here — about a hundred people, guests of the honorees and fellow researchers in the field of energy.

She was glad to be in attendance, especially since hers and Alex's schedule conflicted tonight…

He'd been remote for the last few revolutions, since he'd confided in her about the theft of his work. That night in his den, Celeste had felt, literally, the frustration and resentment bubble out of him. And she almost couldn't contain the sadness, the regret over the fact that she was planning to sabotage his research. His work was going to be taken from him again. Only the vision of the grim environment beyond the Domes and the barren wombs of her time kept her from forsaking her task.

He'd sought her out after she'd returned from jogging out of inside. "I know you have Saturday nights and Sundays off, Celeste, but I was hoping you could swap Saturday for Friday this week. I have plans that, truthfully, I forgot about in all the changes around here."

"Oh, I can't. Ordinarily I would, but I was planning to go to my sisters' house and stay overnight. We've got some things to do that can't be changed." That had been the truth, though she didn't get specific. "I'm sorry I can't accommodate you."

"No apology necessary. Maybe Maddy can sit the boys, and it'll give me an excuse to come home early…"

Staying with her sisters brought an added benefit. She hadn't wanted him to see her dress and have to explain how she was invited to a fancy party like this. To them, she was their ordinary, simple caregiver.

Tuning back in to the present when David was announced, she watched him walk to the podium. He looked big up there, with wider shoulders in the black he wore with that collar thing around his neck. His curly hair shone in the lights.

"Would you bow your heads, please?" he asked in a deep voice.

Alisha rolled her eyes, but Celeste did as he asked.

"Blessed Lord, we come together to honor two scientists who will make a better future for our world." He inserted several remarks about Jess and the other person being honored. "Let us always remember that we have a grave responsibility to keep the earth clean, to preserve our resources and to be good stewards of what God has given us. In God's name, we pray. Amen."

First, one person stood and clapped. Then the entire crowd came to their feet. They were clapping at a prayer? Oh, because of the content of it. They were scientists and knew the importance of the work the chosen two conducted. Once again, she was besieged by the feeling she'd had in New York when David taught a lesson in his church on Earth Day. This society knew what they should be doing but couldn't get it accomplished — resulting in a disastrous future.

Feeling bad, she went to sit back down and her gaze caught on a man, several tables away, who was staring at her.

He had wheat-colored hair.

And a surprised expression on his face.

The man was Dr. Alex Lansing.

• • •

"ALEX, DARLING, WHO are you staring at?" The question came from his date, Sherry Manwaring. Sherry worked in an environmental agency in D.C. He'd attended this annual dinner with her a time or two. And he'd never expected to see the exotic-looking woman in a little black dress and stiletto heels four tables away from them. "I, um, know one of the people at an honoree's table."

"Which one?" She tried to look around him.

"It doesn't matter."

But it did. The wholesome widow who didn't even drive, attending a sophisticated event like this didn't add up. And how she was dressed…dear Lord…

Who was here mattered to Sherry, because when she saw Celeste, she stated, "Let's go say hello to them."

"Dinner's being served." Alex was reluctant to identify Celeste as his caregiver. Sherry would have a lot to say about that. Though they dated and slept together, he'd never wanted a commitment from her or any woman since Lila. Sherry knew how he felt because he'd been honest with her from the start; she didn't seem to mind.

Linking her arm with his, she tugged him along. "It'll only take a minute."

He had no choice but to accompany her. The pastor who gave the benediction reached the table just before they did, but Alex could hear what he said. "Hello there. It's so nice to see you all again." His gaze locked on one of Celeste's sisters. "I recognize the dresses."

They all laughed at a joke Alex didn't understand.

When he and Sherry reached the others, Jess Cromwell stood. "Hello."

"Hi, Dr. Cromwell. I'm Alex Lansing. This is Sherry Manwaring. Congratulations on the award."

"Are you a scientist, Alex?" Jess asked, probably trying to be polite while he wondered why this stranger would come up to him.

"Yes, I am."

Alex turned his gaze to Celeste.

She'd gone totally white and gripped the edge of the table. "Hello, Celeste."

"Alex."

Moving in closer to him, Sherry asked, "And you are?"

"I'm Celeste Hart." She recovered enough to say, "Alex, you remember my sisters." She introduced the others at the table.

Sherry asked, "How do you know Alex, Ms. Hart?"

"I'm the new caregiver for his children."

"Seriously?"

"Earnestly," Celeste choked out.

Luke rose and approached the two men. "I'm Luke Cromwell, Jess's brother."

"You must be very proud of him." This from Alex.

"I am. What kind of scientist are you, Dr. Lansing?"

"I'm working a new sexual-enhancement drug. The clinical trials are running as we speak."

Jess nodded. "I thought I recognized your name. I've read about you. Helen has, too. She saw an article you wrote in the *Reproductive and Biology Journal*."

"So you work with infertility, too?" Luke asked.

"No, not anymore."

A waiter bumped Alex's arm. "Looks like dinner's served. We'll get out of your way. Celi, nice to see you."

As they walked away, Alex glanced over his shoulder. For some reason, the others at Celeste's table were no longer smiling. And she was still white as a ghost. They looked almost as unhappy as Sherry, who was displeased, no doubt, at the sight of such a lovely woman, whom she now knew was living in his home.

What a bizarre thing to happen, Alex thought. And wasn't Celeste full of contradictions? He made a mental note to find out why.

• • •

ALISHA SAT FROZEN in her chair. She was so angry she could barely think straight. First, they sprang David Ryan on her, then, there was the debacle of Alex Lansing meeting the Cromwells. No one spoke as the waiters served them salad, then when the staff left, David touched her arm. "Take it easy."

"Easy? I have no reason to *take it easy*." She zeroed in on Luke. "You did that on purpose. Asked him what he researched. You wanted to see how it connected to us because we refused to tell you what our next task was."

Not at all rattled, Luke held Dorian's hand on the table. "I already knew you were connected when he said Celeste worked for him. He had to be your *next task*."

Her eyes narrowed on him.

"But now I can connect the dots to the young woman who received a very generous scholarship to Johns Hopkins to get her out of your way. What was she, their babysitter?"

"Yes," Dorian answered.

Helen sighed. "Is it really such a big deal that we know what you're doing down here, Alisha?"

"It's a *huge* deal."

"Deal?" Celeste asked. "We've bargained with no one."

Alisha ignored her. "Our next task was *not* supposed to be revealed."

"Which is stupid and unnecessary, if you ask me." Luke was baiting her, but Alisha couldn't keep her objections to herself.

"Promises to the Guardians are not stupid and unnecessary."

"He didn't mean to imply that, Alisha." David's voice was calm. "Look on the bright side; maybe we can help. If we all tell Alex what's happened, prove it to him, he'll probably do what you ask, like Jess did."

"Oh, dear Nord, no. He'd never believe us." Celeste gripped her napkin. "He's had a bad experience with people stealing his work. Our task *must* be kept from him."

"What exactly are you doing?" Helen wanted to know. "Helping him achieve success in his research like you did with Jess?"

"No!" Alisha said in a harsh whisper. "This is how important it was...*is*...to keep our mission a secret. We're here to make sure his life's work is *not* successful."

• • •

WHEN CELESTE ARRIVED Monday morning after spending two nights with her sisters, Alex was seated at the table drinking a cup of coffee, thinking about her. She came through the back door and startled. "Oh, Dr. Lansing, I...I didn't know you'd be here."

So, it was *Dr. Lansing* again. "In my own house?"

"In the kitchen. G-good morning." Her smile was a bit uneasy. As well as it should be. The person in the ordinary green shorts and matching top had been masquerading as a sensible, down-to-earth, no-frills woman but had turned into Jezebel in a little black dress Saturday night.

"Good morning."

She gave him a weak smile. "Where are the boys?"

"I drove them to school." This was the last week of the year, and field trips and special events were planned. "Jon had to bring in a project he'd done at home, and Cody rode along."

Her smile seemed more genuine this time. "It will be nice to have them home all the time."

Shaking his head, he watched her. Sometimes it was hard to believe Celeste was genuine. "You really mean that, don't you?"

"Why, yes, of course. Though I wish Maddy hadn't signed up for summer school."

Alex was worried about that. She'd inherited so many of his traits. Overachieving was just one of them. "Many mothers, or caregivers, like it when their children are in school and out of their hair."

Once again, she seemed unfamiliar with the term. She touched her pretty auburn locks.

"Out of the way."

A confused expression crossed her face. "Why on earth would they feel that way?"

"Kids are a bother, I guess."

"Not to me. I love spending time with them."

He sipped his coffee. "I'm glad to hear that." He watched her. "Did you have a good time with your sisters? And your friends?"

"Yes. It was lovely to see the Cromwells again." She crossed to the stove, filled the tea kettle and put it on a burner. "Did you have fun?"

Until Sherry got a glimpse of you. "I did. Is it too personal to ask how you know the Cromwells?"

"No, of course not." She turned to face him. "We're distant cousins of Helen. Very distant, but when we moved to New York City, we reunited."

"Where were you before that?"

Her face blanked. "I thought I told you. We lived upstate."

"That's right. Corning and Rochester." When she nodded, he continued. "Jess's work is highly regarded. I'm glad he received recognition for it this year."

She poured her tea and joined him at the table. "Is recognition important to you?"

"Excuse me?"

"Do you seek recognition for your work?"

"No, I want to make society a better place." Alex rose from the table to get another cup of coffee. He didn't return to his seat, and instead, he leaned against the counter and wondered why he was telling her—*again*—things he didn't normally divulge, not since Lila died. "I explained to you the other night that my earlier work was stolen. I want to do this research myself because I know I'll do it the right way. That sounds arrogant, but it's the truth."

This time, she rose and came to stand by him. For some reason, that simple gesture made him feel less defensive. He stared down into very sincere blue eyes. He noticed her nose was red, so she must have spent some time outside this weekend.

"It sounds to me as if you have confidence in your work, not that you're arrogant. And you love research. I understand. Truly."

He nodded.

After a few moments, she turned away and glanced at the calendar on the wall. "Cody's birthday is soon. You celebrate the day of your birth here. Do you want me to plan something special for the occasion?"

"Don't you?"

"Please repeat."

"Celebrate the day of your birth?"

"Did I say that?"

"Yes, in a sense."

"I must be fatigued. The three of us stayed up late to watch videos." She gestured to the calendar. "Cody's day?"

"As a matter of fact, I wanted to talk to you about that. I think I have to have your consent for his present."

"Why?"

"You'll understand when I tell you."

CHAPTER 6

ON THE MORNING of Cody's day of birth, Celeste knelt in the garden of flowers and yanked up a particularly stubborn weed. The physical labor felt good, as did the sweat on her brow. She'd had to block out the sun with a wide-brimmed straw hat, though, because it had burned her skin a time or two.

She'd enlisted the kids to complete the task because they were free on their first day of summer vacation. And for other reasons yet to be divulged. Maddy and Jon willingly cooperated.

But Cody, with dirt smeared on his face as well as his hands, grumbled, "Why do I have to do this on my birthday?"

Celeste drew back, resting on her haunches. Was she unaware of customs for the celebration? "What do you mean?"

"Nobody's supposed to work on their birthday."

"Oh, I'm sorry. That isn't my custom."

"Go ahead and just play while we all slave out here in the sun, then." Maddy made the comment but with a twinkle in her eyes. Celeste had learned she was very good at manipulating her brothers.

"Nah. I don't wanna do that while you guys work." Halfheartedly he pulled at another weed.

"I'll play a video game with you when we're done." Jon meant it as a gesture to make Cody's birthday special. But she highly doubted they'd be playing video games or any other kind today.

"I purchased a cake for you, Cody," she said to distract him.

"With my picture on it?"

Not exactly, but one he'd like better. "You have to wait to see."

Jon pulled on a weed so hard, when it was set free, he fell onto his rear. They all laughed.

Celeste went back to her task and sighed. To her, any greenery was lovely, but ridding the garden of certain ones was another wasteful thing they did in this time period. They had no idea how rare and precious even weeds were. People of the future would probably consume them.

Jon nudged Cody. "Maybe we can find the cake somewhere in the house after we finish here, Cody."

"It won't matter then."

Maddy stopped working. "Why?"

Celeste cringed. Had she said that aloud?

Thankfully, a voice called out from behind the fence to the yard. "Hey, everybody. How come you're hard at work on Cody's birthday?"

"I *told* you." Cody jumped up to run to his dad. Celeste held him back. "Wait here, Cody."

Slowly, Alex opened the gate and walked in. Three Lansing mouths gaped, and even Celeste felt a thrill go through her.

"Dad…" Jon's voice held awe.

"Oh, Daddy," Madison said.

But Cody didn't speak. When Celeste looked over at him, his jaw trembled. "Cody, are you all right?"

Eyes flooded, he said nothing, just watched his father cross to them. Then he managed to get out, "Mom said I could. When I finished kindergarten."

"I know, honey." Alex's smile was sad. "Happy Birthday, son. From me and your mother."

The beautiful black lab puppy, with a coat as sleek as the pictures of sealas Celeste had seen, barked. The sound was soft, and the poor little thing backed up a bit.

Cody, Jon and Maddy converged on the animal with exuberance. The puppy began to whimper. Even from where she was, she could sense his fear.

Alex let go of the leash, and the dog bolted around the three children — right into Celeste's lap. From there, he nuzzled into her chest. She caught her breath at the sensations that encompassed her. She couldn't exactly read the dog's thoughts — if dogs had them — but sensed his experiences. Right now, he was terrified and needed to be protected. "Hey, doggy, you're going to be okay." She held the animal close and petted him gently. Immediately, the dog relaxed into her and stopped whimpering. Still, he hid his face from the kids.

"What happened?" Maddy asked. They were all staring at her. "He seemed afraid of us. And now he's okay."

"I think perhaps you frightened him with all your enthusiasm." Celeste's answer was spur-of-the-moment. She hadn't expected this connection with the canine, had no reason to.

"How come *you* don't scare him?" Jon asked.

"Um, maybe because I'm tempering my response." She looked to their dad, who was staring at her, too, with a suspicious expression on his face. "How old is he, Alex?"

"Eight weeks. Just old enough to take him from his mother."

The puppy nosed into her a second time, as if mention of his donor made him sad again.

"Cody, come over here."

He was at her side in seconds. "Touch his back." When Cody did, she said, "Hey little guy, this is Cody. He's your new owner and his love will be yours forever." She kissed the furry head of the pup. She was experiencing her own feelings of awe at holding a real, live dog. An animal. A pet, something she'd never held before. He was so soft even though he smelled... unpleasant. "Isn't that right, Cody?"

Taking her cue, Cody gently ran his hand over the dog. "Yeah, sure." It was cute how he lowered his voice. "I'm going to be really good to you. Feed you." The dog's ears perked up. "Take you for walks. And let you sleep with me."

Alex squatted down next to Cody, his big shoulders blocking some of the sun. Now his scent, something spicy, filled Celeste's head. For a moment, she was totally disoriented by it. He said, "That's yet to be determined. Puppies have needs big dogs don't. We'll play the sleeping arrangements by ear."

Oh, dear.

"Okay, Dad."

"So," Celeste asked. "What are you going to name him?"

Cody's and Alex's gazes locked. Celeste didn't understand the byplay between them. But together they said, "Bruiser."

A hulk of a man? "Why that name?"

Cody's eyes misted again. Alex sat down next to him and slid his arm around his son. Finally, Cody said, "Mom and I came up with the name. She said we'd get a black lab who'd grow up to be a bruiser."

Ah, suddenly, Lila was amidst all of them again.

And Celeste didn't like the emotion that ran through her at the notion. For the godheads' sake, she was jealous.

• • •

ALEX DROVE THE SUV into the parking lot of Virgo Beach and grinned. The day had turned into a scorcher, with the sun beating down on the car and bouncing off the windows. His very excited kids scrambled in the backseats, wired about Cody's birthday and the plans they'd made. And still thrilled about the puppy, who now slept at home.

Alex hit the locks on the doors. "Before we go out, tell me the water safety rules."

Maddy said, "Don't go off alone."

Jon joined in. "Stay in sight."

Cody joked, "Have fun."

"All right. Don't run out to the beach ahead of me. Everybody take something with them, and if we need to, make a second trip to the car."

The first time he took his kids on an outing like this after Lila's death, he couldn't believe how hard it was to get everything ready. With Celeste's help, the preparation went smoother, though. He was beginning to depend on the woman.

"I wish we coulda brought Bruiser." Cody voiced the complaint as they climbed out of the SUV. The heat and humidity was tempered by the cool breeze coming off the ocean, and Alex savored its seaweed scent and the feel of the wind on his face. He glanced over and saw Celeste close her eyes, breathe deeply and smile.

"No dogs on the public beach," Alex told Cody. "Besides, he's so little, he'd be overwhelmed."

"Bruiser was happy to go in his crate," Celeste reminded his son. "He likes the security. And the hot water bottle and clock will comfort him." They'd only planned to stay away a few hours, too.

Alex knew Celeste had researched everything about caring for a puppy on the Internet this week, and he was glad he wasn't alone in this adventure. He was glad he wasn't alone, period. He could still see her in that sexy dress Saturday night and how lovely she'd looked…

"Da-ad. Come on." This from Cody who had taken a pint-sized chair and brightly colored sand toys from the back of the SUV. "I'll get the umbrella." Alex insisted on the protection, even though they'd slathered up with sun screen. Celeste had an odd reaction to the cream. She sniffed it, felt it between her fingers and seemed to relish it on her skin. But then again, she was sensual about everything. He wondered briefly what she'd be like in bed, then banished the thought.

Laden with coolers and beach paraphernalia, they traversed the parking lot, then the grass. When they reached the sand, everybody stopped and kicked their shoes off.

Everybody but Celeste.

"Take your shoes off, Celi. So you can feel the sand under your feet." This from Maddy.

But Celeste wasn't listening. She stared ahead, open mouthed. "It's…it's beautiful."

Cody tugged on her arm. "What is?"

"The water. It…moves so gracefully, and its scent is… salty. And it has this vibrant roar…"

Alex crossed to her. He couldn't see her eyes because she'd put on sunglasses. "Celi, haven't you ever been to the beach?"

"Um, no. Though I've seen bodies of water like this in videos. A real ocean is…quite overpowering. And exquisite."

"I can imagine." He wondered how someone could be forty and never have seen the beach. "Does this mean you can't swim?"

Her eyes narrowed, as if she had to place the word. "It does. I can't swim. But maybe I can learn." She kicked off her shoes. "I'm prepared to go into the sand."

Surreptitiously, he watched her walk ahead of him, her hips swaying in the white terrycloth cover-up she wore. She certainly had been sheltered. He wondered what her life was like in South America. Jesus, it was surrounded by water. Why hadn't she ever been to the beach, learned to swim?

The kids dumped their gear at an agreed-upon spot, whipped off their shirts and headed for the water. Celeste laughed at them. When she saw Alex was unpacking gear, she said, "I'll set everything up. Go play with the children."

"Don't you want to go in with them?"

"Yes, of course. But I'll watch for a while."

"Are you afraid of the water, Celeste?

Above her glasses, her brow furrowed. "I don't think so. Its mass has power, but water contains soothing properties and creates negative ions to replace the positive ones put in the air by chemicals."

"I know. Celi, did you research the ocean, too?"

"I research everything." She gave him a beautiful smile. "Now, go in."

"Let's set up the umbrella and chairs first."

That took about ten minutes. Then Alex ran back to the car and returned with a life jacket. "You can use this when you're ready to join us."

"Oh." He swore she didn't recognize what the thing was.

"Put it on before you come out to the water." Still facing her, he tugged off his shirt.

Her gaze dropped to his bare chest. "You are in good shape," she blurted out. Her mouth sounded a little dry. "Very good shape."

"Why, thank you. I try to use the gym at the company three times a week."

She smiled and her gaze roamed his chest, unabashedly. Turning away quickly, he ran to the water and dived in. Thankfully, it was good and cold.

He rode the waves with his squealing children. He raced in the water with Maddy. And he carried Cody on his shoulders out farther than his son could go alone. Amidst it all, he wondered why they didn't come here more often. This kind of fun, he realized, was one of the many things he'd been missing in his dedication to his work.

Scrambling down when they were in the shallow end again, Cody said, "I'm getting Celi."

He thought of her unfamiliarity of the water. "Maybe we shouldn't push her."

Maddy said, "Dad, you always tell us we need to try new things."

"Yes, but—" There was just something about this...

From the shore, he watched Cody throw his totally wet body at Celeste when he reached her. Instead of getting angry, she giggled and tousled his hair. They spoke. And finally she nodded. She pulled the terrycloth over her head and dropped it on the chair, picked up the life jacket and slid her arms through the straps.

Jesus Christ. Even with the cumbersome floater on, she was perfect. The closer she got, the more curves and muscles he noted. The pink, one-piece suit wasn't at all sexy—except that it covered the body of an athlete, he guessed. Her legs were miles longer than they looked in shorts.

When she reached the edge of the water, and Cody tried to tug her in, Alex yelled, "No, Cody, wait." Walking toward her, he noticed she wasn't secured in the life jacket. "Here, let me help with that."

Which was a *real* mistake. His knuckles grazed her waist, her breasts as he strapped her in. Finally, he stepped back.

"Thank you." Her voice was hoarse.

"Take your time getting in." He went in ahead of her and swam a ways out, then watched from there.

First, she took baby steps into the shallow water. When a little wave came in up to her knees, she stepped back quickly. "Oh."

"Are you scared, Celi?" Madison asked.

"A bit. This is a new experience."

Maddy came out of the deeper water and took her hand. Then Jon did the same on the other side. "We'll go with you," he said innocently.

"I feel foolish."

"Dad says we don't have to be embarrassed by what we don't know. We just have to learn."

A few steps farther. And farther. Finally, she was in up to her waist. "This is wonderful," she said, splashing the water with her hands and grinning like a child.

Alex tore his gaze away to check behind him. Uh-oh. A wave was coming, this time a big one. Before he could warn Celeste—or get to her—it was upon them. He rode the crest, as did the kids, but when he turned around, he did not see Celeste; then she popped up out of the water but stumbled. He swam to her and tugged her up. Her eyes were full of undiluted fear. She coughed, sputtered, spit out a mouthful of water. When she leaned into him, his arms banded around her. "I'm sorry. We should have thought…"

The kids swam to them. Maddy said, "We're so sorry, Celi."

At their contriteness, she drew away from Alex. "It's all right. I just…it encompassed me. Took me under. The sensation was frightening. I'd like to leave this ocean."

They all exchanged looks.

"What?" she asked.

Alex took over. "You can't do that now. You'll never come back in. It's like falling off a bike or a horse. You have to just get back on."

She didn't look convinced. Hell, she didn't look as though she even understood the point.

Reaching out, he gave her a reassuring smile. "Here, take my hand. We'll do this gradually and I won't let you go."

"Earnestly?"

"Yes, earnestly. Trust me?"

"All right, Alex, I'll trust you."

• • •

"YOU TWO SIMPLY must go to the beach. It gave me great pleasure, and the Lansings had so much fun. I was knocked under water, but Alex helped me get accustomed to the waves. And once I did, I was fine."

At the other end of the video on the computeller, Dorian laughed at her. "Slow down." Even Alisha, next to her, was smiling.

"You know what else? We got a puppy today."

"We?" Oops. The smile disappeared from Alisha's face, and disapproval marked her tone.

"Cody did, for his birthday. The animal is so beautiful. He was frightened, though, when he arrived, and he scooted right over to me."

"Oh, Nord, tell me you can't talk to animals." Alisha again.

"Not talk. But I know his feelings."

"I wish I was there to see that," Dorian said.

Alisha managed, "I'm glad you had a nice day."

"I wonder what our birth dates were." Celeste wished they had them to celebrate. "We never knew. We made up ones for our identity cards."

"The custom was lost when society became focused on survival. And we didn't actually get born. We came out of the incubators when we were viable." Here she grinned. "We could have V-days."

Glad to hear Alisha joke—a real rarity—Celeste talked on. Babbled, she thought the word was. "They have cake. Alex purchased one at a place that prepares only sweets. The frosting was white and decorated with a black Labrador Retriever that looks just like Bruiser. Cody loved it."

"Be careful with sweets, Celi."

"I am, Lisha. I consumed one small piece."

Someone knocked at the door. Celeste was so intent on the story of the day of Cody's birth, she didn't anticipate the person's arrival. "I have to go. Someone's come to my sleeping space. I'll phone you tomorrow."

Clicking off the video, she donned a robe over her pink night wear, got up from the bed and opened the door.

Alex and the puppy stood before her. Alex was dressed in pajama bottoms and a T-shirt. "I'm bringing the dog to everyone's room to say good night, so I included you." He rolled his eyes. "I have a feeling I'm not going to get much rest. Cody was mad I wouldn't let them sleep together, but I feel sorry for the little thing. I wanted to ask your opinion on putting the crate in my room."

"Why don't you put it in mine? I seem to calm him."

"I couldn't impose like that."

"You wouldn't be. I'd love it. We never had pets when I grew up and Bruiser's a real sweet for me."

"Sweet?"

"Did I say that? I meant treat. I guess I've been thinking about the wonderful cake."

He grinned at her. "You have an ingenuous attitude toward everything. I wonder why that is."

Ingenuous. Did she know the meaning of the word?

She held out her hands for the dog. "Go get his crate. Bruiser and I will be just fine."

The dog cuddled into her. When Alex left, Celeste crossed to the bed, climbed on and sank back into the pillows propped up on the board head. "There now. You'll be with me; you'll be safe."

The pup's heartbeat slowed. And he'd been shivering, but now he calmed.

"I know how you feel," she whispered in his soft fur." All these new things." She sensed agreement. "We'll experience them together."

Raising his head, Bruiser licked her face.

She giggled. Then she *did* sense someone near. Alex stood in the doorway again, and he was watching her intently. "He does like you."

"And the children. He just can't show that yet."

Crossing to the left side of the room, he bent over, giving her a great look at his butt. Quickly he set the crate up. "Put him in there."

"I will. I want to hold him a bit to calm him."

Alex's eyes burned when he turned around. "He seems perfectly happy now."

Celeste glanced down. Her robe had pulled aside exposing the pink lace of her gown. And the swell of her breast. When she looked up, Alex's expression was still heated.

And a great sexual need shot through her. The masculine appreciation in his eyes made her want to join with him. Here. Now.

He coughed to clear his throat.

She edged the robe closed and rolled her eyes as she'd seen people do when they were embarrassed.

Alex cleared his throat. "I hope you sleep."

"We will."

After he left, she cuddled with the puppy, thinking of how she'd been without sex a long time. It wasn't right that there was no SexLine today.

When the puppy had settled, she rose to put him in his crate. He tensed horribly as she tried to set him inside.

"Don't want to go in there, little guy?"

She got a strong *no* from him. What should she do?

After two more tries to cage him, he reverted to whimpering. "All right. You can sleep with me. But remember, you've got to wake me up if you have to pee. You can't do that in my bed."

Megadamn, it seemed as if the dog nodded.

Happier than she could ever remember being, Celeste climbed into bed, set Bruiser by her side and turned off the light. As soon as she heard his gentle snore, she let her eyes close and her mind drift.

CHAPTER 7

"COMPUTELLER, ON." IN seconds, the device's screen activated, and a voice responded, "Computeller on."

"Spilt screen." Alisha's notes came up on the additional viewing platform.

"Search for the storage site and any backups for Clinical Trial 1309, Dr. Alex Lansing, Equisex. Sponsored by Global Pharmaceuticals."

"Approximate calculation time, thirty minutes."

Alisha let the computeller spin its program and turned to her laptop computer. Rubbing her eyes, she gave it the same command, and the primitive machine booted up.

"How did you do that?" The question came from Dorian, who—when Alisha looked—was standing just inside her room. Dorian wore a white sleeping gown and sipped from a mug. All three of them liked the tea of this time, which was good for them.

"I became tired of manually operating the device. I equipped it with voice activation last night, with a program I retrieved from the computeller."

"Excellent." Dorian came farther into the room and dropped down onto a chair, curling her bare legs beneath her. "Can you fix mine in the same way?"

"Yes."

"Did you stay up all night to do it?"

"Hmm." She kept her eyes on the computer.

"What are you doing now?"

"Trying to find where the results of the Lansing's clinical trials will be stored. And any secondary backup sites, which might be easier to get into if they're in the cloud."

"I've been wondering how exactly we'll alter the data of the clinical trials."

Alisha circled around to face her friend. "We have to get to the raw data and change it before the analysis of the trial is made. Eventually, we'll need access to Dr. Lansing's computer, too, in order to make his calculations on the drug match the results."

"Why is it necessary to change his research?" Dorian asked.

"So no one else can build on his original data, which we know did indeed work."

"But before that, you have to get to the trial results."

"Yes. If I can't find the storage site, I might be able to hack into the primary investigator's email before information he gets to read the results, but the timing would be tricky."

"Almost impossible," Dorian speculated.

"Yes. So finding the site where the testers send the data to be tabulated and changing it before the analysis is crucial."

Sighing, Dorian glanced out the window and was silent for a moment. "Celi seemed happy last night when she contacted us. She liked going to the large body of salt water. And spending time with the Lansings."

Alisha shook her head. This was going to be a problem, she just knew it. "I'm worried about her attachment to the family becoming too great. I have suspected she'd feel this way about them all along."

"I'm worried now, too. She's really taken with those younglings. Perhaps you can warn her not to let her emotions interfere with our task." Dorian laughed. "I'd make the suggestion, but I'm not the one to do that after giving my love to Luke."

"I'm worried about *that*, too."

"Let's not…" She hesitated. "What's the idiom? Beat a dead equine."

Alisha chuckled. She cocked her head at Dorian. "How are you doing on your work?"

"It's tedious accumulating data on the safety of other sexual-enhancement drugs with today's methods. I wish the computeller chips on all that weren't corroded."

"We'll need the information on what makes them viable to determine what to change about Equisex."

"I understand. But these people are so primitive in medicine development…and purpose." Her brows furrowed. "I agree with Celi's criticism that the emphasis on sexual-drug research seems ludicrous when there's so much else wrong with this society."

"People highly value sex here."

"We do too, in the future. But it's organized and clinical. And we're able to participate until we die. If we couldn't, who knows what might happen?"

"At least we had that."

"Truthfully though, Lisha, after what I've experienced with Luke, I think the SexLine matching strangers for sex undesirable. Making love is so much more satisfying."

"May the godheads save us," Alisha commented.

Dorian studied her. "Speaking of the godheads, I saw the books you brought home yesterday. Why didn't you just research religions of the world on the computeller? Or are those chips corroded too?"

Alisha felt herself blush, which rarely happened. "Truthfully, I like the feel and smell of real books, though I'd never purchase them. The waste of trees is horrifying. So I checked them out of the house that rents them. The library." She shrugged. "I figure as long as we're here I might as well find out what I can about something that is so important to these people."

"It's okay to like some of the aspects in this time period, such as those books."

"I suppose. But many things are so sad here."

"Why don't you come back to New York with me next week and cheer yourself up. David Ryan seems to please you when you have discussions with him."

Dorian and Luke had decided to see each other biweekly and since their location and task had been disclosed, Alisha didn't see any harm in it as long as Dorian worked on her part of the plan while she was away.

"I've spoken to him once or twice on the phone. There's been a fire in a local church, and he's helping out with that."

"I'm sure he'd make time for you."

"It doesn't matter. The first report is due in ten days, and I hope to find the statistics and alter the first phase minimally, then more in the second phase, etcetera, so nothing stands out as an abrupt change at the end of the twelve weeks."

"Both the computeller and the laptop computer are portable. You could you do your work from there."

"No, there are too many distractions." She gave Dorian a long look. "Both you and Celeste have fallen victim to those distractions, and *somebody* has to stay on task."

• • •

CELESTE WAS INTENT on her surroundings, as if, once again, they were unfamiliar to her. Her eyes were wide, her mouth forming a perfect O. "This is amazing." She wrinkled her nose. "But there's an unpleasant smell, which pervades the air."

"That's poop," Cody said, taking her hand. "Come on, the tour's starting."

Alex followed her and Cody, glad he'd went along with this June outing to the National Zoo in downtown D.C. His parents had bought the family a season pass, but they'd never brought Celeste here. Maddy was at a birthday party with her schoomates and Jon had gone to a friend's house.

Alex had been careful around Celeste since the night of Cody's birthday, when he'd accidentally caught sight of a creamy breast. Just that small vision had made him so hard, he'd had to abscond quickly from the room. And the pleased look in her eyes made him realize she didn't mind his…appreciation. He had to control himself better around her.

A tour guide gathered fifteen people at the opening to the lion trail. The woman in a tan uniform of the employees stood before the group, smiling. "Welcome to the National Zoo. Millions of people take The Great Cats Tour every year. It will last forty-five minutes and will cover all the basics about our favorite felines."

Alex heard Celeste mumble, "Great Cata…cats."

"Now follow me." As they walked, the guide began her spiel. "The Great Cats exhibit on Lion-Tiger Hill features African lions and Sumatran tigers, huge beasts who roar and stalk, sleep and eat." She stopped at a rocky section with dirt and grass. "We usually see them here, so we'll wait a bit."

Celeste seemed anxious. Cody shifted from one foot to another, antsy, until finally a cat pranced out from behind a tree. Then a second followed.

His son tugged on Celeste's arm. "That one's male because he has a mane. The other one is female."

Alex harrumphed. Even in the wild kingdom, everyone was a couple.

"Is that so?" Celeste always made the kids feel as if they were telling her new things. It was just one of her traits that he appreciated. His gaze landed on her. She wore denims today, ending just below her knees, with a plain, white, short-sleeved blouse that was anything but plain on her. Her hair was pulled up in some kind of knot. It had gotten long enough for the style in the time she'd been with them and the sun picked up its reddish highlights. The skin on her nape looked…appealing.

He focused back on the guide.

"Notice how the lions have extremely strong bodies, from which they benefit. Powerful forelegs, teeth and jaws are used for killing prey."

Cody's eyes were like saucers as she went on to describe what the lions feasted on.

But Celeste was intent on the yellow-gold creatures.

"Adult males have shaggy manes that range from a reddish-brown to black. The length and color of the mane are determined by age, genetics and hormones."

"He's beautiful," Celeste said, her voice full of awe. "With all that bushy hair and those golden eyes."

The guide smiled at her. "I agree. They're my favorite."

For a long moment, Celeste stared hard into the nearest lion's eyes. Alex noticed the animal stared back. Finally, she said, "The male is unhappy."

"Excuse me?" The guide seemed confused.

"Oh, um, he doesn't look happy to me."

Then the lion yawned. "They sleep twenty hours a day, so maybe what you're seeing is the need for a nap." The guide went on. "Notice how male lions are bigger than females, at up to ten feet long. Females reach nine feet."

Celeste mumbled, "Wow."

"The average weight of a male is 330 to 550 pounds while female run 265 to 400."

She shook her head. "I've never in my life seen a creature that big."

The tour continued, and Celeste had the same reactions each time they came upon something new. She was startled by baby cubs and backed away from the Sumatran tigers as if they scared her. The sun was bright and the day clear, as was Alex's mind, at least about one thing: Celeste had never been to the zoo.

Because he was right next to her, he noticed how her eyes clouded when the guide informed them, "The beautiful animals, of course, are endangered. The Gir Forest population has dwindled to only three hundred lions."

Her face paled at the fact.

"Celeste?"

"Such a waste." Her head snapped around to him. "Why would your society kill these magnificent creatures?"

"*My* society?"

"Ours, I mean."

He stuck his hands in the pockets of his jeans. "We didn't know what we were doing."

There was the world-weary look she got in her eyes sometimes. Suddenly, he had the feeling that he didn't really know this woman. "That is so true, Alex. In many things in the past, people didn't know what they were doing."

When they finished the tour, Cody grabbed Celeste by the hand. "Let's eat in Mane Grill." He grinned. "Get it. Mane as in lion."

She gave him a weak smile.

Because they had to wait for a table, fifteen minutes passed until they were seated in the outdoor eating area on Tiger and Lion Hill. Cody babbled on, but Celeste kept glancing back at the lion area.

She picked up the menu, and Cody asked her to read aloud to him because he didn't understand all the words. "All natural-angus burgers, chemical-and hormone-free grilled chicken sandwiches, hot dogs and chicken tenders." She raised her eyes to Alex. "Earnestly? People can eat animal meat named after those beautiful beings." She clapped her hand over her mouth. "I-I'm not feeling well. I'll… Um…" She looked around wildly. "I'll meet you at the carousel in thirty minutes. Go ahead and eat."

"Listen, if you're ill…"

"No, I'll be fine. I need some time alone."

Standing, she walked away quickly but not in the direction of the restrooms. Instead, she headed back to the lions.

"What's wrong with her, Dad? She never eats much meat, but she seemed upset."

What's wrong with her indeed? "I agree. And I don't know what set her off."

But he was determined to find out.

• • •

LATER THAT NIGHT, Alex found Celeste sitting outside on the patio. She'd been more herself after lunch at the zoo, though she hadn't eaten anything. She took in the Panda

Exhibit and Great Apes with interest, but seemed to be tempering her responses to them. And she hadn't again spouted the accusation of the animals being unhappy. Still, he had questions he didn't have a chance to ask until he joined her outside after the kids were settled in their rooms.

She turned to him when he made his presence known and handed her a cup of tea. Her hair was damp as if she'd just showered, and the scent of jasmine wafted up to him. "Thank you, Alex. This was thoughtful."

"For your upset stomach."

"Ah." She put her hand on her belly. Right below breasts encased in that material they called islet. He had to drag his gaze away from her chest. "I'm sorry I didn't behave well at the zoo."

Dropping down on a chair, he stretched his feet out for a casual pose. "Why not, Celeste? The zoo, especially the lions, upset you."

In the light from the lamp on the house, he saw her bite her lip, the action affecting the lower half of his body. To avoid the tense moment, he probed. "Celeste, why did the zoo upset you?"

"The notion of putting animals on display for humans to gawk at repulses me. They're creatures of nature, just as we are."

"Gawk?"

Now she stared at him. "Did you ever think that they don't like people staring at them all day long?"

"I know that's a theory held by animal lovers. And there are groups that work toward eradicating animal cruelty. I just never thought of housing endangered species in a zoo as cruel."

She frowned.

"Besides animals don't think."

"Maybe not, but they feel. I know Bruiser does. They sense things. And they experience negative emotions."

"Some researchers say that."

Abruptly, she looked back up at the sky, where stars dotted the inky black background. She took a long breath and let it out slowly.

"Celeste, haven't you ever been to a zoo?"

"Not like this one. But I've been to a version of one. A long time ago, though."

"The scents, even the food in the restaurant seemed to make you ill."

"The entire experience was unpleasant for me."

That made him…sad. He sipped from the coffee he'd brewed for himself. "Then, I'm sorry for suggesting a trip there."

"Don't say that. I'd been looking forward to going to the zoo. We never got to visit one in New York, so I was thrilled when Cody asked me to come along. But instead of joy, the experience filled me with sadness."

He said to make her feel better, "I guess we don't always know what's best for us."

She held his gaze. "That's very true, Alex. Very true."

Suddenly, he wondered if they were still talking about the zoo.

• • •

AS HE SWERVED into the parking lot of the baseball field, Alex heard a shout go up from the parents who weren't late to the game and who had probably attended all the previous ones. He got out of the car, and as he headed to the field, he rolled up the sleeves of his dress shirt. Once again, he'd be out of place with all the other parents dressed for a summer ball game. Something, he admitted to himself, that didn't sit right with him anymore. His life needed changing and he knew it.

Still sunny and hotter than hell at six at night, he put on his sunglasses. When he reached the field, he stood at the end of the bleachers as he watched a batter from Jon's team take a pitch.

"Strike!" the umpire called out.

Alex glanced at the scoreboard. Jon's team was behind by two runs.

"Oh, good," he murmured to himself as he watched his son take the plate. At least he hadn't missed one of his kid's at-bats.

Jon was a good ballplayer but didn't do well in tense situations. Celi said he'd struck out twice in the last game because the win was on the line.

The pitch was fast. Jon seemed focused as it sped to him. He drew his arms back…swung…and holy shit, he hit the ball. Alex tracked its trajectory as it zoomed out of the park.

"Yes!" Alex pumped his fist in the air.

The crowd rose to their feet, cheering and clapping. But Jon was startled, and it took a few seconds for him to start circling the bases.

As he rounded first, Alex saw an utter glee on Jon's face that he hadn't seen from the boy since Lila died.

When the spectators settled down, his son turned toward the bleachers and gave a thumbs-up. Alex tracked Jon's gaze. Celi sat between Cody and…Madison? She never came to Jon's games. She was always too busy.

Like him.

In truth, he'd been *trying* to keep himself busy as he awaited the go-ahead for the second phase of the clinical trials for Equisex by writing some long-overdue articles for journals he'd committed to. Because he'd been keeping his research out of the limelight, he didn't write about what he was working on. Instead, he concentrated on a series of articles based on the course he taught on ethics in scientific research. But when he saw Maddy, he realized he should be more like his daughter and take breaks from his work.

At the end of the inning, he jogged up the bleacher steps.

"Hey, there," he called out to them as he reached their row, which was, thankfully, in the shade. The three of them did a double take. No one expected him to attend. The knife of parental guilt twisted deeper in his gut.

"Daddy, hi." Madison stood and kissed his cheek.

Cody high-fived him from where he sat on the other side of Celeste. "You missed Jon's home run."

"Nope, I didn't. I saw it from below." He sat and leaned over his daughter. "Hi, Celeste."

Her eyes brimmed with joy. At his son's success? She seemed to be genuinely attached to his kids, and they'd seemed to blossom in her presence. "I'm so glad you saw his run to home."

"Me, too." He pushed away the recrimination of his neglect, vowing to do better.

As if she sensed his feelings, she reached over Madison and touched his hand. "It's only the third inning. There is much more time in this contest."

Her support made him feel better. With a lighter heart, he turned his attention to the game.

Two hours later, the play ended—his son's team won—and they trekked down to the field. Jon ran toward them—and right to Celeste. "I was good enough, wasn't I, Celi?" he asked humbly.

She hugged him right there in front of everyone, and Jon didn't seem to mind. She also whispered in his ear.

"No kidding?" He looked behind her. "Dad! You came." He circled around to Alex and hugged him, too. "Did you see it?"

"I did, Jon. A homer. With two on base. You were a star."

When Coach Bacon brought the team together for handshakes with the others, Celeste cocked her head. "Why do they do that after every game?"

"To show good sportsmanship."

"But they play like enemies."

"Which should be left on the field." Huh! She'd seemed fairly familiar with baseball when they played in the yard, but she didn't know some of the terminology or customs. "Celeste, why don't you know that? It's an age-old tradition and you have to have seen it before."

"Oh, of course, I have. I just never knew the source of the tradition."

Coach Bacon promised to buy the team ice cream, so they headed to Cones, a local stand. Alex was standing in line with Cody to pick out his family's cones, talking about the game, when he saw, out of the corner of his eye, the coach approach Celeste. She was sitting with Maddy at a picnic table out in the warm night air.

He carried a small cone of what looked like pistachio, her favorite. What the hell? The coach bought her ice cream? And knew what to buy, because she'd asked Alex to get her one, so she obviously hadn't told Bacon.

He studied the guy. A jock with big shoulders, muscles revealed in his red team shirt and shorts, dark hair. Did Celeste prefer that or lighter hair on men? An athlete's muscular build or a runner's body?

"Hold my place, Cody," he said and jogged over to the two of them. "Hey, Coach Bacon."

"Call me Nick," the man said. He braced his foot on the bench Celeste occupied, invading her personal space.

Alex held out his hand so the coach would have to move. "Nice to see you, Alex. Did you catch Jon's homer?"

So everybody knew of his inadequacies as a parent. "I did."

"I've been working with him." He winked at Celeste. "So has Celi."

"Hmm, I didn't know that."

Her face brightened. She'd gotten some sun today, and her cheeks had a healthy glow. "I read up on the techniques of batting and gave Jon a few instructions when we played in the yard."

Which was exactly what Alex should have done.

"Are you sure you never played ball, Celi?" Nick Bacon asked.

"No, I haven't. But I love sport."

Feeling like an intruder, Alex nodded to her cone. "I thought we were supposed to pick up our own cones."

"Oh, well." She looked flustered. "I have one now, so don't buy me another." Her tongue came out and licked the icy treat. Alex felt the gesture in his gut.

"Beat you to the punch, Lansing," the coach said, smiling at her.

In more ways than one, Alex thought, walking away from the couple. In more ways than one.

• • •

CELESTE REVIEWED THE list she'd made in her head of how to complete this upcoming task.

Step 1: go to the store.

She glanced over at Maddy. "Thank you for driving me."

The girl's return smile was genuine. She was so glad Maddy had accepted her. "You're welcome."

"I like spending time with you, Maddy."

"I feel the same about you. It's fun to have a girl around to do things with."

Maddy's words thrilled Celeste. Still she had to concentrate.

Step 2: walk up and down the aisles and choose food. Would there be a lot of it? She'd had no time to visit a market before this, even in New York. Alex had asked her last night after the game to go grocery shopping with Maddy. Mrs. Kramer had completed the task previously, and apparently, Alex had been picking up food they ran out of. But they needed to restore their bounty.

"Here we are." Maddy cruised down the line of cars situated next to each other. "Wow, it's crowded."

As Maddie sought a parking space, Celeste finished her mental list.

Step 3: get in a line; purchase food with a plastic card, which she did know how to use because Helen had taught them.

Step 4: carry bags back to the car. Drive home.

How hard could it be?

"This is in no-man's land," Maddy commented when she found a vacancy.

"Please, repeat."

Maddy shot her a look but only said, "We're far away from the entrance."

No-man's land. She'd have to research the idiom on the computer.

As they exited the car, Celeste put her hand over her mouth and nose. So many vehicles in one area had tinged the air with a scent of gasoline. Most people probably didn't smell the subtle odor, but Celeste's senses picked it up. She and Maddy walked for a bit, and Celeste noted Madison lagging. "Are you fatigued, Maddy?"

"I guess. We have a book report due tomorrow, so I stayed up late to read. I shouldn't have gone to the game with you last night."

Oh. Celeste had engineered that. She'd gone to Maddy's room before she, Jon and Cody left for the park ball to check on the girl…

"Are you well, Madison?" she asked after the girl had told her to come in. "Can I do anything for you before I leave?"

Maddy glanced up from her novel, *A Farewell to Arms*. "No, I'll just be stuck here reading when you get back." Her tone was sad.

"Why don't you accompany us?"

Maddy glanced out the window. "I wouldn't mind watching Jon play. I've seen you practicing with him."

"If you drive, you can leave right after, instead of participating in the custom of ice cream, and we can ride back with the neighbors who were going to drive us."

Her mood had lightened. "Yeah, it'll only be a few hours…"

"Where'd you go, Celi?"

"Go?"

"What were you thinking about?"

Celeste noted they'd reached the door to the building. "I was thinking about how I convinced you to attend the game, causing you to stay up late."

"I had a good time. Don't worry about it."

They walked into the store. In the outer area, containers on wheels were stacked one behind the other. "We'll need two to get everything." Maddie headed toward the carts. She yanked one out for her, and Celeste followed her actions.

They rolled them into the store, and Celeste stopped short. What she saw practically robbed her of breath. Crowds of people with their own carts, wheeling hurriedly in every direction. Someone bumped into Celeste with his cart, stinging her elbow. "Sorry," the man said, not sounding contrite. "But you can't stop like that in the aisle."

And then there were the smells—too many to separate, too strong, too strange. Celeste tried not to gag.

Madison had started down the aisle.

Gathering herself, Celeste followed. Maddy stopped at a counter, took a slip of paper from a little machine and waited.

"Number thirty-six," someone yelled.

Voices crowded Celeste.

"That's me." This from one of the other patrons.

From another, "Jesus Christ, Fred, we can't afford that cheese."

Unpleasant dialogue bounced around her, and Celeste felt her head spin.

Maddie read from a list. "We need cold cuts."

Celeste just nodded. She didn't know what several things were, nor did she have time to look them up at home. Cold cuts were among those she couldn't identify.

"What do you like, Celi?" Maddy waved to the glassed-in spaces.

Celeste studied the food in the glass containers. Meat from animals. Counter after counter of it. After her experience at the zoo, she'd steered away from most of it, favoring cheese, grains, fruits and vegetables. "I don't have a preference."

Except to get out of here.

So Maddy made the choices and they moved on. Celeste's stomach turned queasy when they reached another counter. "Daddy likes salmon. That's on the list."

Celeste stumbled backward and her hand clamped on her mouth. "The smell…" was all she could get out.

"Of the fish? It's not too bad."

"I must walk away."

"Okay, go get some crackers. Saltines." She pointed down an aisle. "I'll meet you there."

Swallowing hard, Celeste moved quickly. She bumped into someone and said, "I seek your forgiveness."

The woman stared at her. "Oh, well, okay."

Celeste circled around. She stood near counters, where a crowd gathered at a sign that said, "Buy one, get one free."

She stopped to find her bearings. The sign down the aisle read, *canned fruit.*

She pivoted to look behind her. She was not near the food from the sea nor the crackers. She was in front of a glassed-in compartment with cow products.

Celeste began to breathe really fast. She felt her face redden. And her heart pound. Oh, Nord, what was happening to her?

• • •

THOUGH IT WAS too hot to be running even in the later morning, Alex took to the four-mile trail that surrounded the housing development. The path wended around a pond, a copse of trees, up and down slight inclines. He couldn't believe how the development had matured since he and Lila had built a home here.

But he was running in the heat because the results of the first three weeks of the clinical trial on Equisex would be determined in two days. He'd sell his soul to the devil to see the actual findings, but they were kept confidential until the end. Interim results were not shared with those conducting or sponsoring the trial for fear that the knowledge might bias the outcome by influencing the rest of the analysis. He *would* however, hear if there were any serious side effects of the drug, which in turn could stop the study. If so, years of research would go down the proverbial drain. Sure, he could start over and try to counteract the effects, but he didn't know what he'd do differently. He'd been diligent in the development, testing and retesting, and he doubted he'd overlooked anything. His professional life was on the line with this phase.

Think about something else, darling, or you'll go crazy.

I know. I have to cope better.

Problem was, if he let his mind wander, it turned to Celeste. He'd actually considered suggesting she go jogging with him this morning, but instead, he asked her and Maddy to go grocery shopping. He'd been glad to be relieved of the duty as Ann Kramer had done it in the past, and Celeste had been too busy getting used to the family to take on that task before, too. Even now, she'd seemed hesitant to go, just as she'd been skittish about many other things. Particularly the zoo. Sometimes she was so inexperienced it shocked him. Maddy often seemed more knowledgeable about daily life. Then, on other occasions, she was supremely wise and offered good, solid advice. It was confusing.

She seemed to fit right in at the ball field, though. She watched the play and shouted to the players like any one of the other spectators. It was obvious she took total joy in Jon's success. And in Coach Bacon's attention. He scowled. The coach was interested in her; his overt comment and attention to her was proof. Was she attracted to him? Would she date him? And what business was it of his?

You're interested in her.

Lila, no, I won't talk to you about her.

You're not talking to me, love. You're trying to figure this out in your head.

Shit, he was really losing it, if his dead wife was giving him dating advice.

Sweaty and sore, he returned to the house after an hour run, just as Maddy pulled the SUV into the driveway.

Jogging up to them, he reached the car as she climbed out. "Hi, sweetheart, thanks for taking Celeste…" He saw the worry on his daughter's face. "Honey, what's wrong?"

"I don't know what happened."

"What do you mean?"

"Celeste got…sick, I guess, at the grocery store."

He darted to the passenger side, where Celeste still sat, and yanked open the door. Her head rested against the back of the seat, and her eyes were closed. "Celi, you need to get out of the car. You'll overheat."

"I, um, I need a moment." She didn't look at him.

Reaching over, he took her pulse. It was alarmingly fast. He felt her cheek. Her skin was hot. "Are you ill?"

"I…" She trailed off.

He turned to Maddy, who was behind him. "Tell me exactly what happened."

"I'm not sure. We got inside the store and she was supposed to follow me. But she seemed…like she didn't really know where she was, I guess. We went from counter to counter and she got more and more confused. The store was really busy and I could tell the crowds bothered her. But when we went to buy some fish, she looked like she was going to barf."

He turned his attention back to Celeste. "Celi, do you feel like vomiting?"

"Not any longer." She opened her eyes. "I think I'm okay now."

Taking her hand, he assisted her out of the car. She wobbled on her feet, and Maddy made a grab for her too.

"If I could just lie down."

He said, "Let's get you inside, where it's cool."

She looked at him. "I'm sorry. We didn't purchase the food."

"Don't worry about that now."

Once inside, instead of trying to climb three flights of stairs, they led her to the couch, where she dropped down and stretched out. "Maddy, get a cold cloth for her head." Alex took her pulse again. It had slowed some.

When Maddy returned, she asked quietly, "What's wrong with her, Dad?"

"She's either got a bug or she had a panic attack."

• • •

ALISHA ASKED, "WHAT'S wrong? You look terrible."

Celeste stared at the screen, still queasy inside. "I feel terrible."

"What happened, honey?" This from Dorian. She'd taken to using terms of endearment, as Luke did.

Slowly Celeste relayed the horrific experience of shopping for groceries with Madison. Even recounting the incident made her stomach pitch, though she felt remarkably better since they'd gotten her upstairs and she'd had a chance to rest in blessed solitude. She'd called her friends as soon as she could.

"Are you ill, physically?"

"I don't ache or feel pain. I tried to use the handheld Multimed over my stomach, but it did not change much."

"They aren't made for such conditions. We never have them in the future. What did you feel at the store?" Alisha asked.

"Fear. Deep confusion. Anxiety." She shook her head. "What's more, all the people there were experiencing the same things. Grocery shopping is not very pleasant for anyone."

"I'm sorry." This from Dorian. "What did you do?"

"I managed to get myself lost and couldn't find my way back to Maddy." Even repeating what had happened caused Celeste to shiver.

She could see Alisha reading her computeller. She said, "You had an attack of panic."

She's either got a bug or she had a panic attack. "What *is* that? Alex mentioned it."

"A sudden episode of intense fear that triggers severe physical reactions when there is no real danger or apparent cause."

Closing her eyes, she recalled the situation in the store. "I think it was the crowds and the smells. Neither was pleasant."

"Why didn't you call us so we could have gone through a practice run?" Alisha's voice was gentle despite the chide.

"I couldn't. Alex never mentioned purchasing food would be one of my duties. His request came suddenly. I could find no way of refusing."

"Did you explain the attack to the Lansings?"

"No. Maddy was terrified, poor girl, and Alex simply tried to calm me." She gave a brief smile. "That's usually my job."

"They'll need an explanation," Dorian said.

"All right, let me do a little more research on why these come about."

A half hour later, after Alisha had given her some suggestions, Celeste sensed someone at the door. "Come in," she said when the person knocked.

Bruiser bounded inside. He leaped on the bed and nuzzled into her. He stopped abruptly. Moved away. Looked up at her. Megadamn, if he didn't know she wasn't feeling well. Finally, he cuddled up next to her, his head nudging her hip, offering silent comfort.

"Hmm. He must sense you're sick."

"I'm not sick, Alex."

Alex dragged a chair over to the bed and sat down. "You had a panic attack."

"Yes. I am not comfortable with grocery stores."

His brows narrowed. They were thick and sculpted beautifully for a man. "Why?"

She recited the *cover story* Dorian and Alisha had come up with. "My mother took me grocery shopping in South America when the other two girls were in education. I never liked the place, with the people speaking a different language, rushing, feeling hurried. But one time, she sent me for milk. *Leche.* I knew where it was, but I got turned around, I guess."

"You got lost."

"I never felt such fear in my whole five years. I cried and tried to ask for help, but no one understood me. Finally, one of the workers in the store came upon me and took me to the management, who sought out my mother." She bit her lip to accent the playacting. "But I've had problems with grocery stores since."

Hellor, her explanation sounded stupid. Sounded as if she was some weakling who couldn't control her emotions. Pretending to be so was a part of this charade Celeste detested.

"I'm sorry." Alex's eyes deepened in color, a sign of regret. "Why didn't you tell me?"

"I'm embarrassed."

He shook his head. "Panic attacks are a very real condition and can't be taken lightly."

She smiled. "Yes, Doctor."

"Can I ask, when you were married, why you didn't get used to grocery stores?"

"Mitchell shopped. And after he died, I ordered groceries. Then I went to live with my sisters, and they took care of the chore."

Reaching out, he grasped her hand. Cradled it in his. Even in a weakened state, she felt the connection skitter up her arm. "I'm so sorry." And he was. It emanated from him. But it was accompanied by strong feelings for her as a person.

"I thought I could do this." *Of course she did. It was just a silly task.*

"No worries. Either I'll go to the store, or Maddy can."

"Oh, Alex, not Maddy. She's overburdened as it is."

"We'll figure something out."

Briefly, she closed her eyes. *Play on his sympathies. We can't let him fire you for not being able to do household chores.* "Perhaps you wouldn't have hired me if you'd known this about me."

"Celeste, I hired you to take care of the kids. Which you're doing extremely well. That's more important to me than buying food."

"There are so many things I can't do. Swim. Drive. I feel inadequate."

"You are so much more than those things." He gave her hand a squeeze, let go and stood before she could determine what all those feelings were.

She moved to sit up straighter. "I can come down and assemble dinner now."

"Nope, we're ordering out. Is your stomach better?"

"Somewhat."

"I brought you a menu for a local restaurant that we often do takeout from. Pick something for dinner and I'll come up when I'm ready to order."

She clung to his hand. Though she tried not to be, she was still shaken. "Thank you for understanding, Alex."

Leaning over, he brushed his knuckles down her cheek. "We love having you here, Celi. Those other things don't matter at all." She felt the soft wisp of his lips on her forehead. He meant to be comforting, but Celeste, feeling a hellor of a lot better *now*, wanted to fling him to the bed and join in the worst way.

Instead, she closed her eyes and savored the sensation. When she opened them, he'd turned away. She watched him walk out the door, then drew Bruiser closer. The animal responded by licking her face. He made her laugh, as he always did, but she knew what had happened today was serious. And it wasn't her reaction in the grocery store. Megadamn, she was overwhelmingly attracted to Alex Lansing.

And, worse, his ministrations, the look he gave her and the feelings she read in him confirmed something she knew in her heart all along—that Alex was attracted to her, too.

CHAPTER 8

CELESTE WAS ALONE in the house for the first time since she'd come to live with the Lansings. So today, she was determined to get into Alex's computer. She hadn't told Alisha or Dorian about her plan, but she knew she had to seize the opportunity.

Her recognition of his feelings and hers had catapulted her into action. If she let her emotions for the man grow, she would never complete her task. She had to take steps soon toward accomplishing what might save her society.

First, she'd get into his computer, access data they needed to alter in order to match the results they would change. Then, she'd alert Alisha of her progress. Next, she'd put into place the second part of her plan to get some distance between her and Alex. She'd already begun the process...

"The people to clean the house are coming today, Alex."

"Good, the rooms need sprucing up."

They needed trees?

"I don't understand why I cannot clean." That way she could gain access to the office easily. "I don't drive, and I'm not a good cook, but cleaning is one thing I'm capable of."

"No way. I wouldn't let Mrs. Kramer do it, and I don't want you to. The house is too damn big." He'd smiled wistfully. "Lila hated the job."

"I'm not Lila, Alex."

He'd faced her fully then, his face relaxed. "I know that, Celi. I know exactly who you are."

Another bombardment of irony.

"So, you'll need the key to the office to let the service in. And I'd like you to remain in the office with them as they clean."

"For security purposes?"

"Yes. I'm sure it sounds paranoid to you, but I need the comfort of knowing my work is safe."

"Protecting your work is anything but paranoid." Her tone was heartfelt.

Crossing to her, he'd grasped her shoulders. "Thank you for understanding. No one else seems to see the measures I take as…well, sane."

She had to step back because the gratitude, caring and attraction, too, poured out of him and transferred to every cell of her body. Gathering her strength, she followed him to the living room.

Behind a picture of dancers in feathery, little costumes was a locked box. It was called a *safe*, which for once in this culture, did make sense. She'd seen them on the video box and discussed how they worked with Alisha. She hadn't known of the existence of this kind of device, because in her time, material goods meant nothing to them and no one in the known world, small as it was, kept scientific research a secret. Everything was shared for the greater good regardless of who got credit.

There was an added bonus to the discovery: what else did he keep in there?

She stopped a good distance away so as not to alert him. "I keep the spare keys to the office in here." He glanced over his shoulder, and smiled self-effacingly. "Thanks again for not thinking this overkill." He shook his head. "I guess we all have irrational fears."

Celeste's stomach clenched. His were anything but irrational.

But she maintained her alertness for when he opened the safe: Thirty-three to the left, fifty-six to the right, fifty-five to the left. She could hear the clicks, and once she knew the combination of numbers, she could get into the safe, then into the computer when she had the opportunity.

After the cleaners had done their job, she'd locked up the den and given the keys back to Alex...

She waited three days (she'd finally gotten used to the term) until all the children had medical appointments. They'd be gone from nine this morning to about one, as they were having lunch out. So, at ten—just to be sure she waited for sixty minutes after they left—she headed to the living room. The huge space was not put to use. Thinking of her tiny dwelling in 2514, she wondered again why people built homes so much larger than necessary.

Shaking off thoughts of a time she could never return to, she crossed to the picture, signed, she saw now, by a man named Degas. She wasn't totally familiar with the art of the time but was gradually making her way through its history.

What she was about to do was such an invasion of privacy she hesitated in front of the metal box. Then she drew in a deep breath and opened it. First, she secured the key to the office, then she shuffled through the rest of the contents. Passports—papers to travel with—for all of them to visit a world that was incredibly large. Birth certificates, a box with jewelry in it, which might have been Lila's. Currency. Stacks of small envelopes that she didn't have time to peruse.

Deciding to close the safe and replace the key after she used it, she made her way back and unlocked the office door. The room seemed empty without Alex in it. She sniffed; the air held a hint of male—some aftershave or cologne that he preferred. Trying to ignore the signs of his presence (which exacerbated her guilt), she hurried to the desk and booted up the computer. Tapping her fingers on the sleek wooden surface, she waited. This machine was so slow! When the screen finally came on, she said, "Megadamn!" Access was password protected. She tried all the kids' names. Nothing. She tried Lila's. Nothing.

Then intuition kicked in and she recalled the stack of envelopes in the safe. She rushed back to the room, opened the thing again and found the envelopes. Inside the one marked *computer* was a list of passwords. At the top was *Lila Ann Baker*. This had to be what Celeste needed. Back inside the den, she punched in the letters on the archaic keyboard, and the computer files opened.

Once again, she was besieged by guilt. How badly she would hurt the Lansings slammed into her like a sandstorm. She forced herself to think about that storm, about the gray curtain of air surrounding her time, preventing the wonderful thing called daylight. She made herself remember the barren women and men and the pervasive sadness everyone carried because of their inability to produce younglings.

More determined, she turned her attention back to the icons. She bypassed several things: his email, because Alisha had gained access to that, pictures of children, correspondence. Ah, there was one named *Bright Future*. What he thought his work would bring with this miracle drug. "Oh, Alex, you were so wrong." Her heart ached with the thought.

The list of files for Equisex came up. There were nearly fifty of them. She clicked on the one called *Lab Results*.

Access denied!

She and Alisha had predicted this. So Celeste got to work. She kept an eye on the time as her fingers flew over the keyboard, searching for a way to break the code. After two hours, she managed access. The clock with a pendulum chimed twelve times. Another hour of safety. She'd just begun to read the high points of his research when she heard, "Celi, where are you?" Cody's young voice.

Oh, dear Nord. The family had returned early! She clicked out of all the files and shut the computer down. She exited the office and locked the door. In the hallway, she heard Cody's thundering steps above. She'd just reached the stairs when he came rumbling back down.

His face was reddened. "Celi, where *were* you?"

"Out in the yard's back."

"I checked there and I didn't see you."

"I was off to the side." She tousled his hair. "You must have missed me. Why are you back so soon?"

"We got done with the doctors and we're going to lunch at the park. Dad wants you to come with us. Please."

Dad wants you. Her heart leaped at the notion that Alex desired her company at the same time that the key to his safe, which she'd just illegally entered, dug into her palm. A word came to mind, one she now knew well—betrayal.

Her conflicting emotions disoriented her for a moment, but she managed to say, "Sure. Let me get a sweater. Go tell your dad I'll be right out."

She didn't dare access the safe again to put back the key, nor did she reenter the office. She could only hope everything was put to rights and she could replace the key safely at another time before Alex needed it.

Cody ran back to the car to deliver her message and she climbed the stairs with a heavy heart, knowing that her plan to destroy Alex's life had just moved a little farther down the road.

And this time, it was all because of her.

• • •

ALEX SMILED AS Cody waited by the door. When Celeste came out, the two of them came toward the car. As Alex watched, a quick flash of anxiety went through him. Was the Lansing family getting too close to her? Himself included? He had to admit she'd frightened him yesterday with her frailty. *Him*, a doctor, who at one time had treated people with serious illnesses, was thrown by a simple panic attack.

And today, he couldn't stop himself from suggesting they take her to lunch with them; it was indicative of how much he was coming to care for her. Already cared for her. But it felt so damn good to have these feelings spark inside him again, ones he thought died with Lila.

"Hi, there," she said climbing into the passenger side and Cody joined the others in the back. "I don't have to sit up front."

"It's okay," Jon called out from behind her. "We want you to."

Maddy leaned forward. "We're going for a picnic at this park that has a huge play set. Even I like it."

"Oh." She glanced down. "I hope I'm dressed correctly." She wore sandals, white shorts and a multicolored, sleeveless top. "You look fine. Doesn't she, Daddy?"

She always looked fine. More than fine. Today, the knit of her shorts clung to her hips and the cut of the top accented her generous breasts. He cleared his throat. "You look great. I hope a picnic is okay. We got done with our appointments and decided to have lunch outside."

"It was kind of you to think of me."

He glanced at her as they drove down the street. He'd left the windows open for her because she loved the air coming in. But right now she seemed...down. "You okay, Celeste?"

"Oh, yes. I was reading a book and I think I'm still in that world."

Maddy leaned forward again. "I do that, too, Celi. Maybe sometime we can read the same book and discuss it."

"That would please me very much."

In fifteen minutes, they arrived at the park. Celeste glanced around before they exited the car. "Will we purchase food here?" she asked.

"We stopped at a deli that packs lunches. We got you vegetarian. You don't seem to like meat much anymore."

"I like some of it. But I prefer vegetables from the earth."

"Yuck, your sandwich has tofu." This from Cody.

"Ah. A healthy substitute." [1]

The playground sprawled out before them. Since it was early July, the place had filled with people. "Will the crowds bother you, Celi?" Madison asked. "You've been okay since the grocery trip."

"I apologize for that, again. But this park is out of inside and I'll love it."

"No apologies for the other day." Alex reached over and put his hand on her knee, just as he used to do when Lila sat in the front seat. The memory caused him to pull back. "Illnesses come in a variety of ways."

They settled under the shade of a big oak, on a table that was just being vacated. As they unwrapped sandwiches, potato salad, chips and cookies, the kids bubbled away with stories about the doctor visit.

The boys teased Maddy because she hated shots. "Did you cry when you got shots, Celi?" Jon asked.

For a minute, that damned confusion flitted across her face. Come to think of it, she'd been awed by their stories about the doctor. "Um, no."

"Dad says we have to get them so we won't get sick." Cody wrinkled his nose. "We all got rooster ones."

"Rooster?"

Alex smiled at his son. "Boosters, Cody."

The other two dissolved in laughter. Celeste didn't even laugh, maybe because she often misspoke… No, she *misunderstood* things frequently. He still couldn't figure that one out.

Cody gobbled up his food, then stood. "Can we go on the set now, Dad?"

"I'm not done yet." Alex held up his meatball sandwich. "Neither is Celeste."

"I'll watch them, Dad." Maddy climbed out of her bench, too. The play set was in sight of where they'd eaten but too far away to keep track of Cody.

"All right, then. We'll be over soon."

When the children left, he transferred his gaze to Celeste. Her perfect teeth bit into the sandwich and she licked her lips with her tongue. The site of that tongue and what it might do in other circumstances deprived him of breath.

She didn't seem to notice. "The tofu is acceptable and I like the texture of this vegetable."

"That's eggplant."

"It isn't yellow."

"Excuse me?"

Her eyes widened. "We never had this growing up. I was…" Laughing at herself, she waved her hand. "Never mind. I do like it."

"You like all sensory things, I think." He stared at her. "You missed a spot." Reaching out, he wiped the sauce off the corner of her mouth. But he couldn't draw his hand back. Instead, he brushed his thumb over her lower lip.

Her eyes dilated. As a doctor, and as a man, he knew why.

Swallowing hard, he shifted away from her. "I guess I'm done. We should get going."

"You're right." Flushed, she cleared her throat. "We should."

They disposed of the trash and he said, "Want to hit the bathroom before we go over there? We'll be playing for a while."

"Yes, I would."

"Me, too. I'll walk you over."

They strolled side by side in the breezy air, birds chirping and voices of children off in the distance. When Alex thought about the times he'd done these things with Lila, he felt an acute sense of loneliness invade him. And realized suddenly, he wanted this again. He glanced at Celeste. She wasn't looking at him, but he could feel her attraction to him. Did she want those things from *him*?

Just as they reached the little green-shingled houses, she stumbled on the step up from the grass to the concrete. Alex lunged to grab her. He caught her around the waist and pulled her up hard to keep her from tumbling over. She came flush with him. He remembered that night he skidded off the road and he held her in the car. Why did this feel so different? So much…more?

She didn't move away. His arms tightened. In his brain, he knew this wasn't an advisable path to go down. She was his caregiver, important to his children, in some ways more important than he was comfortable with. It could gum up the works if he started something with her. Still, he couldn't let go.

She placed her palm on his chest. He felt the light touch all the way to his groin. The sunlight caught on her hair, making reddish highlights on her head. Her blue eyes glimmered like gems when they locked gazes.

"Alex," she said throatily. "You can, um, let me go now."

"Should I?"

She drew in a deep breath. "I think so." She bit her lip as if she doubted her words. "Don't you?"

"I guess." He dropped his hands, stepped back and thought, *I hope I can.*

But as they started to the lavs, he wondered if it was already too late.

• • •

"WHAT AM I going to do?" Maddy whined at nine that night. "I'm supposed to go on a field trip to the Holocaust Museum with my American History summer class tomorrow." She sat in bed, her foot elevated and iced. Earlier today, she'd taken a tumble off a high board on the play set and landed on her ankle.

Alex shook his head. Now he was just Dad, but he'd gone into doctor mode when his daughter was hurt. "It's a bad sprain. I don't think you'll be walking on it, with or without your old crutches, for a few days."

"I should have been more careful. I shouldn't have climbed that high with Jon."

Sitting down next to Maddy on the other side of the bed, Celeste took her hand, hoping to calm her. Draining her anxiety only worked minimally, she was so upset. "I know how much you were looking forward to the field trip."

Maddy sighed. "I made plans to sit with"—she stopped short and looked at the two of them—"some kids on the bus and have lunch with…them."

She'd tailored her words. Suddenly, Celeste knew she had someone specific in mind. She sensed *guy* vibes.

Intent on his daughter's condition, Alex was oblivious. "I'm sorry, baby. There will be other field trips, though."

"Not like this." Maddy was immovable.

"I guess if a miracle occurs and you're better tomorrow…"

"Our family doesn't get miracles, Daddy. You know that."

Alex drew in a breath. "I'm sorry about that, too." Standing, he kissed her head. "Get some rest. You're overwrought now."

Standing, too, Celeste left the room with Alex. Tonight, simply his presence overwhelmed her. He seemed big. But breakable.

She grasped on to his arm. "I'm sorry your life hasn't been filled with better things, Alex." Megadamn, he was feeling so bad, she almost couldn't tolerate it. She siphoned off as much negative emotion as she could.

Stopping, he leaned against the wall a few feet from Maddy's room. "Bad things happen to all of us." He raised a hand and brushed his hand down her hair. "To you, too."

"We were right there and couldn't keep her from harm."

"My kids play hard. Accidents happen."

Still, she'd been so consumed by what occurred with Alex when they arrived at the play set, she'd barely watched over the children. She and Alex had almost kissed outside the bathing rooms. When she'd hesitated, he left it up to her. Had she said yes, who knows where that might have led?

"I hope she can handle being kept down." Alex continued speaking. "She never was a good patient. We used to have to corral her in bed whenever she was sick or hurt."

"It's because she's such an active, hard-working person." She decided to float an idea. "Who do you think she was planning to sit with tomorrow?"

"Her friends. Kelly, maybe. Why?"

"Did you ever think it may be a boy?"

"God, no. She's way too young."

"She's seventeen." Celeste had joined with a man by that time.

"Don't even say that. I can't deal with it tonight."

"All right." Celeste just shrugged. "Before the mishap, I had fun today."

He raised his chin, and his gaze was unflinching. "We could have had more."

"Alex…"

"No, I'm sorry to have verbalized that." He glanced at his watch. Hours had passed since supper and getting Maddy settled. "I'm beat. I'm going to go check my email and go to bed."

While he'd been tending to his daughter and the boys were occupied, she'd managed to slip the key back into the safe, but she hadn't had a chance to make sure she'd left the office as she'd found it. Godheads, she hoped she had.

"I'm going to bed now. Good night, Alex."

He just watched her, then shook his head. He left without speaking again.

When Celeste reached her room, she was overcome with despondency. She'd wanted Alex to kiss her today, join with her, right out there in the open. She wanted to invite him up to her room, touch him all over, be with him all night. Nothing else seemed to matter.

She lay awake, thinking about her options. Around two a.m., she came to the conclusion that she had to talk to Alisha again about Alex. Soon. But she also decided something about Maddy. The girl was in pain, angry and disappointed. And *that* Celeste could affect.

Since everyone had been in bed for hours, she tiptoed out of her room, down to Maddy's and eased open the door. The girl was sleeping deeply. Alex had given her some kind of sedative. Celeste crept to the bed and drew back the blanket from her foot.

Slowly, she ran the small Multimed over the entire area.

As she left the room, she thought, *At least I could do that for them.*

• • •

SUN. BLUE SKIES. Puffy little clouds. The day was lovely again, though thunderclouds hummed in Celeste's heart. Alisha walked beside her on the outing Celeste had suggested when she'd called her this morning. Celeste wished Dorian was with them but she'd gone to see Luke, so they were alone. And it was time for a frank discussion.

"I gained access to Alex Lansing's computer, Lisha."

Her friend stopped short. Eyes rounded, she asked, "Why didn't you tell me when you phoned?"

Celeste shrugged. "I...I'm not sure." Which was an outright lie. She dreaded telling Alisha the progress she'd made. "Some other things have happened at the house."

"Tell me about his computer. Did you find Equisex documents?"

"Yes. I was beginning to read them when the Lansings returned home."

"You risked getting caught?" Alisha's hand fisted in her lap. "Celi, this is too important to be careless."

"I wasn't careless." Her voice held a note of annoyance. She immediately said, "I seek your forgiveness for snapping at you."

"You never snap. What's wrong to make you do it now?"

She explained how she'd accessed the data. How she'd gotten out barely in time. How she'd gone with the family on a picnic while the key that she'd used to betray Alex sat in her drawer upstairs.

"What happened with the key?"

Suddenly, she remembered the terror she felt at having to replace the key while they were home, and her heart started to beat faster. "I put it back when I had the chance."

"You should have made a copy."

"There wasn't time. What if Alex found it missing?"

"In any case, you got in. Were you able read enough of his analysis to find a way to prepare for our alterations in the clinical trials?"

"No. I'd just cracked the password when they came back to get me." Celeste sighed. "The results of the first part of the trial will come in tonight, you know."

"I'll access those findings through the email he'll receive from Ravel. We'll use them as a benchmark on what changes to make in Alex's data, too." Alisha waited a moment. "We're making progress. I've discovered several general sites where Clinical Trial Data is stored. Now I need to dig deeper into them to find the Equisex trials."

They walked for a while in silence. Passing a small pond where flish swam, Alisha asked, "Are you still getting closer to the children?"

"Yes, too much so, I guess."

Nord, Celeste didn't dare tell Alisha she'd used the Multimed on Maddy. The risk was worth it, though. The girl had come running downstairs this morning…

"Daddy, Celi, look! My ankle's all better."

"Honey, that's highly unlikely."

"Here, check it out."

When he examined her, Alex had been astounded that the swelling was completely gone and ligaments seemed to be fine. Of course, Celeste was the only one who knew why…

"And Dr. Lansing? You're getting too close to him, too."

Ah, so her friend had sensed something. "Yes."

You can let go of me, Alex.

Should I?

And later, in the hallway, he said, *I would have had a better time if…*

When they reached a set of benches, Alisha suggested they sit down. Uncharacteristically, Alisha took her hand. Celeste could feel strength emanating from her. It felt good. "You can tell me, Celi. I won't scold you. I want to be your confidante, like Dorian is."

Celeste hadn't realized that. She wondered if Alisha felt left out. She squeezed Alisha's hand and discovered she *did* feel excluded. "I don't want to do this, Lisha. I don't want to destroy their lives."

Alisha's light brown eyes darkened. "What do you want, Celi? To allow his drug to be improved upon so much that people in the future pop it like vitamin pills and then can't have babies a hundred years later?"

"No, I want to stop that from happening another way."

"Is there any other way that you know of?"

She'd been awake all night thinking about this. "I want to tell Alex what and who we are. But I know we can't. He's so security conscious. So distrusting. He wouldn't believe us."

"It's too much of a risk anyway, Celi. We absolutely can't take that chance."

"I guess."

"For what it's worth, I seek your forgiveness…I'm sorry that you feel so bad about what we must do. Truthfully, so do I."

"Thank you."

A woman pushing a stroller came up to a bench across from them. Grinning broadly, she picked the baby up and cuddled him to her chest. He wore a little, blue, one-piece thing and a small hat to match. "I know you're hungry, sweetheart. I know."

Celeste watched in awe as the woman slid her hand to her blouse, then opened a few buttons. Oh, by the godheads, she put the child to her breast. Never had Celeste seen this act, not even on video boxes. It tugged on her own womb.

The woman said, "There. Eat away." She looked up and must have seen them staring. "Oh, I…I can put a blanket over my shoulder if this bothers you."

"No," Alisha said, her voice strained. "You're fine."

Celi's throat closed up and she couldn't speak.

Alisha took her hand again. "I guess that says it all, doesn't it?" she whispered.

"Yes. It does."

"You have to distance yourself from Alex Lansing."

"I know," Celeste murmured staring at the tiny life sucking nourishment from another. Their world in the future deserved to have this.

CHAPTER 9

THE DAY AFTER her discussion with Alisha, Celeste awakened to a nudging. Then some squeals. She sensed, rather than heard, *Outside. Now.* Oh. She bolted out of bed along with Bruiser and hurried down three flights of stairs to the kitchen, where she let the dog into the backyard. Bruiser bounded through the grass to a spot where she'd taught him to go. While he did his thing, she brewed coffee for the others and made herself tea, then returned to her room, and since she'd showered last night, dressed in pink shorts and a white T-shirt. Back downstairs, a quick glance at Bruiser romping in the yard told her he wasn't ready to come inside, so she sat down at the table and sipped the tea, watched him play.

And thought about Alex. He would have gotten the first results of his clinical trials last night. They had to be good, given that he succeeded in releasing the drug the first time around and Alisha and Celeste had altered nothing. Her heart clenched in her chest at the thought. She was going to ruin all that for him.

Alex, who'd touched her knee in the car yesterday when she'd sat in front as if he had a right to.

Alex, who'd caught her, then held her in his strong, very powerful hands when she'd almost fallen.

Alex, whose glistening eyes told her he would have kissed her if she'd given him permission.

No, she couldn't think about her feelings for him. About what had almost happened. She had to control her thoughts, even if her emotions ran wild.

Turning her attention to Bruiser, she saw a squirrel scamper down a tree and into the yard; when the dog noticed, he began to bark and run after it. She was watching him chase the tiny furry thing back up the tree when Maddy came into the kitchen, in a cute sundress made of bright green material.

"Up already?"

Maddy smiled and poured herself some coffee. "I'm heading out early."

Odd phrasing. "Today's one of your holidays. You don't have summer school."

Taking a quick glance behind her to the entrance of the room, Maddy sat down. Her face was animated and Celeste noticed the girl wore a bit of face paint. "I don't want to make a big deal out of this, but someone's picking me up for breakfast. I'll be back for the neighborhood barbeque."

"Someone, as in Kelly, your friend?"

Madison blushed. "No. A...boy."

"A boy? I asked you about that the other night."

"I know. I didn't want to tell you anything in front of family. My brothers will tease me, and I have no idea what my father will do. I've never...seen boys much."

"Did you meet up at the field trip?"

"Yes. It was so fun, Celi."

Like a mother watching her daughter blossom, Celeste's heart was full at Madison's reaction. "How long have you been friends with him?"

A shrug of her delicate shoulders. "We've been hanging out for a few months. Talking a lot on the phone."

"It's normal to be interested in boys at your age, Maddy."

Again, Maddy's cheeks became rosy.

"What's his name?"

"Cameron."

"Is he attractive?"

"Yeah, he's cute." Her eyes lit with teenage mischief. "He's got mag hair."

Mag as in magnificent?

For a moment, Maddy stared at Celeste. "Do you, um, want to meet him?"

"Sure."

"Okay. Come out to the car."

When Cameron arrived in a small, dark vehicle she recognized as a Prius, like the one Maddy drove, he exited it and crossed to them. Celeste noticed he touched Maddy's shoulder when he said, "Hey." Then he turned to Celeste. "I'm Cameron Crawford."

"Nice to meet you, Cameron. I'm Celeste." She held out her hand. When she shook his, the boy's emotions were clear. He was nervous but excited, and when he glanced at Maddy again, he experienced a swell of positive emotion.

"I know who you are. Maddy's told me all about you. She says you can do almost everything."

"What a sweet thing to say about me."

"Well." He shuffled on his feet. "I guess we should be going."

"Enjoy your breakfast." She turned to Maddy. "Maybe when he brings you back, he can meet your father."

Maddy's expression darkened again. "We don't disturb him in his office. He'll probably be working."

Touching Maddy's arm to reassure her, Celeste said, "I'll bet he'd make an exception for this."

"Maybe. Will you ask him?" Translated, *Will you tell Dad about this boy?*

"Of course. I'll see you later."

Back in the kitchen, Celeste had just opened the door to let Bruiser inside when Alex came in through the hallway, dressed in jogging shorts and a T-shirt. His hair was messy and he hadn't shaved yet.

As he bent over to rub Bruiser's head, Celeste was bombarded by a bolt of lust so strong that it silenced her, set her off-kilter. Now that she'd admitted her feelings for him, and recognized his for her, her desire surfaced acutely. She wanted to feel that scratchy stubble everywhere on her body.

"Good morning." His tone was stiff, though. Distant. Their situation had caused a strain between them. She'd been the one to refuse the kiss, to refuse anything *more* between them.

"Good morning, Alex. Everything okay?"

"Of course." He crossed to the pot and poured coffee. He nodded to the cup Maddy had placed on the counter. "Did you use this cup?"

"No. It's Maddy's."

"Is she up already?"

"Up and gone."

"Where? Today's the fourth of July."

"Sit for this, Alex."

With a puzzled expression on his face and clear frustration emanating from him, Alex dropped down adjacent to her. "What is it?"

"Maddy's having breakfast with a friend."

"Kelly?"

"No, a male friend."

His cup hit the table, sloshing liquid onto his hand. "Shit." He wiped it up. "What the hell is that all about?"

"She'd made arrangements for him to pick her up for breakfast. I met him. He's very nice. He—"

Alex's eyes flamed. Despite the gravity of the situation, Celeste wondered if they looked that way during joining. "Let me get this straight. You allowed my daughter, who is only seventeen, to get in a car with some strange boy."

Celeste drew back at his sharp tone. "I guess I didn't see this as *letting* her do anything. It was all arranged."

"You're the adult in the situation." His tone was harsher than she'd ever heard. "You should have woken me up when you found out and let me handle the situation."

"There was no situation. She went to breakfast with a boy."

Now his hand slapped on the surface. "This is unacceptable."

Again, she recoiled back. Uneasy with male anger, especially when it was directed at her, she nonetheless tried to be rational. "I don't agree with that. She's—"

"It's not your place to agree or disagree. She's my daughter. I'll make the decisions regarding her."

His outburst and his words didn't make sense. "I always admired you for letting Madison make her own decisions, Alex."

That silenced him for a moment.

Though her anger was spiking at his outburst, she reached out for his hand. He drew it back before she could read what was going on inside him. "Aren't you making this out of proportion?"

He stood abruptly, the chair loudly scraping back. "No. I realize you're infiltrating every aspect of our lives, but I'm in charge of Maddy."

Her anger winning over understanding, she arched a brow. "Then maybe you should spend more time with her." Which was a mean thing to say in response to his equally mean comment because she knew the guilt he was feeling these days about his time at home.

"Don't criticize my child rearing. You've never had any kids, so you don't have enough experience at—"

It was like getting hit with a jutzi ball. "I see." She stumbled to her feet. "Then be sure to be home when she comes back. Because I made the very real mistake of telling her you'd like to meet him."

With that, she swept out of the kitchen, Bruiser at her heels. She was halfway up the steps when she realized she and Alex had just had their first fight. And because he could hurt her with his unkind words, she affirmed again that her feelings for him had to stop, not simply be controlled.

Because they were increasing exponentially, no matter how much she pushed him away.

• • •

FEELING LIKE AN idiot, Alex knocked on Maddy's bedroom door later that night. When there was no answer, he called out, "Maddy, it'd Dad. Can I come in?"

"No!" was the curt reply.

"Please, honey."

A few seconds passed. Then, slowly, the door eased open. She kept it ajar, a shield against his entering her domain. He said simply, "I'm sorry. I overreacted today."

She just stared at him. He always thought she resembled Lila, with her blond hair and blue eyes, but her likeness was accented tonight by the disgusted look on her face that his wife used to get when he did something stupid.

He leaned back on his heels and shook his head. "I should have been saner about a boy driving you to breakfast."

Cocking her head, she asked, "Why weren't you?"

Because I was spoiling for a fight with Celeste. Because the results of the clinical trials came in last night and I wanted to share them with her but couldn't. You were a convenient scapegoat for the anger and frustration I'm feeling.

Yet there was more to his reaction about the boy. A kernel of truth he could tell her. "I guess I'm not ready to see my little girl dating. Hell, Maddy, I don't even know if seventeen is too young or just right for you to go in cars with guys."

Her face got that sadness in it he saw all the time after Lila died. "Mom would have known."

"I realize that. I never expected" —God, emotion welled in his throat and he looked heavenward—"to be doing this alone."

"Oh, Daddy." She walked into his arms. They hugged for a long time and he savored the feel of his child, the scent of lemony shampoo reminding him of when he used to bathe her when she was a baby.

Mention of the word reminded him of the unconscionable comment he'd made to Celeste and he winced.

Finally, he drew back. "You're not grounded."

"I figured. Cody didn't even know what it meant."

A smile. They'd had a pretty good run since Lila died. Except for his not being home enough. And now, maybe he could alter that, especially since there was good news with the trials, which would be proceeding. Time to spend less time worrying about work and more on his kids.

"Listen, another thing. I haven't been home enough for you three. I'm going to be better about that."

Her gaze was knowing. "Me, too."

An arched brow.

"I go out, do more things, because Mom died, too."

Jesus. He hadn't known that. "Oh, honey."

Maddy was distracted by something over his shoulder. "Hi, Celi."

He pivoted. There she stood, dressed in some knit bottoms and a T-shirt. He wondered briefly if that's what she wore to bed. "Hi. I was looking for your father, but I can tell I'm interrupting. I'll just go downstairs and wait for you to finish."

"No, that's okay." She gave Celeste a smile. "He's better now."

Alex faced Celeste. "I want to talk to you, too, Celi. To apologize for jumping all over you about Maddy." He'd also ruined hers and his time at the barbeque, which he'd been hoping to enjoy with his family.

"Don't concern yourself about it." Her tone said the opposite. Men quickly learned to decipher certain words and phrases if they wanted to survive women.

Jamming his hands in the pockets of his shorts, he asked, "What did you want to talk to me about, then?"

"I should leave," Maddy said.

"No, stay." Celeste's face was totally blank, but something simmered in her blue eyes, like a low flame from a lighter, burning hotly. "I won't be home tomorrow evening, if you were planning on going out."

"It's your night off."

"Yes, I realize that. I simply didn't want any more confusion about my responsibilities."

Bingo. She *was* still pissed. Or maybe more.

"I—"

She interrupted. "I have a date. With Jon's coach."

Goddamned son of a bitch! "I see." Maybe she could decipher *his* tone, too.

"I'm looking forward to it." She gave his daughter the smile he hadn't gotten from her. "Madison, I was hoping you'd help me pick out something to wear."

"That'd be cool." She looked at her father. "Even though I'm not grounded, I'll stay home with Cody and Jon if you want to see Sherry tomorrow night."

Staring at Celeste, who had a date with the fucking coach, he quipped, "I'll take you up on that offer, Maddy. There's a work cocktail party I wasn't planning to go to, but maybe I will." He added meaningfully, "Now."

CHAPTER 10

CELESTE WAS STILL home at seven that night when Alex left on his date, and she found herself untenably stirred up. Damn that man, he was driving her crazed.

The phone rang. The boys were at friends' houses until nine and had taken Bruiser. Maddy said she was Skyping with Cameron on the hour. So Celeste hurried to the house phone in the family room. "Lansing residence."

A pause. "You must be the new caregiver. I'm Jeff Lansing, Alex's dad."

"Hello, Dr. Lansing. I'm Celeste Hart."

"I've heard a great deal about you, Celeste. Every time I talked to the kids from our cruise, they sang your praises." His voice, like Alex's, was deep and masculine. There was a serenity in his tone, though, that Alex didn't have.

"That's very sweet of you to say. Alex is out. On a date!"

"Oh. With Sherry?"

I'm afraid so. "Yes."

"I just wanted to check in with him about coming up to the beach house tomorrow. Do you know if he's all set?"

"He is." Alex was leaving for a week to drop off the kids at his parents' house, go to a conference, then pick them up on his return. "Are you still joining us?"

"I...I'm not certain. My throat is achy, so I may stay back and recuperate." She wasn't sure she could spend time with his dad. Even across the phone lines, she could tell the man was very intuitive.

"There will be three doctors here." His father chuckled, putting her at ease. "I'm sure we could take care of a simple sore throat."

Were *all* the Lansing men stubborn?

"I wouldn't want to impose. But let's wait until we see how I feel in the morning. I'm sure you'll have a nice time with the children."

"God, I miss them."

"They're wonderful, Mr. Lansing. Maddy is so smart and kind. Cody's a full hand, but I adore him. And Jon couldn't be any nicer."

"I do believe you mean that. And please, call me Jeff. I'm sure we're going to be seeing a lot of each other."

Don't count on it, Dr. Lansing. Jeff. With any luck, I'll be out of here soon.

The minute the words entered her head, her heart tightened. This was really going to happen. She was really going to sabotage Alex's research, then walk out on him, Maddy, Jon and Cody. Alex would do fine—obviously—but how would the kids fare?

They were going to be another casualty of the completion of her task.

· · ·

ALEX DIDN'T REALIZE he'd made a mistake by jumping into a date with Sherry until he walked into Ed Johnson's huge townhouse in Georgetown. The place was stately, with cherry wainscot, dark wood flooring in the foyer, which led to a large living room off to the left. Not his taste at all.

Sherry had been pleased to get his call, and when he told her about this shindig, she'd been delighted to accompany him, even on such short notice. At some point, he'd have to deal with Sherry because his feelings for her had diminished — since Celeste came into his life. Now, though, she clung to his arm, her French perfume cloying and her slinky dress unappealing. All Alex could think about was holding Celeste at the park and being treated to the scent of her bath splash and the feel of her curves through her plain shirt and shorts.

Shit, this was going to be a long night.

The president of Global Pharmaceuticals, Johnson, caught sight of them and headed over. A tall, powerfully built man, his physique matched his demeanor and position. He carried a drink, probably the double-malt Scotch he preferred. "Alex, this is a surprise. You said when we talked this morning about the clinical trials you couldn't make it."

"I unexpectedly became free. Ed, you've met my friend Sherry Manwaring."

"Of course, at other work events." Alex liked the guy, even though Ed spent most of his time at fundraising. That would kill any enthusiasm for work for Alex.

"Come on over and meet some people from the Clintons' party. Their Foundation is looking to back avant-garde research, and you might be able to convince them to pick us."

"All right. Let us get drinks first."

Ed led them to the bar, and Alex ordered a manhattan for him and martini for Sherry. She sipped it and tugged on his other hand. "Isn't this fun? The Clintons. Can't get any more snazzy than that."

"Yeah. Snazzy." He approached the crowd with dread. This was so not his thing.

• • •

"I'M SURPRISED YOU wanted to come here."

Celeste looked over at Nick Bacon. They both stood in front of the rock-climbing wall at Rockin' Times.

"Jon told me about it. He said you mentioned this activity was good exercise, and I value that."

She'd been at about eighty percent of her normal exercise since she started work for the Lansings. She needed to think about herself more. Do things that would keep her body in shape and her mind sharp for her task here. And stay away from Alex. Who'd made a megadamned date just to spite her. "I also wanted to try it out for the children. If it's fun, I can bring them here."

Picking up a harness, Nick approached her. He'd already snapped one on over his groin and chest. Thankfully, Maddy had warned her not to wear a dress tonight, which she preferred, but simple, light blue capris and matching top. Maddy had also pulled Celeste's hair up in some kind of knot on her head. Nick had commented on the style.

"Those Lansing kids are lucky to have you, Celi." He frowned. "I always felt bad about Lila dying. She was a great person."

"I'm sure she was." Celeste didn't want to hear about Lila, the love of Alex's life.

"Here," he said, handing the strappy thing to her.

Or dear. She glanced around. No one was in the process of fitting themselves for her to mimic. She smiled flirtatiously at Nick. "I have no idea how to wear this."

"My lucky day." His grin was infectious, and his brown eyes sparkled. He was a truly handsome man with dark hair, a strong jaw and nice, wide shoulders. He looked cute tonight in jeans and a shirt that said Syracuse, a higher-education institution in upstate New York.

She pictured Alex's light hair and eyes, his slimmer but muscular physique. Tonight, Sherry would get to appreciate that, and probably more. She sensed from the vibes between them that they had joined many times.

Nick adjusted the harness to resemble a cradle. "Now, step in with one foot and hold on to my shoulder with your hand."

That seemed easy, she thought as she did as he instructed, then repeated the process on the other side. Nick's body was hard, she noticed when she braced herself. And he smelled great, like some sexy scent he must have put on.

"Want me to help buckle it?" He pointed to her breasts.

She laughed. "No, I think I can figure that out from how yours is secured." She should have let him help her — touch her accidentally, flirt more with her. She should join with him tonight. The godheads knew she'd been without sex for nearly three months, and the Vagino was not satisfying enough after such a long time without real contact with a man's body. From that thought, she imagined Alex naked and beautiful.

When she was ready, she donned tight-fitting gloves and walked toward the wall. She estimated it stood thirty feet above ground, meaning if a person fell, some damage could be done to him, hence the harnesses. Several climbers were ascending at various levels. First, they placed their hands on the farthest rungs they could reach, then, their feet in the lower slots. Moving their feet up farther caused their reach to extend, and that's how a climber ascended.

"Race you to the top?" Nick challenged.

"Not this time." She winked at him, as she'd seen Luke do with Dorian. "Maybe when I get the hung of it."

His look was blank.

Megadamn.

"Oh, you mean the hang of it."

"Isn't that what I said?"

"No, but don't worry about it, babe. Just be yourself around me." His grin was infectious. "I'm a very uncomplicated man."

That would be nice, for a change.

• • •

ON THE STOOP of her front door, Sherry wrapped her arms around Alex's neck. Lifting her head, she kissed him. Her body, lush and feminine, pressed against his. His first impulse was to step away. Why couldn't he fall for this woman who'd always reminded him of a young Elizabeth Taylor, who was chic and sophisticated enough to converse easily with an ex-president. But this wasn't who he wanted to be holding. Kissing. Making love to.

Damn it, he'd try. He drew her closer and angled his head. Normally, it didn't take long for him to fall in the sexual haze of desire, but tonight, he was unmoved. So he pulled back.

She took his hand and brought it to her lips. "Come inside." Her voice was a purr, meant to entice him.

"I can't, not tonight. Maddy's babysitting and I want her to go to bed at a decent hour since we're going on a trip tomorrow. She'll wait up for me."

"You could call her and tell her to go to bed."

"Not this time."

In the light from the porch, he could see a look come into Sherry's eyes that reminded him of the lionesses at the zoo. "Where's Celeste tonight?"

"That's a non sequitur."

"Is it?"

"Why would you ask about Celeste?"

"Curiosity." Not.

"She had a date." He tried hard not to show the distaste he felt for the evening she was enjoying.

Sherry lifted her chin. "Is that what this is all about?"

"What do you mean?"

"Alex, we haven't made love in weeks." She counted on her fingers. "Since that woman came to live with you."

"You know I've been focused on the clinical trials, getting the kids set for summer, acclimating our new sitter."

"Is that all you've been doing to her?"

Anger was easier. He stepped farther back. "Give me a break, Sherry. She's there for my kids. I couldn't *do anything to her* if I wanted to."

"Do you want to?"

"This conversation is over. Thanks for coming with me." He circled around her.

"Alex, wait."

But he didn't. He trundled down the steps, blocking out the fact that he'd just lied to Shelly, even if it was for her own good. He hated any kind of deception.

• • •

"ARE YOU SURE you don't want to come back to my place?" Nick made the comment after he pulled his Bronco—a big truck emitting horrible fumes that made her gag—into the Lansings' driveway. The light from the street lamps cast them in a semi-glow.

"Not tonight."

He grabbed her hand. "I'm not asking for sex. I know some women wouldn't consider it on the first date. We could just hang out."

She almost laughed out loud. Any sex she'd ever had was on the first date. "No, but thanks. I had fun rock climbing and loved the pizza."

He tugged her close. "How about one kiss?"

Alex has to be the first man to kiss me.

"Maybe next time, Nick."

"All right. I'll see you at Monday's game."

"You won't. Remember, Jon's going to miss this week's play. He's visiting his grandparents."

Nick grinned. "Does that mean you're free?"

"I'm going with them." Maybe. "Good night."

Climbing out of the vehicle before he could ask her more questions, she slammed the car door and sprinted to the house. Turning at the porch, she waved. He really was a nice man. Under different circumstances, she'd readily join with him. But her emotions were so tangled up in Alex that she couldn't imagine being physical with Nick. She checked her watch before she opened the door. Maybe she'd go to Alisha's tonight and cancel her plans to visit the Lansings beach house with the children, as she'd hinted to Alex's father. Acting as if nothing was wrong between her and Alex around them all would be torture. The kids would enjoy their grandparents without her.

With that goal in mind, she let herself into the house. The interior was quiet. Solemn. No children sounds rambled down the corridors. No smells emanated from the kitchen. She wondered if the kids had eaten the tuna casserole she'd prepared for them tonight or talked Maddy into a pizza.

She was just about to head upstairs when she saw a figure coming down the dark hallway from the back of the house.

She automatically went into a defensive stance she'd learned from Rhea.

"So, did you have a good time tonight?" he said without greeting her.

Her body deflated. "You frightened me, Alex."

"Sorry." He didn't sound sorry. "So, did you?" She tried to place his tone, his stance, outlined from the light in the back of the house. Both, she decided, were stiff and unyielding.

"Yes. I had a good time."

He didn't move. "What did you do?"

"Listen, can we turn a light on? You're all in shadows."

His answer was to move in closer. His scent—cologne and alcohol—encompassed her, and his body seemed threatening. *This* she did not need tonight. Easing back from him, she crossed into the living room and switched on a lamp in the corner. Her eye caught on the Degas picture that hid the safe, and guilt swamped her. She could have nothing with this man while she was betraying him so badly. Walking to the window, she stared out so she didn't have to look at him. The warm air soothed her.

Then she felt his hands on her shoulders. She could read his touch clearly. Strength. Confusion. And acute desire. No, no, he couldn't hold her like this. She wasn't strong enough to resist how much he wanted her. Already, the threads of his need were reaching into her.

"Celi." He breathed out the word like a caress. His body was so near, she could feel its heat. "Turn around."

She shook her head.

And jumped when his lips brushed her bare nape. Her entire body went liquid. She heard herself moan but couldn't stop the sound from coming out.

"You feel it, too." His breath fanned her ear, making her knees buckle.

Recovering a bit, she tried to stand tall and gave her head a hard shake again. "I don't know what you mean."

"Don't lie." His lips tracked their way across her neck, to one side of her face, then back again and to the other side.

"Alex, please." The hoarse plea seemed to make his hands grip her tighter, move in closer. That was when she felt his erection, strong, stony and potent.

Never in her life had she wanted anyone more.

"Please what? Kiss you? Make love to you?"

"We can't."

Forcefully, he tugged her around. Cupping her face, he whispered, "Yes, we can. We're both adults. Unmarried."

"The children could get hurt."

His eyes were wide. And so sincere she wanted to weep. "We can deal with whatever happens between us."

All Celeste wanted was to melt into the man. He brought her to his chest, and his arms banded around her back. Her arms, of their own volition, circled his neck. His head lowered.

Shield yourself. Shield yourself.

Celeste tried. She really did. But he was too strong. Not physically, but his emotional pull was a magnet to her. When his mouth pressed hers, Celeste felt the touch to her bones. Every nerve ending pulsed with one brush of his lips over hers, then a second. He groaned and deepened the contact, angled his head for better access. His groin thrust into hers and she felt his steely length again. Felt *herself* go damp.

The air left Celeste's lungs when he probed her lips open, and his tongue entered her mouth. She had to hold on to him to stay upright. She was consumed, controlled; her heart squeezed tightly, feeling as if it might burst with the pressure.

He didn't stop. He swept her mouth with his tongue. His grip tightened, now on her waist. She was drowning in him, like when she'd become submerged under the water in the ocean. And just like then, she was powerless to stop it.

Suddenly, he pulled back, all except for his hands on her shoulders. She opened her eyes and he was staring at her. "You…you're shaking like a leaf."

Her fingers went to her lips. She sucked in air. Felt her body tremble as if she was ice cold.

"Celeste, honey, what happened?" He began to rub her arms up and down. His actions only made the shivers worse.

"Y-you kissed me."

"But your reaction…"

She rubbed her lips. "This is a first for me."

"I should hope so. You're quivering all over. Badly."

Not that, she hadn't meant that.

Leaving her to grab the blanket off the couch, he slid it around her; she sought solace in the cozy fleece.

Gently, Alex touched her shoulders again, making her shudder. "I don't know what to say about this."

"It…it shouldn't have happened."

"Not the kiss. I mean, your reaction."

A potent weakness invaded her. Every limb, muscle, even her nerves were saturated. "I need to go to bed." She started away.

"No, Celeste, you can't leave me like this."

She turned around. "I have to. I need to rest."

Again, he reached for her. She practically stumbled back and held up her hand. "Please, I beg you. Just let me go."

Finally, he stepped away.

Celeste leaned heavily on the railing as she climbed the stairs. Her eyes leaked, and tears streamed down her cheeks.

Each step was painful. She managed to reach the top and staggered down the hallway to her door. She just made it to the bed before she collapsed.

• • •

EARLY THE NEXT morning, Alex headed to Celeste's room. When he knocked on the door, she didn't answer. He turned the handle—a big invasion of her privacy—but he was worried about her. She'd been so...fragile last night, something he'd never associated with her. The door opened. He scanned the room. The bed was made, the windows closed, blinds drawn.

And Celeste was gone.

He noticed a note propped up on the pillow. So she knew he'd come to see her. Jesus, he'd been awake half the night, trying to figure out what had happened between them. He ripped the paper open:

"Dear Alex,

I'm not traveling to your parents' beach house with you today. I left for my condo early this morning. Please don't try to contact me. We need time apart. I'll return to the house when the children do, of course, but hopefully with more perspective. Tell them I'll miss them."

Gripping the paper, Alex sank to the bed. His gaze traveled over the pillows providing small touches of color. A low dresser/desk was covered with lotions and other feminine accouterments. Her scent hung in the air. She'd put up pictures. One, in particular, contained abstract shapes, but damned if he didn't see a man and woman coming together in it. She was everywhere.

His hand crumbled the note. To say he was disappointed was a gross understatement. He didn't realize how much he'd needed to see her this morning, make sure she was well, examine what had happened between them and where they could go from here.

He'd also been looking forward to the drive to his parents' beach house with Celeste and his kids. The loving warmth of his family would be good for all of them.

And he wouldn't be the only one who was sad about her absence.

The kids rose early and dressed before they even came downstairs. They each entered the kitchen carrying a suitcase. Bruiser, who'd slept with Cody, tagged along but didn't bound outside as usual. Maddy had to coax him through the door.

"Hi, Dad." Jon spoke first.

Cody stumbled to the table and sat.

"Hi, Daddy." Madison looked around. "Where's Celeste?"

Casually leaning against the counter, he sipped his umpteenth mugful of coffee. "Something came up with her sisters. She isn't going to see Grandma and Grandpa with us."

"No fair." This from Cody, who bolted up from the chair. "She *has* to go."

"Sorry son. We can't do anything about emergencies."

Jon scowled, seemed to turn inward in a way he didn't do much anymore. Since Celi had come to live with them.

Maddy shook her head. "Too bad for her, too. She told me she really wanted to come with us." His daughter was thoughtful. "Did you see her last night, Dad? How was her date?"

He practically crushed the mug handle. "She didn't say much about it. She was tired." *And had the craziest reaction when I kissed her.* He couldn't think about anything else.

But he had to. "All right. I'll cook us breakfast before we go."

Unenthusiastic grunts greeted him.

Join the club.

They hit the road about nine. The kids were silent for about an hour, and when Alex glanced in the rearview mirror, he saw Bruiser staring out the window, quiet, too. The second hour, they played a traveling game, and by the time they arrived at his parents' beach house, they'd finished moping about Celeste's absence.

She shouldn't have done this to them.

She shouldn't have done this to him.

His parents' second home, a white clapboard, triple-level structure, rose up from the ground and overlooked sand and dunes that led to the ocean. He remembered coming here as a child, too, and playing on the third level, which was all his. His mom and dad had their friends over frequently, and he enjoyed the company of their children. Sometimes, when no kids came, Alex used to hide out in the hall and listen to them talk about medicine.

They exited the car, and Alex hadn't realized how much he'd needed to see his dad until Jeff Lansing walked out of the side door. As tall as his son, with a still-young face and a full head of white hair, he crossed directly to Alex. "There you are." His dad grabbed him in a bear hug. Whispered, "I missed you, son."

"I missed you, too. Welcome home."

As Bruiser scampered around everyone's feet, his father bent down and said, "Wow, you're a beauty, boy."

"Grandpa, what about us?" Cody whined.

This was the routine his dad followed. He always greeted Alex first, kissed Maddy, then Jon, then swung Cody up in his arms. "You've gotten so big."

Cody gripped his dad's neck. "I *missed* you, Papa."

"We'll have to catch up." Still holding Cody, he led the way inside, and Alex was immediately comforted by the familiar surroundings—a large, sunny kitchen, the stuffed couches and chairs in the great room off of it, and even the piano in the corner had been staples of his early life.

His mother, a spry sixty-eight, came running in from the deck. Tall and slim, too, her hair was tinted blond and her clear blue eyes focused on him. "You're early. I was walking on the beach." She flew to Alex and threw herself into his arms. "Hi, honey. I missed you."

Alex breathed a sigh of relief. Maybe, just maybe, this trip could be salvaged.

• • •

ALISHA DIDN'T BELIEVE for a second that Celeste had a headache when she showed up at six a.m. She'd gone straight to bed, and now, it was almost noon. With a tray of tea and toast, Alisha walked down the hallway to Celeste's room and knocked lightly. "Come in," a soft voice replied.

She found Celeste still in bed, the covers pulled up to her waist. Her hair, which was longer, was messy, her eyes dull and her face pale. "What time is it?"

"Noon."

"I slept a long time."

"Must not have gotten much rest last night." Alisha smiled, though she recognized right away that whatever had happened to her friend was not good. She asked anyway, "Did you have fun on your date? As in *joining* fun?"

Tears welled in Celeste's eyes.

Setting down the tray, Alisha rushed to the bed. "Celi, what is it? Are you really sick?"

Celeste put a hand over her heart. "Here."

Alisha studied her. "It's Alex Lansing, isn't it?"

"I'm sorry, Lisha, yes, it is. I know you warned me not to get involved with him, but I'm afraid I have."

Briefly, Alisha closed her eyes. She loved Celi and wanted to handle this right, but so much was at stake. "What happened?"

"He kissed me. I think he was jealous of my date. I know I was of his. He waited up for me to come home."

"Did you enjoy the kiss?"

She rolled her eyes. "You could say that. I fell apart."

"Fell apart?"

"I became weak, like I missed supplements for a few days. And dizzy. Then I started to shake."

"Did you ever have that reaction during joining?"

"No, never." She shook her head. "Nothing even close to it."

"A mere kiss brought that on?"

"Yes. I couldn't block him, Lisha. Even in joining, I block some every time because my partner's emotions resonate so deeply with me. But I tried and I couldn't."

Alisha took her hand. "I'm sorry. I don't know what to say about that. I know how sensitive you are, how much you feel things. It must have been frightening."

"I was terrified."

"I feel bad for you, Celi. Really I do. But I hope you're not thinking of telling him the truth."

"No, we already discussed this, the day we saw the nursing mother in the park. I knew then we couldn't tell him. Last night changed nothing."

Hoping to soothe her friend, she rose and brought Celeste the tea. She expected Celeste to cry, to mourn, to belabor their fate. But she didn't. She sat up straighter, with square shoulders and her chin high. "Loving Alex, wanting him is selfish. I'll still do whatever I have to in order to get the data we need."

"I admire that, Celi."

Celeste sighed. "So, let's make a plan. Fortunately, the Lansing household will be empty for days. That ought to be enough time to complete our task."

• • •

THE EVENING OF his arrival, Alex and his father sat on the porch at eleven o'clock. Crickets sang their nightly chorus, and a soft warm breeze blew off the lake. The children were settled, and his mother had gone to bed. They'd each poured a glass of red wine and drank in contented silence. His dad was the first to speak. "I wish you didn't have to leave for the conference tomorrow. I wish you could stay the whole time with us."

"Me, too." Alex meant it. He was…weary and emotionally drained. "I wish I could skip the conference."

His dad hesitated, then said, "Why don't you?"

"As if you and Mom would have when you were my age."

Jeff Lansing chuckled. "We did once. The time my brother took you for a week and you were ten. You went to Disneyworld."

"Yeah, I…wait a minute. You didn't go to that conference? You said it was important."

His father stared up at the star-filled sky. "We lied. I needed time with your mother. Actually, I needed time with you, too, but Mom and I were having a rough go of it, and we realized our jobs had become too important to us. We took that week to remap our lives."

"Seriously?" Celeste always said *earnestly*. "Did it work?"

"We were about fifty percent better. I did spend more time with you." He smiled. "We also did some estate planning and retired earlier than most doctors, so yes, I think it worked."

Reaching out. Alex clasped his father's hand. "I don't remember you neglecting me, Dad, if it's any consolation."

"Neither will Maddy or Cody or Jon. Consciously, anyway."

Alex shot his father a look. "Are you saying I work too much?"

"Of course you do. Since Lila died, your attention to your research has tripled."

"I—" He stopped his protest. "Why am I arguing? I told Maddy just this week I'd be more available."

"You've got the clinical trials to wait out."

"No, I mean for good. Celeste showed me that."

"Ah, Celeste, who is your nanny."

The wine was tart and went down smooth when Alex took a hefty swallow. Even thinking about her was painful now.

"I spoke with her last night."

That surprised him. "I didn't know."

"When you were out on your date. She seems like a lovely woman."

"That's one way to describe her."

"Is she what's got you tied up in knots, or is it the trials?"

"Am I tied up in knots?"

His father took a sip of wine. "I can see it, even if you can't."

Sighing heavily, Alex knew he needed to share his feelings with someone or he'd combust. "No, I can see it. And yes, it's her. I don't know whether I'm coming or going with her."

"Does she feel the same?"

He thought about how she'd trembled so much when he'd kissed her it alarmed him. A lot. So he told his father about that.

"How odd," his dad commented. "She has no physical diseases or conditions that would cause that reaction?"

"Not that she shared with me. She's very fit, eats well, exercises in the mornings. She's rarely even tired."

"Then her reaction makes even less sense."

"There are a lot of odd things about her. She seems so ingenuous sometimes, and at others, like she knows the world better than I do."

"Ha. I feel that way about your mother."

Alex chuckled. "And she's unfamiliar with some everyday things." Now that he said it aloud, he realized how true the comment was.

"Like what?"

"From a dishwasher to the ocean. She had a bizarre reaction to the zoo." He explained about her growing up in South America and how her dead husband sheltered her.

"Maybe that's all it is. So, you like her?"

"Very much." He leaned forward on his chair. "I want to be with her...sexually...more than I've wanted anything since Lila died, Dad."

His father gave a low whistle. "That's a lot, Alex."

"I know."

"What are you going to do?"

"You tell me."

His father laughed. "Okay, I will. Skip the conference and go back to Fairfax. See what happens when you have some alone time together."

"I can't do that." He waited. "Can I?"

• • •

ON THE NIGHT Alex went to visit his parents, Celeste and Alisha found the file on Equisex and cracked its encryption. They discovered several things: the trial dates, when exactly reports would be sent for each phase and also the location of the specific backup system. They had what they needed to destroy Alex's work when the next results came in.

CHAPTER 11

"I DON'T KNOW what else to do, Rodney." The red-haired woman with blue eyes stared up at the man with a chiseled jaw. "We're doomed."

Rodney grasped her shoulders. "I won't let you go, April. I can't. You're my soul mate."

"We have no choice."

"There's always a choice."

"Arrgh…" Celeste growled and grabbed the remotes to switch off the *LifeLine Television for Women* network. She used to enjoy these videos before she moved to Virginia. When she didn't know the pain and loss that could occur when men and women became attached to each other.

If only Bruiser hadn't accompanied the Lansings to Alex's parents' home. The dog made Celeste feel better, and she could use a warm body to nestle against right about now. She slid down under the covers—the air modifier was on high—and buried her head in the comforter Maddy helped her pick out. The action didn't make any difference. She was still a traitor, a betrayer of the man she loved.

Loved? Oh, megadamn. Could that be true? Did people of today give their love to each other so quickly? She'd only known Alex five weeks. Something this strong and powerful should take time.

What's wrong? You're shaking like a leaf.

Her reaction to the kiss was indeed strong and powerful.

By the godheads, why hadn't she listened to Alisha from the beginning? Celeste had allowed herself to become attracted to Alex before she even arrived in Virginia. She'd been enamored of the idea of a relationship with a man. Now she hated it.

She studied the room. She wished she could end her stay at the Lansing house right away. But Alisha strongly urged her not to, even after they acquired the necessary information to alter the trial results…

"Can we leave Virginia now, Lisha?" she'd asked. The stake in her heart ground in a little deeper at the thought of never seeing Alex again. Or the children. But she couldn't go on seeing them every day and deceiving them so badly.

"No, I seek your forgiveness for it, too. You have to remain in residence so we can access the computer to alter the data Alex gathered from the beginning. And we have to wait until we change the results to know what to do. The timing will be tight."

"I'm not sure I can stay. Knowing I've destroyed his life. How the children will be affected."

"Alex Lansing will find other work. He did the last time his research was sabotaged." At this, she'd glanced away as if she didn't really believe what she was planning to say next. "And children of this time are resilient."

But the thought of keeping up the ruse, pretending to have their best interests at heart, all the while damning their future, made her physically ill…

After they'd gotten the information, Alisha had flown to New York to get help from Dorian in the next part of the task, which had to be completed by July twenty-fourth, the date the second phase of the clinical trial results would be known.

She'd wanted Celeste to go with her, but Celeste couldn't face the others just yet. She'd rather stay here and suck on her wounds. And though she could have—maybe should have—stayed at the condo, she'd been compelled to come here, to the home she loved so much now.

Her eyes drifted shut. Maybe she'd sleep the pain away…

She awoke to gentle nudging. "More sleep, Bruiser."

A deep voice said, "Bruiser didn't come back with me."

Alex? No, no. She turned her face into the pillow. But she felt a gentle brush on her hair. Then he tugged her around.

There he sat, on the side of her bed, dressed in a plain blue T-shirt, jeans, and a smile on his face. "Hey, sleepyhead, wake up."

She drank in his face, classically handsome but drawn today. He must have showered not too long ago, and his scent of soap filled her head. Made her want to weep. "What are you doing here, Alex?"

"I've come to see you."

Swallowing hard, she bit her lip. *You wouldn't have if you knew what I'd done.* "That was not a good idea."

"I think it was. We need to talk."

Her eyes narrowed.

Carefully, he braced his arms on either side of her. "I'll have to insist, honey."

Celeste's eyes teared. No man had ever used a term of endearment for her. It curled inside her.

He swiped at a few renegade tears. "Please, don't cry. It's noon. Why don't you get up and I'll make us some lunch."

She didn't move.

"I'm not leaving you alone until we have this out."

Deep fear seized her. She was going to have to do this. She could see the determination in his eyes. Was she capable of bluffing her way through a discussion with him? What choice did she have? Like everything else, the future depended on it.

So, she made a quick decision. She'd talk out why she couldn't be with him, then move out of the house. She'd come daily, be with the children but not spend time with him. When they were able to alter the data on the trials and on his computer, she'd quit altogether.

• • •

ALEX THOUGHT HE'D be anxious today, taking charge of the situation and forcing Celeste to talk about a possible relationship between them. But a strange calm came over him on the three-hour drive from the beach. He'd gone by her house, but no one had answered the doorbell when he rang it. After trying her cell, he'd come home and been shocked to find a sweater thrown over the chair that hadn't been there when they'd left and a glass in the sink.

And then he felt it—her presence. He didn't know what he was going to say when he climbed the stairs and found her in bed, but the sight of her asleep had made him even more determined.

"Alex."

He turned from where he'd been staring out the window in the kitchen at the hot July day. She was pale as paper. Her blue eyes stood out and her usually animated features were schooled into a blank mask. Beside her sat her three suitcases.

For a moment, he stared at them, then raised his gaze to hers. "You're not going anywhere, Celeste."

She crossed her arms over her chest. "That isn't for you to decide."

"In part it is."

"Why?"

"Because I've come to care deeply for you." Even to his own ears, his voice was hoarse. "And I want to touch you, kiss you, do more, so much that it's driving me crazy."

Her eyes widened further and he realized she was afraid.

"I know this happened fast. I know it's unexpected." He ran a hand through his hair. "Hell, to nobody more than me. I've never even thought of any other woman besides Lila in the way I'm thinking about you."

Still she said nothing.

"I want to pursue this relationship, but I can see you're not where I am on this. So I'm going to ask one thing of you."

"W-what?"

"Stay these three days with me. See what we have together. If it's what I think it is, then we won't need to worry about the kids getting hurt."

She gripped the edge of the counter. "You have no idea what you're asking."

"Celi, I don't understand why trying to forge a relationship with me is such a problem for you." He crossed to her then. "I know in here"—he touched her heart with his palm—"you feel something for me. I sense it." He grasped her upper arms. "Tell me if I'm right in that, at least."

"Y-you're right." She cleared her throat. "I feel too much for you."

"Why *too* much?"

"Because any relationship between us is impossible."

"That makes no sense, honey."

"I know. I can't be any clearer."

What to do? What to say to convince her?

Pull out all the stops, son, his dad had advised.

"Okay. I'll make a deal with you."

162

"What kind of deal?"

"Do you want to make love with me?"

She nodded. "Yes. But I—" He put his hand over her mouth so she couldn't finish the sentence.

"Then let's do it." He brushed his knuckles down her cheek. "Afterward, if you still want to go, I'll let you."

Celeste watched him for a long, few moments. He was offering her the chance to join—to make love—with him, something she thought she'd never have the opportunity to do. Could she do that? Just that? Would it hurt more to join with him and then leave him? Something told her she couldn't hurt any more than she did right now. So she looked him straight in the eye and said, "All right, Alex. Just one time." She slid her arms around his neck and leaned her head into his chest. "Sometimes this was all I could think of."

She was shocked when Alex slipped his hands beneath her legs and around her back and scooped her up. "W-what are you doing?"

"Carrying my girl upstairs."

"Alex, I'm too heavy. I'm not a little woman."

"No, and I love that about you." He kissed her lips quickly. "Don't worry, I can handle you."

She wasn't worried about that. What concerned her was if she could handle him. No, megadamn, if she was going to do this, she was sure as hellor going to enjoy it.

So when he climbed the flight of stairs with her and headed to his bedroom, she blocked out all doubts, all rationale, and steeped herself in the hardness of his chest, his rich clean scent, the beating of his heart.

Inside, the space seemed bigger than when Jon and Cody showed it to her. Gently, Alex set her on the bed with her feet on the floor and knelt before her. "I want to undress you."

She'd seen the custom on the video box, and Dorian had told her about it. "I'd like that." It would be a first, as women and men disrobed themselves before joining.

Slowly, he removed her sandals. Lifting her foot, he kissed the bottom. Never had she experienced a similar feeling. It was like no other. "Ahh…"

He did the same to the other foot.

Next, his hands went to the hem of her shirt. Gently, he pulled it over her head. "Pink lace. This may be my favorite color now."

Her heartbeat escalated. She wondered how mere words could do that to her. Leaning forward, he kissed her though the material of the bra. His teeth closed over a nipple, and she practically ricocheted off the bed. "Celi, what? Why does my touch affect you so much?"

"I can't block it."

His beautiful brows furrowed. "Why would you want to?"

"I—I feel things deeply. When I was a child, people worried about me." That was true. Sensitives like her were a small percentage of the world's future.

"It's fine by me. Just so you don't shiver uncontrollably, like you did when I kissed you."

She pressed her mouth against his. "Stop talking."

He lingered on her lips, and Celeste absorbed him. He tasted of paste tooth. Now that she'd felt kissing once, knew what to expect, she could handle the sensations better.

But when he unclasped the front closure of her bra, and she spilled into his hands, his touch, his kneading of her bare flesh took her breath away. Little bumps of goose raised on her arms. She had to consciously draw in air.

"This is so powerful," he murmured. "So special."

Her feminine side was glad his touching her was different for him, too.

He drew her up to standing so he could unfasten her shorts and push her panties to the floor. Finally, she stood naked before him and she did shiver, mildly in a breeze coming through the window. He stepped back. "Do you know that your body is perfect?"

"I want to see yours."

"I want to touch yours."

"I…want to take your clothes off. I've never…" Godheads, she had to watch what she revealed.

"You've never what?" No answer. "You've never disrobed a man before?"

She shook her head, knowing she shouldn't have told him that but unable to stop herself. Already a sexual haze was descending on her, and she was losing the ability to think.

"I can't imagine why." His expression was very male. "You can tell me later. I'd be honored to be the first."

What a strange experience to lift his shirt over his head. Instinct told her to put her mouth on his chest, which was covered with lighter hair than on his head. The sensation was new and wonderful. For some reason, men of this time had chest hair. She kissed him, inhaled him, and streaks of lust shot to every nerve ending. "You always smell so good, so different…"

"You do, too."

Her hands dropped to his jeans; she opened the fasteners and pushed them to the floor. She'd touched a man's genital parts before, of course, but when her hands slid to his, cupped him, caressed him, she couldn't block the desire, and black spots swam before her eyes.

"I…I need to join, Alex."

"Join," he whispered against her lips. "What a quaint word."

Picking her up again—her head spun—he set her on the bed, then lay down next to her. Tugging her forward so she faced him, he touched her breasts again. Plumped them. And took a nipple into his mouth. Celeste's vision dimmed and she felt dizzy.

They exchanged urgent caresses for several minutes until she said, "Please, Alex, now. Join with me."

Holding her gaze, he scissored her legs. Dorian had told her men today preferred different positions from their time, so she was prepared for a new one. Still, it felt odd to see so much of him, to be able to touch him as he took one of her legs, opened his then drew hers between them.

"Oh, shit, I forgot protection. I think I have some in—"

She cupped her hand around his nape. "Don't go. I'm incapable of conceiving."

"I forgot." He drew her even closer. "Look at me when I come inside you."

She couldn't look elsewhere. Inch by inch, he slid into her. Full. Hot. Hard. The words echoed in her mind. Never in her life had she felt so close to someone, so connected to another person. Not even Rhea. When he was fully inside her, touching her womb, Alex became part of her body *and* soul; the sensation rocked her to the core.

Alex stopped moving and watched Celeste's eyes glaze over. He was so aroused, so overcome by being with this woman, even the slightest movement set off fireworks. Not only did she clench around him tightly, but the connection went deeper. Taking a deep breath, he managed to say, "I'm going to move now. Ready?"

"I hope so."

He slid back to the opening of her, then in again. She arched her back. Moaned the most beautiful sound he ever heard.

The next time, he drew back and thrust forward faster, harder.

The third time he plunged into her and felt her spasms begin. They increased and increased, and Alex was filled with a kind of emotion, sensation he'd never experienced before. But he didn't slow down or stop. Instead, he went faster, harder as her climax began. His own started and he felt her muscles clench around him as his head exploded and he emptied himself into her.

When he came back to consciousness, pleasure like he'd never known still shot through his body. He wondered if she was experiencing that, too. He reached for her. "Celi, do you feel that? It's like we're still…"

She didn't move. Her head was thrown back and she was silent. He pulled out of her and leaned over so he could see her face better. And gasped.

Celeste had passed out.

• • •

CELESTE SAT PROPPED up on the pillows, staring at Alex. Averting her gaze, she caught sight of the night table, where his medical bag sat; it must have contained the strange salts that had awakened her. He'd slid his T-shirt over her head and tucked her into the covers, then climbed on the bed, facing her.

She said, "I seek your forgiveness."

"For what?"

"Frightening you."

"I have to say, having a woman pass out after sex is a first for me."

Her face colored. "For me, too."

He cocked his head. "You've never fainted after making love?"

"No." She hadn't because she'd never *made love* before.

"Then I'm…flattered, I guess." He brushed back her hair, rubbed his knuckles over the softest of skin. "But worried."

Her gaze was far away. "I had a feeling sex would be this way with you."

"Is that why you resisted me? Us?"

"Hmm." Should she take this opening to stop what was between them right now? "Yes. But I've always known I'm too sensitive to you. Like when you kissed me."

"But if it's never happened to you before?"

"I sense things in daily life, too. When the children are sad. When you're upset. Others' emotions overwhelm me sometimes."

"Ah, that explains the grocery store and the zoo. Why didn't you just tell us this about your sensitivity?"

"It's an aberration in my genetic makeup, Alex." Which was partly true. "I'm embarrassed by it, just like the panic attack."

"Don't be." His face darkened. "Does it hurt?"

"Not hurt, exactly. It's just so intense, so acute…" She reached out and touched his bare chest. "I was afraid any intimacy between us would evolve like this." Not until he'd kissed her and she couldn't block him, but the gist of what she said was accurate.

He lay back on his own pillows and took her hand. She startled a bit. "What?" he asked.

"I've still got you running through my veins. Even just a light touch affects me."

He started to disentangle his hand.

"Don't move away. I like it."

"You do?"

"Didn't you? What we did together?"

His laugh was sardonic. "Hell, if I liked it any more I would have had a heart attack."

She gripped his fingers. "Where your heart seizes up and may stop? Really? I could cause that?"

"No, no, it was just a figure of speech."

"One of your idioms." When she realized what she'd said, she added, "I never heard most of them until I came to this country for further education. I'm afraid I still misinterpret them."

"Celeste, I love that about you. Your sensitivity. Your delight in ordinary things. Come to think of it, I've been drawn to you from day one, affected by you every time we've brushed shoulders or you touched my arm."

"As have I with you," she answered truthfully. "What we did together was very special. I'll never forget it."

"I don't understand."

She shifted uncomfortably. He wasn't going to like what she said next, and neither did she. "You said if we did this once, you would allow me to leave."

"After what happened when we made love, you still want to go?" He sounded horrified.

Her eyes clouded. A crystal-clear image assaulted her: life without him, without the younglings she loved. "I should."

"No, no you shouldn't. Stay. We could have three whole days alone together."

Why, *why* did he keep throwing these temptations at her? *Three* whole days with him alone. It would be ecstasy.

Who would know? Not the children. Not Alisha and Dorian. Did she dare take the time with this man who affected her like no other had? No other probably ever would?

The distasteful thought of being with someone else sexually catapulted her into a decision she knew she shouldn't make. "All right, Alex. Three days. That's all I can give you of myself."

"I'll take it."

She wondered briefly why he didn't sound as if he meant the vow. But then his lips touched hers, and she forgot her concerns, forgot about everything but the feel of his hard body against hers.

• • •

SHE POISED ON top of him, smiling down. She looked like some goddess from a different land, her hair wild, her eyes blazing. This time, they took it slow in the foreplay, but Alex had about reached his limit. And he was scared to death she might faint again. He held her hips when she tried to rise up to prevent her from moving too fast.

Leaning over, she brushed back his hair. Her smile was sun-bright. "Don't concern yourself. I withstood the last half hour well."

What she'd done was ohh and ahh and moan and encourage him every time he put his hands on her, every*where*.

"Besides, even if I lose consciousness, it will be worth it."

"I don't want to hurt you."

"Then love me."

Raising her hips, he gently settled her on him. She sighed and closed her eyes. The definition of bliss was written all over her face. Then she began to move. He was hoping if she controlled the action, she could temper her response. The sensation of her muscles closing around him, the feel of her body gently slapping his made him stop thinking and let go with her. When they climaxed, emotions combined with such physical pleasure, it blinded him.

When sanity returned, he realized she was sprawled out on his chest. His hand went to her neck and took her pulse. Fast but steady. He touched her skin. Heated, sweaty, but no surprise there, after what they'd just done. "Celi, are you all right?"

She buried her face in his chest. "I'm drained, but I didn't faint. I have to stay here a minute, though. Okay?"

He chuckled. "Okay by me."

By mid-afternoon, they'd gotten dressed and she was cooking him breakfast, because it seemed like morning and they hadn't eaten all day. The scent of dough and the sweet, brown chips filled the kitchen. She said, "You'll love these pancakes. Dorian showed me how to put bits of chocolate in them."

"Chocolate chips."

She looked over her shoulder. "That's what I said."

No, she hadn't. "Celeste, didn't they have stuff like this in South America?"

"Oh, yes, I'm sure they did. But we weren't allowed sweets when I was a young...young."

There it was again. Words almost said, then changed. He was noticing different things about her today. He wondered if, when they made love, the connection had been so great that he was even more attuned to her.

He watched her graceful movements at the stove. She'd pulled her hair up in that knot thing he liked and wore a plain, peach dress that skimmed her knees. His heart filled at all he felt for her. What would he do…? No, he wasn't going to think about that. Or anything else. He was stunned when that determination led him to realize he hadn't thought about his work or the clinical trials all day long.

She served him the pancakes and refilled coffee for him, tea for her. He watched as she cut into the sweet meal and put a piece in her mouth. She closed her eyes. "Mmm… These are wonderful."

"Jesus."

Quickly, she opened her eyes. "What's wrong?"

He took her hand and brought it to his groin. "This is what you did to me just now. After a lot of sex."

Her grin was…female. Confident. It hit him then she was very skilled at lovemaking. Sometimes, she seemed so innocent about everything else, but the way she touched him, what she did with her muscles when he was inside her, how she moved just right to give him the most acute pleasure didn't fit with her naïve demeanor. Her dead husband must have been a great lover. The notion made him scowl.

"Don't you like that I can do this to you?"

"I love it, honey."

After breakfast that was really dinner, they took a long walk outside. As they neared the park, an explosion rent the air; she startled and covered her eyes. "W-What is that?"

"You're kidding, right?"

"No, I…" She drew in a deep breath as she glanced toward the sky. "Oh, Nord. That's beautiful." A questioning look to Alex.

His jaw dropped. "Celi, those are fireworks. Granted, July 4th passed, but the town voted to show them for a few days in a row."

"We never had them."

This had to be addressed. "No, you might not have had them in your childhood if your parents did missionary work in a remote location, but if you've been in the states since college, you *had* to have seen them."

Her shoulders stiffened where he held them. "I…I don't know what to say."

Deep-seated worry, concern called forth the whole host of things she wasn't familiar with. "Celi, is there something you're not telling me?"

He could see her visibly calm herself. "Like what?"

"I don't know. Maybe you're an android. Or from outer space." He was trying to joke because she seemed upset, but in his gut he knew this wasn't humorous.

"No, no. I'm just…what did you call it, ingenuous." She took his hand. "Come show me these fireworks. They're mesmerizing."

Still disturbed, Alex led the way into the park. Fear accompanied him. Something was definitely off about Celeste, and he could no longer rationalize it away.

• • •

"THE MALL WILL be mobbed later on, but I wanted you to see it. I still can't believe…" he trailed off.

And Celeste knew why he didn't finish his sentence. Now that he'd been inside her, claimed her body and soul, he was noticing too much about her. Intuiting things even when they weren't making love. She should have left him after the first time.

It's only for two more days. Maybe I can keep his doubts at bay. After that, I'll limit contact until I can accomplish my task.

Moving in close, she said, "Thank you for bringing me here."

They strolled along, holding hands like many of the other couples out this early. "What do you want to see first?"

"The monument of Lincoln."

"Ah." They walked toward it. She was immersed in the sites of people jogging, biking, and walking around in the crisp morning air. The scent of coffee rose from vendors, also out early. During this whole week, there would be parades and other celebrations, and Alex had suggested they visit this thing he called a Mall (though it wasn't enclosed and didn't have stores to purchase goods). Now they headed toward Washington's most popular site, the monument of Lincoln.

As they reached the building, Celeste gasped. The structure towered over her. She took the brochure out of the purse she carried. "The building resembles a Greek temple." She'd studied the Greek chips. "And contains a seated sculpture of Abraham Lincoln as well as scrolls of his two most famous speeches."

Beside her, Alex put his hand on her shoulder. "I know that."

"I can't wait to get inside." But once they did, the statue, which rose up on a ten-foot pedestal and was nineteen feet high itself, halted her. She was bombarded by size, strength and a bit of fear, so she stepped back from it.

"What's wrong?" Alex asked.

"I'm... It's so big."

"Big things seem to bother you."

She shot him a questioning look.

"The lions. You reacted similarly to them."

"I suppose they do. My world has been...smaller, as a child and even as an adult." She knew it wasn't enough of an explanation, after all her slipups, but she had to keep trying to convince him.

Turning her attention back to the sculpture, she studied the chiseled features, the detail, the ornateness, which was truly lovely. Though she was still feeling overwhelmed, she had to touch it, and when she did, her skin tingled. Acutely.

She moved her hand on the cold stone, filled with a sudden understanding. "Our society was wrong to subjugate ones of its own species."

Alex's face turned somber. "I know. Slavery was a real blight on our history."

She looked up to the man who'd in some ways come alive for her. "War was hard for him. So many people died." She turned to Alex. "There is much honoring war here in this Mall."

"You're right about that. The Korean War monument, the World War II one. Wait till you see the Vietnam Wall."

"Other wars will come, Alex. Ones that will destroy millions of people." When she realized what she'd disclosed, she said, "I really think that, based on mankind's history."

"No, I don't agree. We have treaties for nuclear disarmament. Hopefully, we can avoid the worst."

But Celeste knew the worst would come. Early in the twenty-fourth century, nuclear war had been averted by sanctions and eventual treaties, and because of mankind's need to build the Domes when the air was becoming suffocating. But before the world was safe, a vast and vicious cyber war broke out, unleashing bacteria and chemicals that killed those who weren't already in Domes. The population had been reduced drastically.

Unless, of course, Dorian had changed the future.

And Celeste did her part. Best not to forget that.

• • •

THEY ATE BREAKFAST bought at a kiosk and devoured it at an outdoor table with a good view of the Potomac. The water sparkled like crystal on this shiny, bright July morning. Celeste selected chocolate croissants and milk while Alex picked a breakfast burrito. He nodded to her meal. "Partial to sweets, are you?"

"Hmm." She licked a bit of chocolate off her lip. "Aren't you?"

"I'm partial to you." Leaning over, he kissed her; she tasted like the treat. When he drew back, she grinned, the expression both delighted and aroused him.

After the fireworks incident yesterday, Alex had done something that went against his nature. He decided to ignore the inconsistencies about her for now. Empirical evidence told him too many things were unfamiliar to her, but in his heart, he knew if he addressed it, he would ruin these two days together. It was hard enough not to beg her to continue a relationship with him, but that would also cloud their days. Tomorrow night was plenty of time to talk her out of ending this between them and get to the bottom of her strangeness.

When they finished eating, he asked, "So, you ready for The Wall?"

"I'm not sure, Alex." A line appeared between her eyes, marring a blemish-free face. "But after reading about its significance, I feel compelled to see it."

"Most people do. Lila started to cry as soon as she walked toward the thing."

A sad smile crossed Celeste's face. "I wish I'd known her. I know that sounds crazy, because I wouldn't be here with you if I had, but Jon and Maddy speak of her often. Cody likes hearing about her, and so do I."

He frowned. "I didn't know that."

"I've encouraged them to tell me things." She watched him as she took another bite. "I seek… I'm sorry, have I done something wrong?"

"No, I should have realized that they'd want to…keep her alive that way. I've been selfish."

"Preoccupied."

"Yeah, but not these last two days." Standing, he tugged her up and tucked her under his arm. She fit perfectly. "All I can see, feel, think about is you."

As usual, her reaction was sensual; her bare skin seemed to sizzle at his nearness. Suddenly, he wanted to skip The Wall and find the nearest hotel.

But they didn't. When the monolithic structure was in view, Celeste halted several feet away. He tried to see the monument from her eyes. The nearly three hundred feet of names of those who'd died rose ten feet high. To anyone, it was intimidating. To someone as sensitive as Celeste…

He said, "Maybe we shouldn't go closer."

"No. I need to." She gripped his hand until she was right in front of the first section of the wall. He watched the marble reflect back on them and was startled to see his face full of hope and love and expectancy.

Slowly, she reached out and ran her fingers over the name Jason L. Benson. Her eyes teared, and her head fell forward until it rested on the stone. From the side, he could see fat tears trickle down her cheek.

And as Alex watched her cry for fifty-eight thousand men who'd died in war, he realized he was in love with this very special woman.

• • •

ON THEIR THIRD night together, Alex suggested he take Celeste to a fancy restaurant, but she asked to stay at home. Celeste had decided she wanted to know everything about this man she'd come to care for. They could order out, have some wine and be close. The idea appealed to him, too.

Again they were out of inside, ensconced in chairs, pushed close enough so they could touch. Though the air was hot and muggy, she nonetheless enjoyed the sultry heat. "Alex, what do you want out of life?"

"Personally or professionally?" A candle on the small table between them let her see his face. In relief, it was sculpted and strong boned.

"Both."

"I haven't thought much in terms of personal goals since Lila died. But I can articulate some of what I want: for the people I love to be happy and healthy." He stared off into night. "For so long, a dark cloud his been over me. It's gone now. I want it to stay gone."

"That's nice."

Taking her hand, he squeezed it. A cricket, louder than the others, chirped out of sync and they laughed. Then he asked, "What about you?"

She shook her head. "Personally, I want something I'll never have."

"What is it, honey?"

This was even harder to verbalize to him, somehow. "A child."

"I planned to ask you about that. You know I worked in fertility and gynecology early in my career, so I wondered if you've had the most recent tests. Maybe something can be done. We've made great strides in sperm rejuvenation and egg viability and in vitro fertilization."

Not nearly enough, she thought. And Alex's own work would not only impede progress in that area more than he could ever fathom, but send it spiraling backwards.

"No, I'm afraid none of that works for me. My womb cannot sustain a child."

"There are hormones for hostile wombs."

"Alex, please don't try to make this better for me. I'm up to date on all the advancements and know I can't have a child. So instead, I enjoy helping the ones that exist already."

"There's a saying: *Teachers change the world, one kid at a time.* So in a sense, you're changing the world."

Oh, godheads, if he only knew.

"What about you, Alex? What would you do professionally if it wasn't for research?"

"I taught some night courses at a college while I was in my medical practice and before I went into research. Now I do one course a semester. As well as write articles for journals. I suppose I'd become an educator if I could no longer research. And a part-time writer."

"I would love to teach." She could hear the wistfulness in her voice. "Young ones."

"You could do that. Or you could open up a day care."

Her heart lifted. "Oh, Alex, what a good idea. That would please me so much."

He leaned over and kissed her nose. "I can see."

They talked until one day turned to the next. It was past midnight when he took her hand and said, "I want you again." Sexily, he leaned over and whispered, "I need to be inside you."

"One last time." It just slipped out.

His face darkened. "Celi…"

She put her hand to his mouth. "Don't say anything. Please."

In his bedroom, he disrobed her with a tenderness she didn't know existed.

He kissed her as if she were more precious than air.

And when he slipped inside her, he brought her to a gentle peak that made her eyes leak, and then he tumbled over the top, calling her name.

Afterward, he drew her to him. "Before we go to sleep, I want to say something. I love you, Celeste."

Half asleep, she murmured against his chest, "My love is yours, too, Alex."

• • •

ALEX DREAMED ABOUT her all night. So when he reached for her the next morning and found the space empty, he frowned. He'd wanted to hold her, to talk about how they'd articulated their feelings of love for each other last night and how they would work out being together, despite her misgivings. For the life of him, he couldn't figure out why she had such strong doubts.

He donned pajama bottoms, then trundled downstairs. The house was eerily quiet. No scents of breakfast. No stir of her in the air. And suddenly, he knew. He bolted to the steps and took them two at a time until he reached the third floor.

Her door was open, so he went inside and once again saw a note on the bed. His heart clamored in his chest as he opened it.

"Dearest Alex,

I'll never forget these three days. My love for you is strong and will last forever. I'm sorry we can't be together, but it's impossible. I'll watch the children until you can find someone else, but I have to move back to my condo. I'll be in touch."

For a moment, Alex felt disoriented. He dropped down on the bed and put his face in his hands. Had he really lost the woman he loved a second time? Could he possibly leave her alone as he'd promised? How could she expect him to after what they'd shared? After what they'd said to each other?

He straightened when he heard a familiar buzz. He reached for his phone to see if she was texting him and realized he didn't have his cell.

Light from the dresser caught his eye. Celeste had left her phone? She must have been truly upset. By rote, he picked it up. Clicked *view message*.

It read: *Come to NY. We must make plans for July 24.*

July twenty-fourth? The date seemed…oh, dear Lord in heaven, that was when results of the safety phase of the clinical trials would come in. What a coincidence.

But how could it be?

Cold dread seeped into him. He stared down at the phone. As if from a distance, he clicked into her text trail. There, he found a myriad of messages from the one who sent today's.

When he finished reading them, he dropped the phone to the floor, put his hands back over his face and, this time, cried as he hadn't since Lila died.

CHAPTER 12

AT THREE O'CLOCK in the morning, Celeste quietly climbed the stairs from the lower floor at Jess's dwelling, trying hard not to disturb Alisha and Dorian. They were gravely worried about her, as she'd burst into tears upon her arrival in New York. They hadn't talked last night about what had happened to her, because Celeste had been too upset.

Quietly turning on the machine for hot water, she stared out at Jess's backyard and remembered the first time the three of them came here. Surrounded by the comfort of another home she loved, she told herself firmly, *Remember how you saved Jess. And how you have to save people of the future.*

The timekeeper ticked loudly in the room and she heard the refrigerator turn on.

"Celi?" The voice came from behind her.

She turned. Helen stood in the doorway, wearing yellow pajamas, with her hair in a braid to her waist. Her complexion was rosy with sleep.

Celeste asked, "Did I disturb you?"

"No, I got up to pee." She put her hand on her stomach. "Then heard you out here."

"Go back to bed, Helen. You need your rest."

Instead, Helen crossed to her. She took Celeste's hand and placed it over the baby in her womb.

I want to have a child…

"Tell me how she is. I didn't want to ask earlier because you were so upset. But I'm comforted like no other time when you confirm she's doing fine."

Smiling despite the yawning agony inside her, Celeste put her hand on Helen's stomach. Joy surged through her when she heard the thump, thump, thump. Very fast. Very strong. "She's happy, Helen. Healthy. She…"

Her hand still on Helen's belly, Celeste felt her own womb contract. As if something inside *her* moved. Suddenly, she became lightheaded and grabbed for the counter.

"Celeste, what's wrong?"

"I…" She placed both hands on her own stomach and pressed. "I…" Water leaked from her eyes.

"Oh, sweetie, did touching Jessica make you sad?"

Celeste shook her head as the tears continued.

"Are you ill? I wouldn't be surprised if you had an ulcer from all that's happened."

"No, it's not a lesion inside me." Still crying, she captured Helen's gaze and gave her a watery smile. "It's a child. In my womb."

Helen jaw dropped. "I thought you couldn't…"

"I thought so, too. I *knew* it to be true."

"Just like me. You got pregnant against all odds."

Her heart was filling up so fast Celeste could barely breathe. Then her knees weakened. "I…need to sit."

They took places at the table. Helen brought over tea and sat back down. "Do you realize what happened when you put your hand on Jessica?"

Celeste shook her head. Emotions, thoughts swirled so fast and furiously in her head she couldn't separate them out.

"Our babies communicated."

Staying very still, Celeste was afraid to move. Afraid she'd wake from a dream and this miracle would be fleeting.

"Is the baby Alex's?" Helen asked.

Celeste nodded.

"You didn't tell us much when you got here. Only that you'd left Virginia. You were so sad. Nobody pushed, but they will today."

Panic seized her. "Helen, promise me you won't tell anyone about this miracle, not even Jess, before I can figure out how this happened."

"All right. When was the last time you two made love?"

"Last night."

"You're a fertility expert, Celeste. You know what happened. Sperm can last up to five days in the womb before conception."

"But I'm supposed to be barren."

"Apparently, only in your time." Helen grinned. "The research I came across when I was still trying to conceive said that some studies show the more intimate the sexual encounter is, the more likely fertilization."

"I wonder if that contributed to our time's infertility. Women and men were never intimate."

"Maybe."

A quick burst of joy bubbled out of Celeste. "I'm pregnant, Helen. I'm really going to have a child."

"Enjoy this gift before you have to analyze the problems with it."

By the time the sun came up, Celeste had managed to tamp down her absolute delight so it didn't show to the others. Dorian made breakfast, which Celeste devoured, then Alisha said, "All right, Celi. We need to know what this is all about."

• • •

ALISHA HAD PROMISED herself during the night that she'd be kind to Celeste. Never had she seen her friend in such pain, and in truth, it frightened her. So she began quietly. "You said when you arrived that you couldn't go back to the Lansings, after we agreed you'd stay until we successfully stopped the trial."

"I was upset. I know I have to go back." She raised bruised eyes to Alisha. "But it's going to be almost impossible for me now. You were right, I wasn't strong enough to do this task. You should have taken my place. I'm afraid my love is now Alex's. If I have to be with him, with the younglings…" Here, her voice croaked. "I fear I won't be able to keep my silence about who I am."

What on this earth could Alisha say to that?

Luke, of all people, spoke up. "Don't berate yourself for falling in love, Celi." He picked up Dorian's hand and smiled at her. "It happens to the best of us."

"It didn't affect our accomplishing our task with Jess, though," Alisha said as calmly as she could.

"No, Lisha," Luke said. "It helped you achieve your goal."

This man always defied her. "Telling Alex Lansing who she is, who we are won't help us at all."

Dorian leaned forward. She looked as though she hadn't slept much either, despite the fact Luke had stayed with her. "Why does she have to go back? You gained all the information and access you needed."

"But we have to have access to his computer to match the results on the twenty-fourth, after we tamper with them."

"Not necessarily. We might be able to access them remotely."

"It doesn't matter." Celeste's voice was empty. "I know I have to follow through. I'm just not sure I can keep lying to him now."

"You're going to have to do your best, Celi." This from Jess. "I know personally how successful you can be."

"Thank you, Jess. I know I've disappointed you, Alisha. And I seek your forgiveness for feeling so unsure about what I can do."

"Then we'll just have to hope for the best," Helen put in. Alisha did a double take at their friend. She seemed unusually upbeat amidst such a serious discussion.

"We have fourteen days to wait. We won't know what to change, in either the results of the trials or on Alex's computer, until the findings are in. Our problem will be with substituting our data for the original on his computer."

"You're the best computer hacker in this century, Alisha. You can do it." Luke seemed so confident.

Alisha was thoughtful. "Just so long as Celi can do her part and go back to Alex Lansing for a while."

Celeste's face paled alarmingly, but there was no other way to deal with this.

The doorbell rang. Alisha, who was closest to the foyer got up to answer. On the porch stood David Ryan. "David! How nice to see you."

Leaning in, he kissed her cheek. It was then that Alisha stiffened. Behind him was Alex Lansing.

• • •

ALEX'S HANDS FISTED when he saw Alisha. For some god-forsaken reason, she and her sisters were *after* his clinical trials. The notion was unfathomable, but for too long, he'd let his feelings for Celeste obscure reason.

"She's here, isn't she?" Alex asked around a clenched jaw.

"Yes." This one, Alisha, was cold and forbidding. "How did you find us?"

"He found me." David shrugged. "The name of my church was in the program for the awards ceremony for Jess. He came to the church an hour ago."

"No use denying what you've been doing, either." Alex held up Celeste's cell phone with the silly pink case. "I read your texts."

With a resigned expression on her face, Alisha stepped aside. They entered and she led them through the big foyer, down a hall and into the kitchen.

Alex saw Celeste right away. Even from this far back, where he was concealed, he noted the lines of exhaustion etched around her eyes. But there was something else about her. She seemed pleased. Fuck, she could at least be suffering over how she'd tricked him with phony words of love and a body that drowned him in pleasure. Had she no feelings at all for him? The thought made him angrier.

Luke said, "David, good morning."

David stepped away from Alex. "Oh, my God." Dorian put a hand over her mouth.

Celi looked past the minister. Her face turned sheet white now, something that happened when she was weakened by an event. For a minute, he worried about her, then he chided himself. "Hello, Celeste." His tone was snarky.

Tears clouded those eyes he used to love. Now, he hated the sight of her. Without preamble he asked, "Why, Celeste, why are you trying to sabotage my research?"

"To save the world," she said immediately, just as Dorian exclaimed, "Don't—" and Alisha snapped, "Celi, no."

He jammed his hands in his pockets. "To save the world. What kind of a fool do you think I am?"

Jess stood. "The kind I was." He pulled another chair up to the table. "Sit down, Dr. Lansing. We have a story so bizarre you're going to have trouble believing it."

"I don't want to sit." He scanned the table. "Jesus, are you all in on this?"

"In a sense," Luke told him.

He zeroed in on David. "Even you? You're a man of God."

"Yes, even me. Please, Alex, let us explain. If you want to accuse us of wrongdoing afterward, we won't protest."

"Oh, I'm going to accuse you all right. First I'm going to sue your asses off, then report you to the police."

"That would be me," Luke said dryly. "I'm a New York City police lieutenant."

The man's statement made Alex's anger recede and logic come to his brain. A minister. An officer of the law. A world-renowned scientist. Something was going on here that he didn't understand.

To save the world.

He didn't believe that, but he'd listen to an explanation. He sat on the chair Dr. Cromwell provided.

Celeste got up and went to the coffeepot. He steeled himself against her. They could tell him nothing—*nothing*—that would make him forgive her. She'd tricked him into falling in love with her so she could destroy him.

"I want Celeste to explain it to me."

Her hand shook as she set the cup down next to him, and he could practically feel her...Jesus...her fear of him. Ignoring her fragile state, he didn't thank her for the coffee, and she reseated herself across from him.

"This is going to sound fetched-far to you, but you have to listen carefully." Her voice was devoid of its usual *joie de vivre*. "Please don't interrupt."

"She means far-fetched," Jess explained.

Alex said nothing. He didn't even nod.

Celeste took in a deep breath. "Dorian, Alisha and I are not from this time period. We backtracked from 2514 to prevent some things from occurring today that cause disaster in the future."

Of all the things he expected, it wasn't that. His gaze flew to Jess Cromwell, the other scientist in the room.

"It's true, Alex." Jess seemed perfectly comfortable with his statement. "They came to stop events from happening to you and me."

"They sabotaged your research, too?"

"No, they kept me from being murdered."

Hell! Could this get any crazier?

"So he could continue his research," Celeste said, "research that prevents the world from becoming so polluted that the entire population must be covered with Domes."

"That's impossible. Millions of people couldn't live under a dome."

"In the future, there's a cyber war between nations that sets off a biological attack. Two thirds of the population is killed off."

As if she'd just spoken them, he remembered her words at the Lincoln Monument.

Other wars will come, Alex. Ones that will destroy millions of people.

No, I don't believe that. We have treaties for nuclear disarmament.

"In any case," Celeste continued. "That isn't the only devastation in the future. There's widespread infertility. Conception is impossible. It has been for forty years, even in vitro."

You know I worked in fertility and gynecology early in my career, so I wondered if you've had the most recent tests. Maybe something can be done. We've made great strides in sperm rejuvenation and egg viability and in vitro fertilization.

"This is where you come in, Alex," she continued. "Because of your progress with Equisex, generation after generation becomes less and less fertile. By our time, we lost the ability to conceive as well as many, many other things."

Seriously? They expected him to buy this story? "Let me get this straight. You want me to believe it's my drug that causes future infertility?"

"Yes."

"How does Jess fit in?"

He develops a way to extract methane from the ground without water or air contamination. It saves us from pollution."

"So two things devastate your world?"

"Yes."

"Christ. No way in hell am I going to believe this science fiction."

"They have proof," Luke put in. "And Alex, I had trouble accepting it, too. But it's true."

"I can't fathom that I'll believe this in a million years." He turned to her and said sarcastically, "That means never, Celeste. Absolutely *never*."

• • •

HE MUST BE delusional. Alex dug his thumb and forefinger into his eyes, gritty from lack of sleep. But still, when he looked again, the computer screen had grown before him; he watched openmouthed. This could still be a hoax, *had* to be, but it sure as hell looked real.

Alisha had taken over. He ignored the fact that Celeste sat off to the side, seeming so fatigued — and hurt, damn her — that he couldn't look at her.

"We've brought with us a series of what you call documentaries from the twenty-fifth and twenty-sixth centuries, in case we had to convince you of the gravity of our mission. The vids provide a history of drugs that mitigate sexual dysfunction." Alisha's voice was authoritative, but he was so damn pissed about all this, he didn't even want to listen.

He glanced at the Cromwells. Jess and Helen were holding hands, their attention was focused on the screen. Obviously, they hadn't seen this chronology, either.

But documentaries could be faked.

A narrator in a grey tunic and pants, short hair and shocking green eyes came on screen. The caption read, *The history of sexual performance drugs*. The woman began, "Sexual dysfunction cures began in ancient Greece and Rome but only for men. Let me clarify that, as crazy as it sounds, women were not always considered equal to men in importance." She smiled. "Those afflicted with the malady in ancient times consumed — actually ate — the reproductive body parts from a variety of animals."

Alex felt his foot tapping. He already knew this. And about the Muslim culture, next on screen, which used drug therapy for men.

The narrator continued. "It wasn't until the early twentieth century when testosterone therapy was initiated." She explained about John Brinkley's experimentation. Also, in that century, vacuum pumps helped men to achieve erections."

"I know all this," Alex said impatiently. Getting warm from this impossible story, he tugged on the neck of his polo shirt. "It proves nothing."

Alisha paused the machine. "Proof is here, Alex." The undercurrent of impatience and curtness in Alisha's voice didn't help his mood. "It's important to see this from the future's perspective."

She switched on the video again. "But the real progress—their term—came in the late twentieth century, with sexual performance drugs, which are phizer derivatives." She named a few. "These are considered the fathers of sexual-dysfunction drugs. The *mother* was developed in the early twenty-first century and was one of the most devastating advancements to occur: the perfection of Equisex by Dr. Alex Lansing. Considered a miracle drug for both men and women, it revolutionized the industry and laid the groundwork for our fertility problems of the future."

"Oh, my God."

The documentary stopped and Alisha said, "Second chip, please."

The freaking thing responded without her touching the keys.

The narrator was a different person, in a different setting. Alisha explained, "I've included many documentaries so you'll realize that we didn't fake these."

"The jury's still out on that one."

"What does that mean?" Celeste asked Helen.

"He doesn't believe us yet."

The narrator gave an introductory speech and Alisha said, "Go to 2050."

"By the mid-twenty-first century, Equisex was in common use for all men and women over fifty. In the twenty-second century, the drug and its derivatives were consumed daily by adults of all ages."

The pictures the pharmaceuticals, which apparently were the offspring of Equisex, displayed on screen. "Then the practice spread to adolescents."

What? He never meant for that to happen. And he noticed something else. He said aloud, "They talk about my drug as a disease."

"In a way," David Ryan said, "it became that."

"Not until 2350 did Equisex, which was discovered and perfected in 2014, become linked to the world's dwindling population. But with the environmental pollution, the building of the Domes and finally the threat of cyber war, this growing infertility was ignored. It wasn't until we were settled in the Domes that the Institute of Fertility and Sexuality was formed. By 2400 we had a clear picture of what had happened."

"What exactly happened?" Alex asked.

Celeste sat forward and spoke. Her hair obscured her cheeks, which were still pale. "Throughout the ages, with consistent use of Equisex, the vaginal walls thinned. Researchers thought the cause was the effect on a woman's hormones. But sperm viability also decreased."

"There's no evidence of that in all my research."

"It didn't show up until many generations after you, Dr. Lansing." This from Jess.

No side effects in this generation, Celeste said the first time they talked about his work.

Celeste, there are no more generations to try it on.

But there were.

When the presentations concluded, Alex sat back in his chair, stunned, not only at the information he'd just gotten, but at the fact that he partly believed the tale.

He stared at the seven people assembled before them. "I don't know what to say." He faced Jess. "Is this what convinced you to go along with them? The computer show?"

"Partly. But I had even more evidence initially. Dorian, Celeste and Alisha materialized in my office. A la *Star Trek's* transporter device."

Alex's gaze swung to Celeste. "You said I look like Captain Kirk."

All responded together, "You do."

Luke leaned forward. "Alex, I'm the one who had to be convinced. After I saw the tapes — chips they call them — my cop's brain denied it."

"How did they make you believe?"

"Logic sunk in." He motioned to the computer. "Do you really think that all this is made up?"

He didn't answer.

Alisha addressed him. "There are contraindications even today that your drug could be harmful. I've read your research which was eventually published."

"The protests are mostly from far right-wingers. Alarmists who think anything to do with sexuality is bad."

"No, Dr. Lansing." Helen spoke to him now. "I read some articles based on scientific research when I thought I couldn't get pregnant."

"Thought?"

"I'm pregnant. It's a miracle."

Personally, I want something I'll never have…a child.

"So basically," Dorian pointed out. "This isn't so far-fetched."

Closing his eyes, he ran his hand through his hair. Then something occurred to him. "Why didn't you just appear in front of me, like you did Jess, and convince me to stop my research?"

Celeste raised her chin. "Because we knew your work had been stolen before. We thought you'd try to stop us instead of helping us, so we decided to complete our task surreptitiously."

He arched a brow. "Even you, Celeste? After you got to know me? After these last three days?" Leaning forward, he slapped his hand on the table. "You should have told me. You should have stayed this morning to explain it all to me. It would have been a hell of a lot easier to hear it from you."

Alisha said, "I don't think I want to know what happened in the last few days, but I take full responsibility for her silence. I forbade Celeste to tell you. I didn't believe you'd cooperate."

"Maybe *you* wouldn't have known that." He faced Celeste. "But you should have. I'll never forgive you for that."

She recoiled as if she'd been slapped. Her head hit the wall and she moaned. Helen jumped off her cushion and rushed to her. "Celi, are you all right?"

Sitting up, Celeste rubbed the back of her skull. "Yes, Helen." She looked at Alex. "I did think you were an honorable man, and I don't expect you to ever trust me." Her voice was shaky. She was vulnerable; he hated seeing her in this state. "And because I know who and what you are, I *do* expect you to believe us now and even help us destroy your work."

Jesus. Alex felt as though he'd landed in Oz.

CHAPTER 13

CELESTE KNOCKED LIGHTLY on the den door. Since she received no response, she opened it. She found Alex in pajama bottoms borrowed from Jess, facing away from her in front of the large window. He was shirtless, revealing his wide shoulders and a tanned, naked back. She remembered how smooth the skin was there. How she'd kissed every indentation of those shoulders.

"Alex, may I come in?"

He nodded, then turned to her when she stepped inside and closed the door. "You know, if I do believe this, and Jess Cromwell pretty much convinced me in the last three hours, everything about you falls into place."

Staying by the door, she shifted on her feet, knowing this was going to be another attack. "I imagine that's true."

"Right from the beginning, you set me up. From the first Skype session. You knew I'd recently lost my sitter."

She closed her eyes briefly. He still didn't know everything. "We, um, engineered Patty Mason's scholarship."

Now those beloved blue eyes widened in shock. "How on earth did you manage that?"

She explained about Jess's friends at the university and that they provided the funds for the scholarship.

Cocking his head, he said, "That's mega bucks. Where did you get the money?"

"We brought enough diamonds with us to use as currency and paid for her scholarship."

"At least Patty benefited from this whole debacle." He watched her. "Where did you get diamonds?"

"Diamonds and other gems mean nothing to us. We have them on display in our Ancient Galleries in most regions. The only ore significant to us are lecci crystals, which provide fuel. Again, it's obtained by from the earth's core by machines."

"How do they work?"

"They're self-recharging light crystals similar to your lithium batteries."

He shook his head and his hair, which had gotten longer, fell into his eyes. "Jess says you're a sensitive for real."

"That part is true."

"It's how you sucked me in." His words were cut-glass cold, and Celeste knew his anger was rising inside him again. "Even the kids."

"I love the children."

"Spare me, Celeste. This has all been an elaborate ruse to you."

"No, not that part. Not the kids. Not you." She added the last hoarsely.

"What is it you say? *I seek your forgiveness* if I don't believe you. You lied badly to all of us."

There was no defensive retort to his statement because what he said was true. She merely wrapped her arms around her middle to withstand the emotional blow of his ire. Her stomach was churning and she was worried about the fetus inside her. The baby. *His* baby.

"Was there really a dead husband back in your time?"

This would be hard. "No, we have no marriage, like you do here."

That stopped him. "What? Jess and I didn't talk much about your customs."

"When we lost the ability to conceive, men and women grew separated. Eventually, outside of work, their only contact was sexual."

"It's why you called it joining. And not making love."

"I made love to you."

"You aren't capable of that."

The emotional blow hit her again, making her recoil back.

"Why do you do that? Move away if I yell at you."

"It doesn't matter."

"Are you so sensitive that a person's negative emotions hurt your...body?"

Swallowing hard, she shook her head. "Not everyone's."

"Then you should go. I'm not feeling kindly toward you, but I don't want to hurt you physically."

"I thought maybe you'd want to know more about our society."

"I know enough. Cyber war. Domes because of global warming. Many scientists today fear exactly that."

Her eyes narrowed. He wasn't the only one who had a right to anger. "But your society didn't stop it."

He watched her.

"Will *you*? Now that you know?"

"Yes, of course I will. After putting the pieces of the puzzle together, I have no choice but to cooperate."

"We plan to alter the findings of the clinical trials. Will you change your research to match it?"

"Yes. Jess and I decided Alisha will help me."

"Not me?"

"No. Not you. I can't bear to be in the same room with you." He took a deep breath. "And obviously, it's harmful for you to have contact with me."

"My love really is yours, Alex."

"Get out of here, Celeste," he spat out angrily." I'm leaving at daybreak. Don't ever contact me or the kids again."

"What will you tell them?"

"That you loved them. That you had a family emergency, causing you to leave. Eventually, I'll let them know you're not returning. Maybe by then, we'll all forget you."

"I hope you do. I don't want the children or you to suffer because of me."

"It's a little too late for that, sweetheart."

"I guess it is." Her heart tightening so badly it ached, she walked out of the room. She'd gotten exactly what she expected from him, but it still sliced her to the bone.

Then she remembered. Placing her hand on her belly, she whispered, "At least I have you, a part of him, little one." And this miracle was a lot more than she ever thought she'd get out of this whole odyssey.

• • •

SINCE THE KIDS would come home tomorrow, Alisha accompanied Alex to Virginia to analyze his research. She wanted his input on where they might be able to change the results of the clinical trials, based on how he'd developed the drug. Jess and the others had convinced him of the necessity to do this, but it was like rubbing salt in a wound. (Would Celeste understand that idiom?)

As he opened the office door in his home, something occurred to him. This had been happening for the last forty-eight hours, when other things about Celeste Hart fell into place. He stopped when he reached his desk and faced Alisha. "How did she get in here? Because I imagine that's what happened — you gained access to my computer to get the data for the trials you want to change and my research itself."

Ever calm and staid, Alisha faced him squarely, though her face showed lines of fatigue. "The key in the safe in the living space. Celeste's sensitivity allowed her to hear the combination when she was in the room with you." Before he could respond, she added, "You know, you have a mean streak."

"What?"

"She *does* love you, and you hurt her terribly in New York."

"I'm not going to discuss her with you."

"Not discussing her won't alter the fact that you were cruel to someone who's as innocent and giving as any I've ever met."

He ignored her and sat down in front of the computer, booted it up and waited for the familiar ping that would allow them to destroy his work. "How do we go about this?"

"We'll review your data from the beginning. You'll tell me things that could go wrong in the clinical trial, make a new file documenting that and then, when I get the results of the trial, I'll know exactly what to change in them. You must have clues in your research showing these factors could occur."

"I was right, though, wasn't I?" He needed to know at least this. "Equisex *was* the answer to sexual fulfillment."

"At a great price." She watched him. "You know, society achieved sexual fulfillment for men and women by my time without any drugs."

"What do you mean?"

"Most people are sexually active until their death. Release is achieved in every encounter, for both men and women."

He pictured Celeste in bed and remembered how she knew so much about giving him pleasure. His stomach turned at how she might have learned that in the future. "I don't want to talk about that." He faced the computer and called up his files. "So, the plan is to screw up my data so nobody else will attempt to duplicate the drug."

"Yes, the computeller predicts a ninety-eight percent chance that altering your data will keep someone from building on your research. At least long enough to change history and eradicate our reproductive problems."

"Then Celeste, all of you, can have children when you return to the future." God, he could barely get the words out.

Pulling a chair up to the desk, Alisha stared at him strangely. "Didn't she tell you last night?"

"Tell me what?"

"That there's a ninety-eight-point-six percent chance that we can never return to our time. This was a one-way trip."

That practically poleaxed him. "So you three are forced to live in a primitive environment for the rest of your lives. And you still made the decision to come?"

She arched a brow. "Wouldn't you have, if it meant saving mankind?"

He nodded. Then she explained the projection — traveling ahead in time — and what they found. His brain went on overload. "All because of me."

"No, not you alone. You are the lynchpin in the sexuality arena. You didn't cause the cyber wars or pollution."

The parameters of her world were sinking in now. "Were you happy in your time period?"

She cocked her head. "I'd say no; no one was really happy. Our lives—those of us left—revolve around survival." She gestured to the computer. "Let's get started."

They worked through dinner and at eight o'clock, Alex's stomach growled. "We need to stop for a while, Alisha. I'm hungry. I can't remember the last time I ate."

"All right." She stood and stretched as he picked up the phone.

"There's no food in the house. I'm going to order a pizza. What do you like on yours?"

"I don't eat pizza. As a matter of fact..." She crossed to her backpack and removed a case. From it she withdrew what looked like vitamin pills. "This is our sustenance in the future."

He remembered how Celeste coveted chocolate. How she savored pizza. And pushed brussel sprouts around her plate. Still, he couldn't imagine a world without food. "Seriously?"

"Earnestly. Think about it. How could we have your food, with no air or clean soil or even water, which is so precious we are allowed a modicum amount, rationed from the earth's core and purified?"

"No wonder she had such a reaction to the ocean. Our world must have overwhelmed her." He struggled not to feel sorry for the woman who'd cut his heart into shreds, but still...

"Go ahead and have your pizza. I'll make myself some of the tea Celeste favors."

While Alex ate—a spicy, cheesy confection that he usually loved but now tasted like cardboard—and Alisha sipped her drink, he thought about the future. "Alisha, tell me about your world. Your government. Your science. You must be so advanced."

She filled him in on the small population, the World Council, how they'd finally achieved world peace. It was hard to take in. "What is your profession?" he asked when she finished telling him they worked until they were sixty — lifespan was 110 — and then taught others to replace them.

"I'm in charge of the Institute of Anthropology, which is why I helped develop the plan to backtrack and accompanied Dorian and Celeste here. I am more acquainted with your customs."

Poor Celeste hadn't been. Jesus, he'd had so many clues and he'd simply ignored them.

"Dorian?"

"In charge of the Institute for Physical Stamina. We all must keep in top shape to survive. We have none of your flab or cardiovascular problems."

There wasn't an inch of fat on Celeste. He remembered her supple body under his hands. "And Celeste?"

She works at the Institute for Reproduction and Sexuality. She isn't head of it, like we are, because it's the largest institute with the most distinguished scientists. She would have been in charge one day, though."

He sighed. "I'm mad as hell at you three for tricking me, and devastated about destroying my work, but I do feel bad that you can't return to your time period."

She shrugged. "Dorian's found Luke; they'll probably marry. And Celeste attracts men like flyers, so she won't have any problem. I'll probably stay single, which is what I'm used to, but I do miss the SexLine."

"The what?"

She laughed. "Oh, you think you're surprised by what I previously told you? Wait till you hear this."

• • •

WHILE CELESTE'S HANDS flew across the keys on the computer in her old room at Jess's house, she was tormented by the events of last week. But she refused to mope or be maudlin. She looked up when Dorian came to the doorway, leaned against the jamb and stared out the row of apertures—megadamn, the windows—and shook her head.

"I cannot believe people today are confined to inside for such long periods because the air outside is hot. In our time we would have given anything to experience this kind of weather."

Celeste watched as the sunlight nearly sizzled on the stones outside. "There is a great deal of irony in this world for us."

Dorian nodded to the computer. "What are you doing?"

"Planning for my future."

"How?"

"Come sit with me." When Dorian dropped down on the bed, Celi scooted closer so Dorian could view the computeller. "Now that we've nearly finished our tasks, we have to find something to do in this time period. We can't keep living with the Cromwells."

"I know."

Celi cocked her head. "You're moving in with Luke, aren't you?"

"Yes. Most of my belongings are already at his apartment. I was waiting until you…" She hesitated. "Celi, you're overwrought by what's happened with Alex. I can tell. I want to be here for you."

Fighting the very strong urge to leak tears, she put up a brave face. "I am, but I must overcome those feelings and move on."

Fluffing up two pillows, Dorian leaned back on them. "You two joined, didn't you?"

"No." Celeste stopped working and faced her friend. "We made love. And it was the most wonderful experience of my life. But it's over. I have to plan ahead."

"Take time to grieve his loss."

"I don't have the time."

"Why? What aren't you telling me?"

"Something." She hated lying to this woman. "But I'm not ready to share my thoughts with anyone, yet." Except with Helen, who promised she wouldn't reveal anything about her baby. The Cromwell men had a way of making decisions for other people. And Alex could never find out about this child.

"I will tell you that I'm studying the methods and procedures of setting up a care facility for children."

"Earnestly?"

She nodded. "I talked at length with Alex about becoming a teacher. When he suggested this as an option, I knew it was a better idea. I can be with babies and other younglings all day long." *And still take care of my own.*

Dorian smiled. "It's perfect for you. Maybe Lisha and I can help."

"You'd be bored to water leakage. You need something more intellectual. More active."

"I talked to Luke about my fake private-investigation business. He said he'd help me make that into a reality if I wanted." She smiled sadly. "But I could help you out initially."

Another reason that wouldn't happen was because Celeste had no intention of staying in the area. She was making plans to disappear. Separation from Alisha and Dorian would be hard, but she had a child to consider.

"Why are you smiling?"

"The thought of the day care." She squeezed Dorian's arm.

"Let's look at the computer and I'll show you what I've found."

"If you're sure you don't want to talk more about Alex."

"No, this is better for me to think about."

Though she knew she'd never be able to forget Alex because his child would remind her of him every day, she refused to be sad at the miracle growing within her.

• • •

ALEX'S NECK THROBBED where he kept all his tension, his eyes stung from lack of sleep and his arms and legs were weak; all he wanted was the oblivion of slumber. But he couldn't get the idea of Celeste having had meaningless sex with men every time she'd been…how did Alisha put it?… *in need*. Not only that, but in her time, sexual activity began when people were about Maddy's age. No wonder she was so skilled. He tried to be angry about that notion, but it simply made him sad.

A knock on the bedroom door told him rest wouldn't happen anytime soon, but it did detour his thoughts of Celeste. "Come in."

He was sitting on a chair, purportedly reading a science journal when all three children paraded inside. "Hi," he said. "Did you need me for something?"

"We wanna know when Celi's coming back." This from Jon whose tone was challenging.

"I told you at Grandpa's that I didn't know. Her family has an emergency."

"Who's gonna watch us?" Cody asked.

"I am. I'm at a low point in my work." Very, very low. "I thought I might take the rest of the summer off to be with you."

Propping her hands on her hips, Madison eyed him like an adult. "So, Celeste won't be back all summer?"

"That could happen."

"No, Dad," Cody said, throwing himself at Alex. "She *can't* be gone long. She *can't* leave us like Mom did."

Oh, God.

He rubbed Cody's back. "Hey, buddy, this isn't like losing Mom."

"We *love* her," Cody said. "And Bruiser won't come out of his cage in her room unless we drag him. I tried to get him to sleep with me, but he goes up there and sits in front of the door."

Alex made a mental note to lock access to the third floor. "We'll deal with the dog."

Celeste probably had an affinity to the animal, too. Jesus, that was no joke. He remembered how, when Bruiser had arrived, he would only settle down with her, nuzzling up to her, sleeping with her and avoiding the usual potty mishaps of puppies.

"Let's go sit on the bed." When all four of them were cuddled in, he said, "I'm thinking we don't need a caregiver anymore. If we get housekeeping help, we can survive without anyone else."

"I like having Celeste here, Daddy. She made things brighter." Maddy's gaze narrowed on him. "Did something happen to make her go away?"

"I told you, she's taking care of a family emergency."

"You seem upset that she's gone, too."

"I'm just tired. From the conference."

"I'm gonna call her tomorrow," Jon stated emphatically. "She gave us her cell-phone number when she lived here in case we needed her."

Which was still in his suitcase. He'd forgotten to give it back to her. "Okay, but if she doesn't answer, that means she's busy."

"She'll answer. She loves us." This from Cody.

Hell, he wished he could just tell the kids at least part of the truth, as he'd told his dad…

She's not who or what she pretended to be. I found this out when I went back to Fairfax. I'm done with her in our lives… No, Dad, I can't explain more. Maybe later…

But Alex never intended to tell any of them Celeste was a sensitive from the year 2514, who'd come back to his time to save the world. The notion sounded preposterous; the authorities would have him locked up. No, his kids and his dad never needed to know the truth about the woman who'd broken his heart—and ruined his life's work. They were better off without her.

• • •

THE CHURCH WAS still and quiet. David liked it best this way. The scents of candles and lemon wax tinged the air, and a slight breeze from the fans overhead cooled him. There was something about the solitude and somberness that brought God to him. He prayed: "Please, dear Lord, take care of Alisha, Dorian and especially Celeste. It's mind-boggling what they're going through. They need your guidance, your comfort, your grace."

"We sure do." Startled, David looked behind him. As if God had brought her to him, Celeste gave him a small smile. "Thank you for praying for us."

"Of course. I'm surprised to see you here."

Her gaze swept the sanctuary. "I like the solemnness of this place." She smiled. "It quiets me. Maybe I'll start attending church regularly."

"I would love to have you in my congregation."

Her face darkened. "About that. Can we talk?"

"Of course. Would you like to sit here or in my office?"

"Here would be good. Maybe He—or is your God a she?"

"God can be whatever we want God to be."

"Maybe God will hear me better in Her house."

Smiling, he moved down on the pew and angled himself so he could see her fully.

She sat, too, and ran her hand over the cool wood. "We have no wooden furniture in the future. No trees, as you'd assume. And here I'm surrounded by such a precious commodity. It humbles me."

"I can imagine." He waited. "How can I help you Celeste?"

"I have to know first if what we discuss will stay between us. You said once you were bound by your law to keep talks private."

"Unless you're going to harm yourself or someone else, it's private."

"Physically?"

"What do you mean?"

"I need help with something that's going to hurt some people psychologically. Emotionally."

"No, I didn't mean emotionally. That's God's department."

She nodded. "I'm pregnant, David."

"Oh, blessed Lord in heaven. What wonderful news." He studied *her* for a second. "Though you said you couldn't…"

She shrugged. "The only things I can think of are, a, we changed the future, so I'm somehow different. Which doesn't make sense, because we're all basically the same on the outside and the computeller hasn't changed and doesn't have additional information. Or, b, with a man of today, conception is possible."

"You don't look very happy about it."

"By the godheads…by your God, I am, David. I'm happier than I've ever been in my life."

"And sadder, I'll bet."

"Because of Alex, you mean."

He nodded. "Is there no chance for you two to get together? Especially if you tell him about the baby?"

She drew in a deep breath, obviously fortifying herself. "That's why I'm here. He can never know about the child. He might try to take him from me, or worse, offer to wed me because of it. I couldn't live with Alex under those circumstances, knowing he hated me and was only with me because of a child."

"You could be wrong about that, Celi. He's upset for obvious reasons, but it's all still new. Give him time."

"What if he tried to take the baby away from me? Because I'm not fit."

"Do you think Alex would do that?"

"No, but I don't understand men of this time period at all!" Her frustration was evident.

"Not many women do. I'm not going to spout platitudes about our sex. But Alex seems like a decent guy."

"He is. He's wonderful. I just don't know the side of him I saw a few nights ago. He's so angry at me."

"Hurt, more like it."

"Regardless, I need your help in making plans to move away, perhaps to another country, where he can't find me. Unfortunately, that means the Cromwells and Dorian and Alisha can't know either. Will you? Help me?"

"Of course. This is your choice and I'm here to do anything I can to make you happier."

Though David sincerely doubted abandoning her friends and giving up on Alex would bring about those results.

CHAPTER 14

ALEX WAS SPITTING nails as he pushed the cart down the grocery-store aisle. Even after she'd been gone for days, he could still picture Celeste when she'd come home from this market, pale and shaken. Since they had no food in the future, the place must have frightened her. Had he known about her world, he would never have sent her here. Had he known about her sensitivity, he would have kept her in a glass bubble. Which was about the stupidest thing he'd ever thought, because she was stronger than he was.

"Hey, Alex. What are you doin' here?"

Alex looked up from the cereal box he was blindly staring at to see Coach Bacon standing next to him with a cart full of groceries. Tanned and rested, he looked a hell of a lot healthier than Alex. "Hi, Nick. I'm doin' the same as you."

"I'll bet you miss Celeste. Boy, I do."

Oh, great.

"I was wondering if you had her phone number. Jon said she went to New York."

"No, I'm sorry I don't have it."

The coach eyed him curiously. "Huh. That's odd. Jon thinks she's comin' back soon."

"Could be."

"Huh! So if you hear from her, tell her to give me a call. I got a sister in the Big Apple I haven't visited in a while. I'd like to go there and see them both."

"She *is* dealing with a family emergency."

"I'd still like to talk to her."

Alex gripped the cold steel of the cart handle. "Fine. If I speak to her, I'll tell her that. Good seeing you, Nick."

Moving away from the coach who had the hots for Celeste, he thought about her and Nick Bacon together. Then he thought about the SexLine again and wondered why she hadn't slept with Nick if sex was merely release to her.

Because she was waiting for you, Darling. You know that.

No, Lila. Not now. Not about this.

I'm just sayin'.

Alex managed to finish the shopping without any mishaps, and when he got back to the house and pulled in the driveway, he stopped the car abruptly. The garage floor was ankle deep with water, which was seeping out onto the blacktop. "What the fuck?" He leaped out of the car and rushed into the area. Water gushed out of the spout full blast. His sneakered feet squishing, he waded through and turned the faucet off.

Then he heard yelling in the yard. He walked to the opening and in the bright midday sunlight, he saw Cody following Bruiser from the side yard to the front. The dog stopped and lay down. Cody shocked Alex when he said, "I hate you, Bruiser. I hate you." His son looked as though he was going to kick the dog, but he didn't. Instead, he bent down and hugged the mutt. "Please eat. We're *worried* about you."

Alex noted the bowls of water and kibbles Cody had set down in the yard. Bruiser took a few nibbles, then got up and walked away, as had been his pattern. He drank and ate just enough to stay alive, but the amount was getting less and less and he'd lost a lot of weight. They'd taken him to the vet, who said there was nothing wrong with him, but a two-month-old puppy had to eat more or he wouldn't make it. Jesus. That was *all* they needed.

"Cody?" His son turned. His face was covered in red splotches—from crying?

"Are you all right?"

Rising, Cody approached him slowly. With big fat tears in his eyes, he blurted out, "He's gonna die, Dad."

Alex squatted down. "No, he isn't."

"He *needs* Celeste."

We all do.

Cody shook his head, his mop of blond hair falling into his eyes. "I been calling her and nobody answers."

Because I have her phone.

"I was gonna ask her to help Bruiser. That we wouldn't bug her if she'd just take the dog so he'd eat."

"Oh, son."

"Dad, we *gotta* help him."

Tears trickled down Cody's cheeks. Alex was at a loss for what to do. So he took the boy into his arms and let him sob out his fear and frustration. Cody's solid little body trembled, and each tear was a lash to Alex's heart. How could Alex have let the kids get so attached to Celeste?

When the boy quieted, Alex hefted him up to take him inside. When they reached the garage, Cody said, "Holy cow, Dad. What happened to the... Oops."

"You didn't leave the water on, did you, buddy?"

"Must be I did when I got Bruiser some." He threw his arms around Alex's neck again. "I'm sorry."

"No worries, honey. At least this is fixable."

Later, just before supper—Alex had made macaroni and cheese, their favorite—Jon came home from his baseball practice. He entered through the garage, and Alex greeted him in the kitchen. "Hey, Jon, did you—oh, dear Lord, what happened?"

His son touched the purplish bruise that circled his eye and was already puffy. His face had dirt smudges in several places. "Nothing."

"Jon, come sit."

"No, I wanna go upstairs." He started out. Alex tugged him back.

"Jon, you can tell me anything."

The boy's eyes clouded and his shoulders slumped, as if he was carrying a burden too big to bear. "A guy on the team said my hitting sucked since Celi left. It does. But I got mad, anyway, and punched him. He punched back."

"Aw, son, you know it's not okay to hit people."

"I don't care. Coach benched me, but I'm gonna quit the team."

"Jon, no. Let me help you."

"You can't dad." He ran out of the kitchen.

Leaning against the counter, Alex wondered how things had gotten so out of control.

At dinner time, Maddy was out, and both boys came to the table, sullen. They pushed around the cheesy meal, which smelled great, and refused to eat the broccoli that they normally liked. Since Alex had never had any trouble with them like this—they had good eating habits—he ignored their behavior. He didn't want the damn stuff, either. Hell, nobody was hungry.

Around eight, he began to worry about Maddy. She was spending the day at Kelly's house and had called to say she was eating dinner at her friend's. Just as he was looking for his cell phone, she walked through the door. He met her in the kitchen. "Hey, Maddy."

She wasn't sullen, but the light Celeste had put in her eyes was gone. "Guess what, Daddy? I got a job."

• • •

TWO DAYS LATER, life at the Lansing household was not any better. The dog had completely stopped eating, and they often caught him lying in front of the door to the third floor. Cody and Jon were sullen, and Maddy was rarely home. Again. At a loss for what to do, he called his dad. Jeff Lansing jumped in the car and met him at a restaurant downtown at noon.

When they were seated in an outdoor area overlooking a grassy knoll, his dad said, "You look as bad as you sounded, son. Tell me right away what's going on."

Alex stared over at his father. A waiter came and they both ordered beers, then Alex began. "I don't know how to even start. It's such a bizarre story, I'm afraid you'll have me committed."

"I'm here for you, as always."

So he told his father the tale…women from the future… infertility because of him, Domes because of pollution…no intimacy…the SexLine…one-way time travel and the miraculous computer. "That's it in a nutshell." Celeste would have no idea what the statement meant.

His dad sat back and stared over the railing for a moment. "It's so lovely out here. All that green grass. The blue sky. We haven't ruined everything yet." He turned to Alex. "I'm sorry to hear we knew about the pollution, and we did nothing. Those three women who came to help must be furious."

"You believe me, just like that?"

His dad watched him. "Alex, you have the most scientific mind of anyone I know. If you believe this story, of course I do."

Alex felt his heart clench. "Dad, my drug…it caused infertility."

"No, son, people who built on your drug contributed to a society so self-centered that it caused reproductive problems." He whistled. "Your mother and I spent a lot of our lives dealing with them. She'll have a fit when she hears about this."

Alex was surprised by his reaction. "I said time travel. Do you believe in that?"

His father gave a grin that reminded Alex of Cody. "You know what a science-fiction buff I am. And there are several theories of time travel in that genre. I've come to believe time is a continuum, with threads running through it and making travel back in time possible. I also believe if you pulled out one of those threads, you could change the future."

"Jesus Christ, that's exactly how they described it."

His father shrugged. "I'm more concerned about the personal side of all this. About you."

Staring down at the little ring of foam on his beer, Alex was more confused than ever. Chatter from other diners went on around him, but all he could see was Celeste telling him how she'd tricked him. "She deceived me badly. She made me think she loved me so she could sabotage my research."

"Did she have to accomplish her task that way? Destroy your work *and* suck you into a personal relationship?"

"It was probably easier."

"How is she?"

Alex shook his head. "She was devastated when I left her a few days ago. I'm afraid I didn't make it any better. I…was cruel to her."

"We do that to people when they hurt us. You're in love with her."

"Of course I am." His hand fisted on the table and he pounded the top. "But it doesn't matter. There's no future for us."

"Alex, because of them, there's a future for mankind. Think about what miracle she actually performed before you banish her from your life."

• • •

CELESTE AND HELEN were lying on the bed, Celeste's hand on Helen's stomach, and vice versa. The open window blew a balmy breeze on their skin.

Helen giggled. "Mine's kicking. Yours is too little yet to do that. But she's communicating with him, I know."

Only yesterday, when the tiny egg was a week old, had he manifested himself as a boy. Suddenly Celeste had just known the gender. "When we do this there's an airiness inside me, not exactly a movement, but something."

"The others would think we're crazy."

"Which is why we can't let them see us. Nobody else is home now." Dorian was staying a few nights at Luke's, and Alisha had gone out for a jog.

Helen gave Celeste a gentle smile. "You'll have to tell them sometime."

"Maybe." But probably not. David had helped her form a plan for where she could go and what she could do. But she couldn't share that with Helen. Godheads, it was times like these she really wished she could talk to Rhea.

"The guys and Dorian and Alisha will love that you're pregnant."

Her jaw dropped. "Alex can never know."

Now Helen grasped Celeste's hand in hers. "Alex has a right to know."

"No, Helen."

"A baby would bring you together. Then you'll be forced to work things out. Sweetie, everyone could see when he came here he was still in love with you."

"I don't want to discuss this." The doorbell rang and Celeste jumped up. "I'll get it."

Preoccupied with Helen's words, she was halfway to the foyer when she stopped abruptly. The visitor was Alex. And… oh, God, oh, yes… She hurried forward, flung open the door, and Bruiser leaped at her, knocking her over on her tailbone. The dog was only two months old but big enough to do this.

"Easy boy." Alex grabbed for his collar.

Hugging the beautiful animal, Celeste said, "It's okay, Alex. I'm not hurt."

A wet tongue licked her face. Bruiser made soft noises in his throat and began to nuzzle her breasts. "I know, I know. I missed you, too. Don't worry, everything's okay now."

She managed to sit up and face Alex. He was unshaven, his hair needed to be cut and his eyes were bloodshot. "Hi," she said softly.

"Hi. I can explain."

She met foreheads with the dog. "You don't have to. He's been sad since I left."

"So much so he won't eat. At first, he took a few bites. Now he's gone without food for a day or so."

"Oh, Bruiser." She put both hands on the sides of his face and stared into his eyes. "You have to eat, sweetheart." She looked up at Alex. "He's hungry."

From off to the side on the porch, Alex picked up the bag of dog food. "I figured you could make him eat."

"Come on inside." He stepped over the threshold and closed the door.

She took the bag and grabbed a handful of kibbles. Bruiser gobbled it and three subsequent ones. But he wouldn't let Celeste stand. He put his head down on her lap. She said to Alex, "What are you going to do? He has to have sustenance or he'll die."

"I knew you could get him to take a meal. My children can't handle the dog dying now."

Finally, she stood, and the dog cuddled at her feet. "What's wrong?"

"Other than what happened to our world because of me?"

"Alex, it wasn't your fault."

"Never mind that. I'm worried about the kids. Jon's quitting the baseball team, Cody alternates between yelling and crying, and Maddy got a job, for God's sake."

Her heart clenched painfully in her chest. These children didn't deserve to suffer because of her actions. "I'm so sorry."

"They miss you."

"I miss them." She swallowed hard. "And you."

"Do you? Aren't you glad not to be playing a part?"

"I wasn't playing a part in the life I lived with you and the children."

His sigh was deep...and painful. "It was all smoke and mirrors."

"I don't know what that means."

"Not important. Look, I've got a plan. Would you listen to it?"

"Of course."

They moved into the living room, where Bruiser jumped up on the couch next to Celeste and settled half on her, half on the cushions. She looked over at Alex expectantly.

He ran a hand through his hair, messing it beautifully. She knew the strands were thick and a bit coarse. It also had streaks in it from being in the sun. "I want you to come back to Virginia with me."

Her throat constricted. "What?"

"I think the problem with the kids is they didn't have time to adjust to you leaving. If you could come back for a few weeks, explain things to them and prepare them for your absence, they might adjust better."

The pain in the pit of her stomach was acute. But what had she expected, that he wanted her to come back with him? Forever?

She folded her arms around her waist to keep in the disappointment. "How long before school starts?

"About five weeks. But we always spend the week before at my parents' home on the beach. Maybe if you could stay until then?"

More than anything else, she wanted to make things better for Alex, Jon, Cody and Maddy, but she had to think of the child in her womb. "I would do that Alex, gladly, joyously, but I couldn't bear to have you…lash out at me while I'm in your home. Not after what we had together."

His face closed down. "Two things — I promise I'll be kind to you. I won't intentionally hurt you, especially since you're doing me a favor. But second, there can be nothing more between us than employer and employee. I can't get close to you again, Celeste. That *I* can't bear."

Again she thought of the baby and how going home with Alex would cause tension. But there were other younglings to consider, too. Those she loved dearly. Taking a deep breath, she said, "All right, Alex. I'll come home with you. For a little while."

• • •

ALEX GLANCED INTO the backseat, where Celeste slept. He needed to wake her as they were almost home. She stretched out on the bench seat with not-so-little Bruiser sprawled over her. She'd started the trip in the front with Alex, and the dog in his cage in the back, but Bruiser scratched and whined so much—apparently, in an attempt to get to Celeste—that they were forced to accommodate him. Which was just as well. Sitting next to him, Celeste had quietly folded her hands on her lap and stared ahead, not making conversation. But her scent had wafted over to him, and the shoulder and leg flesh she bared in a multi-colored sundress tormented him, so he was glad she was out of sight.

A few miles from the house, he said softly, "Celeste, we're almost there."

It was too dark to see her, but he could hear the rustle of clothing, the soft, "Umm," and then, "Hey, buddy. You're heavy."

An answering growl came from the dog. Hell, he'd never get used to the mutt communicating with her.

She must have sat up, because she poked her head through the space between the two front seats. And there it was again, the smell of her lotion, her shampoo, just her. "Thank you for letting me sleep."

"You're welcome. You went out like a light."

She hesitated. "I haven't been resting well."

Him, either.

"I hope it was the correct decision not to tell the kids I'm coming back."

"I didn't want them thinking you'd be staying perma-nently."

"Of course not."

"I wanted to be able to quell that expectation in person."

"A wise, parental thing to do."

He hated that their dialogue was cold, stilted.

A few minutes later, he pulled onto their street. He heard the window go down and Celeste sigh, then felt the coolness. "I love the wind on my face."

"I understand why now." He glanced in the rearview mirror. I'm...sorry about what happened to your time period."

"I wonder if our efforts with Jess changed that. I hope there are no Domes. I'll never know."

Determined not to dwell on all she'd lost, he drove into the garage. "We're here." He turned around and could see her from the overhead lights. "I want you to know I realize what you gave up to come to our time. That you most likely can't go back."

"Alisha told you?"

"Yes, it was quite a sacrifice."

"The kind you're making, Alex."

"No, ending my work is not as drastic as leaving a home you love to help the universe and never being able to go back." Jesus, he couldn't believe he meant that. "In any case, thank you."

They exited the car and a fully roused Bruiser bounded out, circled them and headed for the house. He barked at the door as he hadn't barked since Celeste left. Alex opened it, and the dog leapt into the hallway.

He led them to the children in the playroom upstairs. The area smelled like popcorn, and Alex could see bowls spread out next to the kids. Maddy was at the computer, Jon wrote at the table and Cody had a picture book open on his lap. Bruiser reached them first.

"Hey, boy." Cody practically bubbled. "You got your energy back."

The dog turned and barked at Celeste, as if saying, *yes, and this is why.*

"Oh, my God, Celi!" Maddy bolted up and rushed to her before the boys could move.

They quickly joined the two females for a group hug that made Alex's stomach cramp. He'd actually thought that someday they'd be a family.

"Celi..."

"We *missed* you..."

"I'm so glad you're back..."

"Hold on, guys," Alex put in reluctantly. "This is only temporary."

When the four disentangled, all the children stared at him as if he was Simon Legree.

Celeste took over. "I'm back for four weeks. Then I've got to leave again to take care of my sister." She slid her arm around Cody and told the story she and Alex had agreed on. "She's sick, with breathing problems, so the doctors want her to go to the dry climate to recover. We may be moving to the state of Arizona."

"Aw, no," Cody said. "You gotta stay with us."

She knelt down. "Cody, if Jon or Maddy were sick, wouldn't you do everything you could to help them get better?"

The boy nodded solemnly.

Jon said, "I would."

Maddy agreed.

"So," she said, forcing a smile. Alex could tell this was killing her. "We have to make the most of these weeks. We'll pack them with fun and good experiences."

"Daddy, can you be with us?" Maddy asked. "You said you're at a low point in your work."

"We'll see." Alex turned his back on them. The last thing he needed to commit to was spending time with Celeste. As a family. Depressed, he left the play area and headed to his bedroom.

CHAPTER 15

"I'M NOT SURE I can do this, Alex."

"How long did you spend on the Internet, looking up information after I told you yesterday what I planned for today?"

She shrugged.

"Hours, I'll bet."

From the driver's seat, she looked over at him and shook her head. "It goes against my principles to drive a vehicle."

"It's a Prius, so it's better than most. You're going to have to make some concessions now that you live here." His voice softened. True to his word, he'd been kind to her, though he didn't go on several outings with her and the children. And she figured the deal he came up with last night was a peaceful offering. He'd come to her after dinner while the kids were cleaning up. She'd been outside, enjoying the stars, and even the heat, when he joined her…

"I've been thinking about what you'll need to survive in our time."

She'd wanted to say, *I need you,* but of course she didn't. She'd accepted her fate.

His face was shadowed by darkness falling, but she could still see his eyes. They were full of so many emotions, she didn't know what any of them meant. "I want to teach you to drive a car and swim. I mean, I'll take you to swimming lessons, because I don't know how to help someone else learn that skill. But I taught Maddy to drive."

"Oh, Alex…" She stepped forward without thinking and hugged him. When she realized what she'd done, she stepped back quickly. "I'm sorry. I forgot…"

Forcefully, she banished the memory of how good his body felt close to hers.

"Let's just try this. First, look around."

She scanned the area. "There are no other vehicles in this parking lot."

"The college runs a skeleton crew in the summer."

"A what?"

He actually laughed. "At least I don't have to wonder why you don't understand some things." He explained the idiom. "In any case, we got here early so we could practice here before we go on the road."

"I feel safer doing that." She faced forward and grasped the wheel. At least the inside wasn't leather.

"Turn the key in the engine."

It roared to life, the sound and vibrations under her hands startling her.

"Now, you tell me what to do next."

"Place my foot on the brake and put the shift into drive mode." She did so. "Then ease off and press the gas."

She touched the gas pedal so lightly, they barely moved. "A little harder, honey."

Because of the endearment, she lost focus and pressed too hard. They spurted forward, and she slammed her foot on the brake. "Oh, dear."

"Don't worry about it. That's a common mistake. You have to get a feel for it."

After an hour of parking-lot driving, she turned off the car. "I think that's enough. My stomach is queasy from the lurching."

"We didn't lurch that much. I hope you're not getting sick." Reaching over, he felt her forehead.

Closing her eyes, she savored his touch, clinical though it was. He'd applied some different aftershave this morning, and she'd been inhaling the masculine scent all the while they were in the car. She longed for him to hold her so she could bury her face in his neck. He left his hand on her for a moment, then drew it back. "You're not warm. But let's quit for today."

When they both exited the car to exchange places, Celeste saw a man approaching them. "Hello, Alex. Looks like you were having a driving lesson. How did it go?"

"I thought it went well," Alex replied. "Tom, this is Celeste. Celi, this is Dr. Tom Judson. He's in charge of the science department here."

"Very nice to meet you." The muscular, medium-height man reached out and clasped her hand. He didn't let go for a minute. Then he turned to Alex. "I'm glad I happened to run into you. The funding just came through for more courses in our department, that's why I'm late asking you this. Two sections of the basic ethics course you usually teach filled. Then two psychology and philosophy courses that are tangential to your subject matter."

"They all sound interesting."

"I wondered if you could recommend someone to hire, since you've made it clear you want only one of the ethics classes."

"Hmm. I'll think about it."

Tom held out his hand to shake with Alex. "I hope to hear from you soon." He gave Celeste a very masculine perusal.

"And I hope to see you, too." He winked at her. "Maybe Alex will give me your phone number."

Without saying anything to her, Alex slid into the driver's side and Celeste joined him in the front. Immediately, she felt negative vibes from him. She touched his arm, and her hand practically sizzled. "What's wrong, Alex?"

He faced her, his eyes burning. "Knowing I can't have you, watching Tom flirt with you, is hard."

"I'm sorry. I don't really understand flirting, but I believe his actions were harmless."

Alex drew in a heavy breath. "No, *I'm* sorry. Having you around makes it a lot harder than I thought it would be."

Her eyes danced. "Hmm, I know what a double entendre is, Alex."

That made him laugh as she'd hoped it would. The last thing Celeste wanted was for this man to hurt more.

• • •

SPIRITUALITY AND ETHICS. Do we need God in our lives to keep us from deceit, covetousness and theft in scientific research?

Alex sat back and stared at the words he'd just typed into his computer. He decided to work in the library across from the YWCA, where Celeste was at this very moment taking her swimming lesson. He enjoyed doing these articles for journals, and the college appreciated it, too. Especially Tom. Who had flirted like crazy with Celeste!

Not your business anymore, buddy.

He turned his attention elsewhere. The college was looking for a professor in his areas of interest. Now that his research was kaput, and he couldn't imagine starting over on another project, maybe he'd like to teach full time. Lila always thought he would be great at it. That way, he'd have more time for his kids, too.

Turning back to his writing, he poured his thoughts out onto the paper and in forty minutes had a rough draft. As he'd been writing articles for years, he knew the revision would take much longer, but it was an accomplishment to have gotten this much done.

The icon for his email came onscreen, indicating he had mail. He clicked into it. Charles Ravel. The clinical-trial head investigator. Alex felt as though somebody had stuck a sock in his throat.

The email was short. *Just checking in. One week to go. If no abnormalities show up this time, you're halfway to a stamp of approval for safety. Good luck.*

Closing his eyes, he fought back the bitterness he'd tried to dampen for weeks. This time, Ravel would be disappointed — there would be no positives in the results. If Alisha got to the data in time, she'd change it so that subjects would show vascular issues, unforeseen spikes in hormone levels and diminished potency. They'd succeeded in placing the seeds for those flaws in a new version of his research. The outcome would be negative: Equisex would be deemed too dangerous to pursue. The trials would be publicized, and everyone in the scientific community would know he'd failed. He was surprised to realize the latter didn't matter to him.

Just then another email came through. From Maddy.

Hey, Daddy. Hope Celi's doing good at her driving and swimming lessons. Cody, me and Jon were wondering if you knew when her birthday is.

He sat back. He wondered if Celeste had a birthday. For God's sake, she was conceived in a petri dish, gestated in a lab and spent the first weeks of her life in an incubator. Did they even consider her…formation…a birth?

He was stunned by a realization. So much had happened to change the future, much of which had started with him. It would end badly if he hadn't cooperated. He stared at the other emails in his inbox, looked at Ravel's again and felt some of the devastation he'd experienced moments ago lift. For the first time, he truly wanted to change the data in his research and prevent the future from developing as it would if he didn't.

A half hour later, with wet hair and rosy cheeks, Celeste got in the car after her lesson. She smelled of chlorine. He couldn't help but smile at her. "You look happy."

"Oh, Alex, it was so much fun! I got the hung of it right away, swam submerged easily and even managed to complete some strokes on top of the water."

"I'm not surprised." He perused her yellow top with shorts to match and how she'd pulled her longer hair into a ponytail. A few wispy strands escaped, kissing her cheek. "You're in great shape and you learn fast. I do think the species of mankind and womankind in the future is healthier than we are now."

"Of course we are. Were. Would be." She giggled, then stopped abruptly. "Oh, I seek your forgiveness. I shouldn't joke about the future."

"We could all use a little levity right about now." He started the car and listened to the engine purr for a moment. "And we're going to have more at home."

She cocked her head.

"Maddy emailed me to ask when your birthday is. I said I didn't know. She sounded excited. So I wanted to warn you to plan something to tell her. You said you didn't know when you were…what was the word you used?"

"Produced?"

"Yes."

"Well, be prepared."

She was quiet as he pulled out of the Y parking lot and headed home. He asked, "What is it?"

"I do know the date of my production. Dorian and I were intrigued by the custom of birthdays. When I went back to New York, so sad after I left here, she tried to cheer me up. One of the fun things we did was searching the computeller for the dates. We don't count days, months, like you do. But we came up with what would be our birthdays in your time."

"What are they?"

"Dorian on October twelve, Alisha on June five. Both in the yearling 2474."

"What about you?"

Her eyes filled with sorrow.

"Celi. What is it?"

"My date. It's…" her eyes clouded "It's July twenty-fourth."

• • •

CELESTE ENTERED THE house with trepidation. The knowledge that her birthday fell on the date when all of Alex's dreams would be dashed was like adding injury to insult. Or was it the other way around? The knowledge sat heavily in her heart. As if he knew, Alex sidled up to her and whispered, "No long faces, Celi. Let's just enjoy this."

His selflessness made her love him all the more.

They reached the kitchen, Celeste first.

"Surprise!" three voices called out in unison. A bark followed the shout.

"Oh, my," she said, as heartfelt as she could.

"What's all this?" Alex asked easily.

Maddy stepped forward. "Since we don't know when Celi's birthday is, we thought we'd celebrate it today."

"I see." The entire kitchen was decorated with pink and white crepe paper and a big Happy Birthday sign. A somewhat lopsided chocolate cake, emitting a sugary scent, sat on the table, and hats and streamers were off to the side. The entire area was bathed in sunlight streaming in from the wide expanse of windows and the patio door.

Celeste gave them a broad smile. "How sweet of you to do this for me."

Jon had been holding on to Bruiser—who wore an adorable red bow around his neck—and when he let go, the dog rushed to Celeste. Instead of hurdling himself at her, though, he nuzzled her stomach gently. In an unbelievable development, even to Celeste, Bruiser had stopped jumping on her—because he knew there was a child growing inside her. Talk about miracles.

"Hey, buddy." Bending over, she cuddled the dog. "Thanks for the surprise."

He barked in answer.

"When is it really, Celi?" Maddy asked.

"The day? Um, July twenty-fourth."

"So you'll be here when it comes. We'll have another party," Cody proclaimed. He walked to the table and picked up a big, pink cardboard and crossed to her. "Look, Celi. We made you a giant card."

Alex moved in close and read over her shoulder.

"Ten Reasons We Love Celi

1. She understands us. (That must be Cody's entry.)
2. She knows how we feel, sometimes before we do. (Now that was the truth.)
3. She's so fun.
4. Bruiser loves her.
5. Dad smiles more when she's with us. (That observation hurt her heart.)
6. She's different from anybody we've ever known.
7. She'll try anything we ask.
8. She's smart, like Dad.
9. She's moral and knows right from wrong.
10. She loves us."

The words blurred at the end.

Alex touched her shoulder. "I fully agree, guys."

All at once, they ran to her for another group hug; this time, Alex got caught up in it.

When they drew back, Cody frowned. "You're crying, Celi. Why? Doesn't this make you happy?"

"Very much so. My eyes leak sometimes when I'm happy."

She saw Jon capture Alex's gaze. "Women!"

Maddy poked him. "Don't listen to him. He's a boy. What do they know?"

The joking continued until Celeste could control herself. Finally, she said, "Who made the cake?"

"Maddy, mostly," Cody told her. "But we helped."

"They frosted it." Maddy looked at Alex. "Can we have some now, Dad?"

Checking his watch, Alex gave them a sham frown. "An hour before supper time?" Even Celeste could tell he was kidding. "Oh, all right."

They took seats at the table, and Jon put on his party hat. Celeste remembered these from Cody's birthday, but she didn't know what to do with the cone-like thing.

Alex picked it up and blew. A terrible noise came out. After she took his cue, Celeste followed suit and laughed at the silly toy. But she became saddened when, as she perused the children, she realized that she wouldn't be here to celebrate Jon's and Maddy's birthdays. Beneath the table, her hand cradled her stomach. She'd have to console herself with the knowledge that she'd know how to give her child a proper birthday party. The child who was their brother. Alex's third son.

Maddy served the cake, and the boys dug in. Celeste tasted a bite. Its sweetness was calming. She continued to take small forkfuls as they all chatted. When the cake was eaten, the horns blown again and the streamers started to droop, she scanned them all. "Thank you so much for doing this. I don't ever remember having such a good time."

Alex stood. "I'll clean up. The party givers can go chill. And I imagine Celi wants to shower after her swimming lesson and rest after her driving…attempts."

That set off another round of discussion, forcing her to relate every detail of both. Finally, she was able to leave the kitchen. She climbed the stairs and entered her room, Bruiser at her heels. Once she got there, she flopped on the bed and he leapt up to join her.

She cuddled into the dog. "Oh, Bruiser, how am I ever going to give you all up?" Tears came in earnest then as she buried her face in the dog's fur.

• • •

ALEX ABSCONDED TO his den as soon as he finished with the cleanup. The sight of the kids fawning over Celeste, the very real joy she took in each of them pierced his heart. And those ten sayings from the kids were so true. He stretched out on the couch and closed his eyes. How on earth was he ever going to let her go?

CHAPTER 16

AT ELEVEN O'CLOCK on the night the second phase of the clinical trials results were to come in, Alex sat at the computer, waiting for the email from Ravel. The first report had been sent to him around midnight. He already knew tonight there would be no celebration. A whole ten years of his work life would...be gone.

He thought back to his comments to his wife about his work in the field of sexual-enhancement drugs...

I think good sex will lead to happier people, he'd told Lila. *I'm going to pursue that research.*

I'm veering off from the standard drugs. I'm including women.

Why, thank you, dear, she'd responded.

Lila, I got the money from Global Research.

The chemists are combining the elements I've chosen.

The drug needs alteration.

I've received the go-ahead for animal testing.

She was dead before they learned the drug was safe on animals...

Tonight, it was once again difficult to believe that in the original version of history, the drug had gotten FDA approval and been manufactured and widely distributed. He wondered what he'd felt then? At the same time, he mourned that it had been the root cause of the future's infertility.

"That's not happening, as of today," he murmured to himself.

Alisha had phoned him at nine tonight to tell him she'd gotten the data a few days ago before it was sent out to be analyzed, and she'd altered it according to the specifications they'd built in to Alex's notes. She'd said she was sorry. Huh! Him, too.

A few minutes earlier, he'd poured himself a double shot from the bottle of bourbon on his desk. Now, he sipped the amber liquid, enjoying its tart taste. And wondered if Alisha had called Celeste, too. Had Celi cried? She'd done so off and on since she'd come back. She seemed more emotional these days. But hell, so was he.

Was she still tortured about what she'd done to him? He knew he didn't want her to be. He didn't want to hurt her anymore. Now that everything was over with his work, he let himself finally admit that she didn't deserve his animosity.

"Alex? The door's ajar. May I come in?"

Could he handle receiving the news with her here? Would it make the results harder or easier to digest? What the hell... "Yeah, but lock the door. I don't want the kids to see this if they get up."

He heard the lock snick and she approached him. "I just checked; they're asleep. Even Maddy."

"Another big day for them--the actual day of your birth."

She grinned. "I had fun at the amusement park, though I was afraid to go on the coaster that rolls."

"And the Ferris wheel."

"Please." She placed a hand on her stomach. She did that a lot now, probably because being here again, dealing with the emotional upheaval was making her queasy. She'd never been quite this sensitive before she'd come back from

New York, though, and he vowed from now on not to make it worse.

Her gaze darted to the computer screen. "You're waiting."

"Uh-huh."

"Alisha said it's done."

"I need to see the final confirmation."

When she placed her hand on his shoulder, he immediately felt better. He brushed it off. "Don't do that. Don't take on my grief."

"I caused it."

"No, no you didn't. In any case, please don't harm yourself because of me. I can handle this."

"All right."

"You can block what I'm feeling, right?"

"I can."

"Promise me you will or I'll insist you leave."

"I promise."

He realized in that moment that he trusted her again.

"So it's all right if I wait with you?"

How ironic that he wanted her company to endure the very thing she'd come to make happen. "Yes. Pull up a chair." As she did, he asked, "Want a drink?"

Her cute nose wrinkled. "No, thank you."

Silence descended. He'd turned his desk light on, but the rest of the den was dark. Shadows hung in the corners.

A few emails came in and the ping of the notification startled them both every time. At exactly 11:59 p.m., Charles Ravel's missive arrived.

"Alex,

I'm sorry to tell you there are serious concerns about the safety of the drug for both men and women, more for the latter. So much so that I've been forced to cancel the trials. I'll send a full report about it tomorrow. Again, I'm sorry. I know how much of your life you put into this.

Charles"

Leaning his head back into his chair, he stared at the screen. "So, it's done."

Celeste didn't respond.

He thought, *All I wanted to do was help people.*

As if she read his mind, she said, "You've changed the course of history, Alex. By this act of bravery."

Her words were true. It was just so hard to cling to them now that reality had arrived.

She reached for his hand.

"No, don't."

"I'll block the transfer. I promise."

He opened his palm and she put hers in it. He laced their fingers. Neither spoke. They just sat there.

• • •

CELESTE'S HAND WAS cramping. Her heart hurt and her shoulders ached. After a very long time of sitting with Alex, she knew she had to move. The tension, the sadness wasn't good for the child within her. Briefly, she wondered if she told Alex right now that she carried his child would the knowledge alleviate some of his pain? Probably not. More likely, it would cause him increased grief. And *that* she had a choice in. So she disentangled her hand from his. "My fingers hurt."

"Oh. I didn't realize."

"And I should go."

He didn't respond. She stood and took a few steps to the door. From behind her, she heard, "Wait."

Celeste halted. *Please, God,* she prayed to David's deity. *I don't know how much more of his suffering I can take.*

Coming up behind her, he put his hands on her shoulders. Pain was inside him, which she quickly blocked, as she'd promised. But something else swirled there, too, something that she didn't want to go away. He confirmed it when he whispered, "Make me feel better, Celeste. And not by siphoning off my grief. Replace these bad feelings for me, if only for a little while."

Forcefully, she pushed away the notion that what he wanted might not be the best thing for her. Instead, she let his presence envelop her. Turning, she locked her gaze with his and ran her hands up his chest. The muscles beneath her fingers leapt at her touch. He wore a light blue shirt, which had buttons. She undid the first, the second, the rest. She ran her hands over his chest again, feeling the coarse hair there. Leaning in, she inhaled him. The scent that was Alex filled her with such joy, it startled her.

He tipped her chin. His eyes were blazing with need, with want, with lust. She felt the same emotions rise up inside her. Slowly, not breaking eye contact, he brushed the straps of the sundress she wore down her arms. The top fell to her breasts. He helped the material along to her waist then filled his hands with her flesh. Celeste moaned at the wonderful relief his touch brought. Pregnancy hormones combined with the deep love she felt for this man to stir her as no other had. Then his mouth was there, suckling. His hands drifted to her hips. He pushed the dress to the floor, along with her panties. He slipped his hand between her legs, ground his palm into her.

She started to spiral with only light stimulation. When he slipped two fingers into her, she came with volcanic force.

Her face was buried in his neck and he bore the full weight
of her. For several moments, he didn't speak and neither did
she. Finally, when she could move, she drew back. His face
was a mask of conflicting emotions. But his need for her shimmered off of him.

Slowly, silently she led him to the couch. Pushing on his
shoulders so he settled into the leather, she dropped to her
knees and, as he'd taught her to the night they made love,
unbuckled his belt, undid the zipper on his shorts and lowered her head.

• • •

A HOT, HARD knot of desire pulsed within him. Celeste mas-
saged his penis expertly, finding a variety of ways to incite
him. She licked the tip with her very clever tongue. Then she
took him into her mouth. She brought him to climax so fast,
shock combined with bursting pleasure rushed to every part
of his body; his mind blanked.

When he came to, she was still on her knees, and her head
was in his lap. He brushed his hand down her silky hair, and
a soft tenderness replaced the lust he'd experienced only a
few minutes ago.

Sensing that, he guessed, she stirred and came to her
knees. What a lovely sight she was — hair all tangled from his
hands, cheeks red and eyes shining. She stared at him with
every emotion she felt etched on her lovely face. But he didn't
want to think about feelings yet. He didn't want to think at
all.

She asked, "Feel better?"

He cocked his head. "You know, not quite." He gave her
a sexy wink. "Not yet. Stand up."

She seemed puzzled by his request but stood anyway. He stood, too, and shed his clothes. When she realized what he was after, she gave him a temptress's smile. Naked, he pulled her to him and held her close. She didn't block this time, he knew it in his heart, because he felt the deep, deep connection.

After moments of closeness, he drew back and settled her out on the couch. Since the cushions were wide, he was able to cover her and support his own weight with his arms braced on either side of her.

By arousing her a second time, he got hard. Moans slipped from her mouth and she moved restlessly. She was ready in minutes. So was he. Staring her in her eyes, he said, "Watch as I do this." Slowly, incrementally, he slipped inside her. A sudden peace swept through him, followed by the quick slap of desire. Before he started to move, he said, "There, now I feel better."

• • •

ALEX AWOKE TO the sun shining through the slats in the blinds. He was covered with a light blanket, still naked, so he knew he hadn't dreamed last night. But he was alone.

Lying where he was, he raised his arm over his head and thought about what had happened in the past few hours. He and Celi had come together as though they'd never *joined* before. It had been hot as hell, but more so, they'd linked on a level so deep, so spiritual it made him forget his work.

He glanced at the computer. But that had happened, too. His life's work had been destroyed by a few clicks of the mouse.

After a bit, he threw back the cover and headed to the john off his study. He cleaned up, brushed his teeth and dressed in his wrinkled shorts and shirt from yesterday. Then he made some coffee in the Keurig he kept in his office. Taking a seat by the window, he watched the backyard come alive with birds flitting from one branch to another on the oak tree, and squirrels scampering for food.

One notion prevailed. Not how devastated he felt about his work. But...how was Celeste? She hadn't passed out but matched him need for need. Afterward, she'd shifted to his side, where he'd held her while they both slept.

His mind went next to how much she'd given up in her life to travel back in time to save them all: her home in the future, her work, friends, family. She had a mother there, though they called her a donor. And Celeste had selflessly forsaken it all to save the world.

You've done the same, she'd told him.

And in the end, he had. In a sense, though, as he'd said, his sacrifice hadn't been as great. If she'd just told him the truth....

It hit him then like a direct beam from the sun she loved. Christ Almighty, she *could* have told him who she was, why she was here. She *could* have warned him and risked the future for her own happiness, because ultimately, he might have dismissed her concerns. But instead, she'd sacrificed again: the kids, him—he knew she loved them—and her personal chance at a life as a family. Was there a better definition of selflessness?

Slamming the cup down on the table, he stood and hurried to the door. When he found it locked, he fumbled in his haste to get to her. He'd just reached the foyer when, through the windows, he saw a car pull up to the house. *Hell, not now.* No more delays. But when he recognized who exited the van, he sighed in resignation. Six people strode to the front porch like gunslingers looking for a fight. He opened the door before they could ring the bell.

"What are you?" he asked without greeting. "Her posse?"

Luke Cromwell stepped forward. "If we need to be."

Demure little Helen joined her brother-in-law. She just topped five feet, but she lifted her chin. "Something's wrong with Celeste. We're here to see her. And take her home, if need be."

He stepped back. "Come on in."

Once inside, they moved to the living room where he'd interviewed Celi what seemed like eons ago. Jess, his wife and Pastor Ryan sat. Luke, Dorian and Alisha stood next to the couch.

"Why do you think something's wrong with her?" he asked, stepping back from them.

"You idiot." Alisha's voice rose a notch. Her tone and the expression on her face indicated she'd like to take a swing at him. "Celeste is in love with you, and you blackmailed her into coming here. Of course she's not all right. Especially after the finality of our task last night."

Dorian touched Helen's shoulder. "Tell him."

Helen said, "I *felt* she wasn't all right. I couldn't sleep because of it. I convinced everybody to come here and see her."

"Are you a sensitive too?" Alex asked.

"No, just someone who loves her."

David Ryan cocked his head. His body language was more benevolent, his expression kinder. "Alex, please think about what these three women gave up to come to our time period, how Celeste sacrificed her own happiness with you and the kids to do what's right."

Jamming his hands in his pockets, he nodded. "Actually, the notion just dawned on me."

"What does that mean?" The gentle voice full of feeling came from the doorway. He looked over to see Celeste standing there, fragile in a soft, pink skirt and a T-shirt. Her hair was beautifully mussed from sleep.

Before he could explain, Helen bolted up and rushed to her. They hugged. He watched Celeste close her eyes and savor the contact. They held on for an unusually long time. Chest to chest. Belly to belly. Finally, Helen stepped back. "Celeste is okay."

"Yes, Helen, I am."

Luke, the tightest strung, crossed to her and put his arm around her. Tugged her close as they faced Alex. "No thanks to you, Lansing."

Alex couldn't take his eyes off Celeste. Her cheeks were rosy, her expression puzzled.

She asked, "What did you mean, Alex, that the notion of what I gave up had already dawned on you?"

Hell, he couldn't stand not touching her and walked over. Taking her hand, he drew her away from Luke, who only let go when Celeste nodded to him. "I don't really want to do this in front of an audience."

"Too bad." From Alisha.

"We're not leaving." Luke again. "Say what you have say to her and then we'll decide whether to take her back with us or not."

"Move back at least." His tone was exasperated. When they gave him some space, he grasped her shoulders. They felt strong but feminine. "Honey, I see the light now. That means I've come to an understanding. Exactly as David said. You've given up so much. I...seek your forgiveness that I didn't see it before."

To his shock, Celeste burst into tears.

• • •

"NO, NO." CELESTE hiccupped through her tears. "Not now, don't forgive me *now.*"

"If you think it's because of last night, it's not." He smiled. "Earnestly."

Luke growled, "What the hell happened last night?"

"No," Celi went on as if Luke hadn't spoken. "It's because…" Tears continued to leak from her eyes. She glanced at David for help.

David said, "Go ahead, Celi. It'll all work out. Have faith."

Still crying, she took Alex's hands. His eyes were full of concern. "I…I haven't been honest with you. About one thing."

"Don't tell me this was all a hoax. I won't believe you."

"No, not that." Her hand went to her stomach where her child lay. Where his child thrived. "You'll hate me for keeping this from you."

"No. I won't. Tell me."

"I'm pregnant, Alex."

Dorian and Alisha said together, "That can't be, Celi," and "What the hellor?"

She glanced at them, knowing the significance of the fact she'd just uttered. "I am."

They stared at her, hands clasped, misty-eyed, even Alisha.

Alex stared at her, too.

Before he could speak, David stood. "Alex, can you blame her for keeping quiet about this? Please, think before you say anything. Words can't be taken back."

"I don't have to think about it." She couldn't determine his tone. He gripped her hands tighter. "You expect me to be mad that you didn't tell me about this little miracle"—he freed one hand and placed it on her belly — "when I've been acting like such an ass these few weeks."

"Yes, I… Well, no you're not an ass. I thought…"

He placed his fingers on her mouth. She was less frantic now, and his thoughts, his feelings flowed into her. "Oh, God, you're happy about him."

"Him? A boy?"

She nodded.

"Of course I'm happy. Of course I want him. And you."

"Are you just saying that because I'm going to have your baby?"

"Nope." He nodded to the group. "They're witnesses, like they said. I'd already decided I had to have you in my life and was on my way upstairs to see you."

A surge of undiluted joy swept through Celeste, like the cool wind coming in through the car window. She leaned into Alex. Collapsed, really, against him.

His hand went to her neck, anchoring her there. "You're not going to faint again, are you?"

"Celi fainted?" Dorian asked. "When?"

Holding her close, he faced them. "*That* I'm not going to share with you. Now will you all please go into the other room so I can be alone for a few minutes with my future wife and my son."

"Your wife?" Celi croaked out.

"Of course." He shot a meaningful look at the others.

"Took you long enough," Luke said, hostility still lacing his voice as he headed to the kitchen. "I need coffee."

Her friends filed out.

Alex tipped Celeste's chin and stared into her eyes, his own full of love. "Please forgive me. I love you so much."

"Oh, Alex," she whispered, her eyes filling again.

He was lowering his head to give her the kiss she craved, when there was activity in the foyer. Three bodies rushed into the living room.

Maddy asked, "Daddy, what's going on?"

"Why are there all these strange people in our house?" Jon wanted to know.

Cody crossed into the room and looked up at them. "You're crying again, Celi. Are you happy or sad?"

Still holding on to Alex, she whispered, "Oh, Cody. I'm happy. Very, very happy."

Maddy gave her father a knowing look. "Dad, you are too. Why?"

"Let's sit down, and we'll tell you." He leaned into Celeste so just she could hear him. "Only part of it, though."

She smiled, he smiled, then they faced their children.

And for the first time in…forever, Celeste looked forward to the future.

• • •

FOR NOTIFICATION OF Kathryn's new work and information about her books, be sure to sign up for her newsletter at http://on.fb.me/12dhOtc.

If you liked PERFECT TIMING, you might want to post a review of it at amzn.to/JLox7O

Visit or Contact Kathryn at
www.kathrynshay.com
www.facebook.com/kathrynshay
www.twitter.com/KShayAuthor
http://pinterest.com/kathrynshay/

AUTHOR'S NOTE:

WELCOME TO BOOK two of my new series, Portals of Time. This trilogy has been a labor of love for me as I've always been a science fiction/time travel aficionado. But since my first love is romance, there never seemed to be an opportunity to combine the two genres until now. I came up with the original concept for the trilogy years ago, and at last it's come to fruition. Since all the stories take place in the present, I think I was able to keep the books classic Kathryn Shay with a twist. I thoroughly enjoyed creating the new world of the future, playing around with language, and at the same time building a great romance and saying something important about society.

In PERFECT TIMING, I have to say my heart simply broke for all Celeste went through. The sweetest of the three women, the most open and honest, it was hard to make bad things happen to her. I'll just bet every reader adored her and wanted her to have the best. It took a while, but eventually Alex wanted that, too. I didn't blame Alex for being so hurt he could barely tolerate her presence, though. He fell hard and fast for her and she *did* betray him.

Which Lansing child—or youngling—did you like best? It's really difficult to say, isn't it? And wait until the third book, regarding them. I'm not sharing any spoilers, but it will be really fun for readers.

Be sure to read the concluding story to this trilogy, ANOTHER TIME, and if you missed the first, grab a copy of JUST IN TIME.

Excerpt from book #3 in the trilogy, ANOTHER TIME…

PROLOGUE

ALISHA WATCHED AS David Ryan smiled benevolently at the two couples standing before him in the splendor of the Lansings' garden. Flowers grew from in the ground, and the entire area around him was a mass of summer blossoms. Nature still boggled her mind.

"Will you, Lucas Cromwell, cherish Dorian, love her and care for her, during your time together?"

Contrary Luke grinned at the same time his eyes filled. "I will. Oh, I will."

"Dorian Masters…" David asked the same question and she answered, "With all my heart."

Smiling still, David turned to Alex Lansing. Alex's face was already wet with tears, and he could barely respond to David's query. Finally, he muttered a yes. Celeste, looking up at him, scrubbed her hands over her cheeks, then took her vows solemnly. When she finished committing herself to him, she glanced over his shoulder. Her new family looked on, their faces alight with joy. The older one, Maddy, wore a dress similar to Alisha's—pink, Celi's favorite color, though Celeste's was darker and more fitted than the girl's. Both boys were clothed in suits, like Alex and Luke.

Celeste finished, "And I promise to cherish, love and care for you three with all that's in me."

The smallest youngling, Cody, pumped his fist in the air. "Yes!" he said, and everybody laughed.

David confirmed them married for life, and the couples kissed. Enthusiastically. Glancing at Alisha, David winked. She'd come to like the pastor and, in some ways, depend on him for his clear thinking and generous spirit. Especially since she was alone in the world...

What will you do now, Lisha? David had taken to the nick-name, too.

I have no idea.

Come back to New York. We all want you there.

Jess and Helen, in attendance along with Alex's parents, reiterated the notion several times. *Stay with us, at least for a while,* Helen coaxed.

She'd agreed. *What will I do with my time, David? Now that our tasks are completed.*

We'll find something for you.

When he said the words, she'd been disturbed by the use of *we.* Though she liked him, she didn't want to get too con-nected to David. To a minister. Alisha was the ultimate athe-ist. Though she'd made a myriad of adaptations to this era, believing in a god wasn't going to happen.

She was distracted from her thoughts of the past when the ceremony ended. Everybody hugged — something Alisha accepted from the women but still couldn't get used to from the men.

A sudden wave of sadness swept through her. Would she ever, truly, become accustomed to this world? She knew now she had no choice. Originally, she'd hoped that the rest of his-tory might have stayed the same or similar enough so that someone, perhaps Rhea, would find the record of their mission. It was possible that only those two threads—the ones involving Jess and Alex—had been pulled from the fabric of time. Though they'd been told by the Guardians that they'd most likely never be able to return to their time period, Alisha was wishing for another outcome.

But after they'd destroyed Alex's research, no one from the future had appeared to announce society had developed differently, but they remembered the women's assignment and the three of them could go back to their time. She'd clung to the notion, but now, nearly three weeks after their tasks were done, all hope was dashed.

As people gathered to congratulate the newly wedded couples, David approached her. "You're sad," he said, studying her face.

It unnerved Alisha that he could read her so well. "Why would I be sad? I love Celi and Dorian. They've found happiness."

His hazel eyes filled with understanding as they sparkled in the sunlight. "You're not alone, you know."

"Of course not. I still have Dorian in my life, especially now that I've moved back to New York. And Jess and Helen."

"And me." Just then, his phone vibrated. "I'm sorry, I have to take this."

Alisha wondered who would be calling David during the ceremony. A woman? She knew he'd dated, that archaic custom that still—what was the idiom?—winded her mind. Briefly, she wondered what kind of woman he preferred.

He returned quickly. Now his features were strained.

"Is everything all right?"

"I'll tell you later. I don't want to spoil the day."

Grasping on to his arm, she drew him farther away from the picture taking. "I won't say anything. People of your time feel better sharing things."

As if he couldn't help himself, he blurted out, "There's been another church fire. One of my minister friends was hurt. Honestly, this confirms someone in Brooklyn is torching churches."

Alisha could believe it. From her research on religion of today, she'd found that a lot of unbalanced people used this god they loved as an excuse to hurt others.

Which was another reason to reject the notion. Still, she liked David. "I'm sorry. I hope he's all right."

"She."

"What?"

"The minister is a she. Kerry Mackenzie. I know her well."

Huh! Alisha wondered why the notion of his female friend bothered her.